# Francis King

is a former President of I... Switzerland, he spent his ... his father was a governm... ......... While still an undergraduate at Oxford, he published his first three novels. He then joined the British Council, working in Italy, Greece, Egypt, Finland and Japan, before he resigned to devote himself to writing. Until recently he was drama critic of the *Sunday Telegraph*, and he reviews fiction each fortnight for the *Spectator*. He is a former winner of the Somerset Maugham Prize, of the Katherine Mansfield Short Story Prize, and of the *Yorkshire Post* Novel of the Year Award for *Act of Darkness* (1983). He lives in London.

From the reviews of *Visiting Cards*:

'Francis King is a cunning craftsman . . . *Visiting Cards* slips through the fingers as lightly as a feather. There are no great villains and no great heroes here, but instantly recognisable humanity.'      *Literary Review*

'Francis King's brilliant comedy will crack the ribs of those who, like him, are conference veterans. For those who are not it serves as a word to the wise . . . Read it at home, or you may, as I did, attract unwelcome attention to yourself by laughing uncontrollably in public.'      *Observer*

'Francis King in the highest of spirits and excellent literary form . . . *Visiting Cards* is very funny indeed. The plot is skilfully organised and ends with a brilliant harlequinade, from time to time crossing the borderline between comedy and farce in a way that reminds one of Evelyn Waugh. *Visiting Cards* strikes me as something new and fresh and delightfully diverting.'      *Tablet*

By the same author

Novels

*To the Dark Tower*
*Never Again*
*An Air that Kills*
*The Dividing Stream*
*The Dark Glasses*
*The Firewalkers*
*The Widow*
*The Man on the Rock*
*The Custom House*
*The Last of the Pleasure*
   *Gardens*
*The Waves Behind the Boat*
*A Domestic Animal*
*Flights*
*A Game of Patience*
*The Needle*
*Danny Hill*
*The Action*
*Act of Darkness*
*Voices in an Empty Room*
*The Woman Who Was God*
*Punishments*
*The Ant Colony*

Novella

*Frozen Music*

Short Stories

*So Hurt and Humiliated*
*The Japanese Umbrella*
*The Brighton Belle*
*Hard Feelings*
*Indirect Method*
*One is a Wanderer*
   (selected stories)

Poetry

*Rod of Incantation*

Biography

*E. M. Forster and his World*
*My Sister and Myself: The*
   *Diaries of J.R. Ackerley*
   (editor)

Travel

*Introducing Greece (editor)*
*Japan*
*Florence*

# FRANCIS KING

# *Visiting Cards*

Flamingo
*An Imprint of HarperCollinsPublishers*

Flamingo
An Imprint of HarperCollins*Publishers*
77–85 Fulham Palace Road,
Hammersmith, London W6 8JB

Published by Flamingo 1992
9 8 7 6 5 4 3 2 1

First published in Great Britain by
Constable and Company Ltd 1990

ISBN 0-00-654470-3

Set in Palatino

Printed in Great Britain by
HarperCollins Manufacturing, Glasgow

*To*
Peter and Albert

# 1

>:> <:<

'Isn't lunch ready yet?'

'Yas*sir*! Just killin' 'im!'

Through the half-open door, Amos had momentarily glimpsed the black face above the white robes blotched with the stains of what might have been iodine but now seemed more likely to be blood.

'Semba,' Naylor grunted, scratching at his crotch with the hand in his trouser-pocket. The other hand held between thumb and forefinger the miniature torpedo of an evil-smelling cheroot.

'Semba?'

'Brought her with me.'

'From England?'

'Good God, no!' Naylor's pink-rimmed eyes squinted morosely at his guest. 'From Nigeria. My last posting.'

Why should anyone decide to bring a servant from Nigeria to Malindi?

Although Amos had reluctantly decided not to ask that question, Naylor answered it. 'Semba has one outstanding talent. She can iron a shirt better than anyone I've ever known. Not much good as a cook, as you'll duly discover. Hopeless as a cleaner, as you must already have noticed. But give her a shirt – even one as crumpled as that one of yours . . .' He sucked on the cigar. 'Still and all, I mightn't have brought her here if the wife hadn't waltzed out on me with a Greek bum she met in a Lagos supermarket. Not that *she* was any use at ironing,' he added.

From the kitchen came a brief, frantic squawking. Amos hoped that Semba had wrung the chicken's neck, not chopped off its head.

'Now she'll have to pluck it,' Naylor sighed in lugubrious resignation. 'And then dismember it. And then cook it. I hope you've nothing to do this afternoon.'

'Not much. The Malindians are surprisingly efficient – so one just leaves them to it.'

Naylor looked at his watch. 'What's happened to that wife of yours? You did say you were bringing her along with you, didn't you?'

'She went on a shopping trip with the wife of the President.'

'The wife of the President! Good God!' Naylor jerked up in the chair in which he had been lying almost horizontally, with such violence that he scattered cigar-ash over the front of his shirt. 'Why the hell should the wife of the President take *her* on a shopping trip? *I've* never even met the President – let alone his wife.'

'The wife of the President of the Malindian Centre of WAA.'

'WAA?'

Amos always felt embarrassed by having to say the acronym. It was as if, muzzy with drink, he were trying to say 'What?' Hurriedly he explained, 'The World Association of Authors.'

'Oh, your little show!' Naylor was appeased. 'Tell me about it.' At that he shut his eyes, as though in preparation for sleep.

'Well. Well. It's a world association. Of authors. And I happen – for my sins – to be its President.'

'Yes, I know about that. But *why* should you be its President?'

'Why? Well, I had the bad luck to be elected.'

'Yes, but *why* . . .? Oh, never mind.'

Amos was glad to be spared having to explain. It had all been a mistake. Their mistake and, worse, his mistake.

Naylor was now, to all appearances, asleep. The ash lengthened on the cheroot which stuck up from the hands clasped over his stomach. The stomach rose and fell, and from time to time he made a curious gobbling sound. Amos watched him, when he was not reaching out for the glass of Malindian gin and tonic on the table beside him. Surely someone in the British Council should have access to supplies of English gin and tonic?

Naylor, convulsed with a sudden hiccough, opened his eyes wide. 'Where *is* that wife of yours?'

Amos wanted to retaliate by asking: 'Where is our lunch?' There were sounds of sizzling and a smell of onions coming from the kitchen. For some reason, he found both singularly unappetizing. The bell rang out.

'There! That must be her.'

'Semba!'

'Yas*sir*!' Frying-pan smoking and spitting in her left hand, Semba rushed out of the kitchen. To the dry, iodine-coloured stains on her robe there had now been added wet, scarlet ones. All too plainly, the chicken's neck had not been wrung.

Laura coughed on the doorstep as she inhaled the smoke, waving a hand before her face. Then, voluptuous and majestic, she advanced into the room. 'You're Mr Naylor. And you're my husband,' she playfully added to Amos. 'I'd recognize you anywhere. Oh, Mr Naylor, do please give me a drink. I'm as parched as the Gobi Desert. The weeniest amount of tonic and the largest amount of gin.'

'Don't you mean the other way round?' Naylor enquired, going over to the table of drinks.

'No, I mean exactly what I said.'

'Good for you!'

Seated, Laura opened her bag. 'There you are, darling. A little present. A watch to replace the one you dropped into the loo. Rolex.'

'But . . . this must have cost a fortune!' Amos was appalled.

Laura chuckled into her glass, then gulped and gulped again. 'Fifteen dollars. And that's for you too. And *that*.' She dangled first a fake Cartier and then a fake Longines watch before him. 'You can match your watch to your clothes. Or vice versa.'

Amos was examining the Rolex watch. 'Darling – the second-hand of this watch is moving in sudden jumps . . . Oh, now it's stopped completely!'

'You can't have everything. Can he, Mr Naylor?'

'Bob.'

'Can he, Bob?'

'Not for fifteen dollars. No, he can't.'

Laura had begun to inspect the room. 'This is not at all what I'd expected from a British Council home.'

'Why's that, Mrs – ?'

'Laura.'

'Why's that, Laura?'

'No books. Not even one of Amos's.'

'I'm an ELT expert. You can't expect an ELT expert to indulge in the luxury of books. Not even of one by your husband.'

'ELT?'

'English Language Teaching.'

'Oh, good! Then that's all right then. Isn't it?' She gulped again at her drink. 'Tell me – '

'Bob.'

'Tell me, Bob, what exactly is your age?'

'Forty-one. But people say I look older.'

'For once people are right. I'm thirty-seven. But people say I look younger.'

'For once people are wrong,' Amos said, disgruntled at having been left out of the conversation.

'*He ready, sir!*'

'He? Is there another guest?'

'Only the one we're going to eat, Laura.'

*

10

Amos had known all along that Laura would eventually tell Naylor the story of how, to everyone's astonishment, he had come to be elected to the International Presidency of WAA. It was a story which she told as often as the one of how, no less to everyone's astonishment, she had at last come to accept his proposal of marriage while he was on a donkey-tour, eventually to become the subject of one of the least successful of his books, in the Highlands of Scotland. 'It was all the result of a hilarious mistake,' Laura said – as she would also often say of their marriage. 'But I was certainly not going to correct it – and I absolutely forbade Amos to do so. Amos usually does what I tell him,' she added, frowning down at the chicken thigh at which she had been unsuccessfully sawing with a bent and blunt knife.

The election had taken place almost three years previously at a WAA Congress in Tokyo. Members of the executive committee of the English Centre of WAA, meeting in London, had been either not in the mood or not in the funds to participate in it. Who was to represent them? Then a publisher among them had suddenly remembered that Amos Kingsley ('Amos *who*?' more than one person had asked) was at that moment in Japan, writing for his firm a history of *bunraku* ('Bun *what*?' more than one person had once again asked). Was Amos a member of WAA? No one knew, but everyone agreed that he could be made one if he wasn't. 'We certainly ought to be represented at so prestigious a Congress,' the Chairman said. 'Even if it is only by this – this Amos Kingsley.' Heads nodded round the table.

Amos, who had long felt that he ought to get round to joining WAA, was flattered when a cable from the English Centre arrived at the Kyoto inn against the low beams of which Laura was constantly banging her head. 'Why should they want *me* as their delegate?' Amos wondered aloud. Could the Chairman, a successful biographer, be an admirer of *My Ass and I: A Journey by Donkey in the Highlands*? Might he even be a knitter, impressed by *Fairest Fair Isle: A Pattern of History*? The Chairman asked for a 'telephone or cabled answer soonest'. Having failed to take an accurate account of the time difference, Amos's telephone answer soonest found the Chairman, roused from sleep at three-thirty in the morning, in irritable mood. 'Amos *who*?' he asked, and then answered the question before Amos could do so: 'Oh, yes, of course, you're the chappie in Japan.'

Laura and Amos were pleased to move from the Japanese inn – could those weals that had appeared all over Amos's body be due to nothing worse than an allergy to soy sauce, as Laura kept assuring him? – into the luxury hotel in which the Congress delegates were accommodated. Exhausted from an interminable bus journey from Kyoto to Tokyo (it was so much cheaper than even a second-class, slow train), Amos misheard the number of their floor as the third. The diminutive bell-boy, Laura's rucksack on his back and Amos's sleeping-bag at his feet, pressed the lift-button and they shot skywards. Later, in the suite, the boy demonstrated how one turned on a bath, flushed a lavatory, and activated a television set. He refused a tip with a pitying smile. 'One doesn't tip staff in Western-style hotels in Japan,' Laura said. 'Or one tips them more than fifty yen,' Amos said, more wisely.

Amos then rushed over to the vast window, floor to ceiling and extending the whole of one side of the room, to jerk back the curtains. He gave a piercing scream. He was looking down from not the third but the sixty-third floor at a grey waste of parking-lots and hovels.

He threw himself on the bed, burying his head in his arms. 'Can't . . . can't . . . can't . . .' He was once again the child who had sat down on the narrow staircase up to the highest gallery in St Paul's, blocking the way for all the other visitors, and had refused to climb any further.

'Don't be so silly! Pull yourself together!' It was an aunt, one of the many who acted as his foster-mothers, who had said the words then. It was Laura who said them now. Amos stopped being silly. He pulled himself together.

Laura went over to the minibar and opened it. 'Oh, look at all these lovely drinkies they've left for us.' Later she would have to borrow money from the elderly delegate from Colombia – clearly, to judge by his behaviour to her, a man with an irresistible appetite for beautiful giantesses – when it became apparent, at the end of the Congress, that all those lovely drinkies were not, like the soap, the shampoo, the bath-essence and the sewing-kit, courtesy of the management.

Soon after the Congress had started, Amos discovered a gift which, until then, he had never known himself to possess. He could 'come up with a formula'. Had the Bulgarians, to the fury of the Greeks, proposed a resolution of censure about the treatment of the Slavophone minority in Thrace? Had the Puerto Ricans, to the fury of the Americans, proposed a resolution of censure about United States suppression of Hispanic culture on their island? Were the West Germans and the East Germans, the South Koreans and the North Koreans, the Finns and the Swedes, the Indians and the Sinhalese at loggerheads? Amos would rise, raise his hand and declare: 'I think I can come up with a formula.' The formula was so ambivalent in its meaning and so fuzzy in its expression that, reluctantly, both sides would agree to it. Soon, at times of difficulty, the then President, an excitable French novelist, would turn to Amos: *Monsieur le délégué de l'Angleterre – vous n'avez pas une petite formule pour nous?'* 'Oui, oui,' Amos would squeak. '*Un moment*, please!' And he would at once get to work, with Laura peering over his shoulder and

13

sometimes coming up with some *petite formule* of her own.

'The English have a genius for compromise,' the chief American delegate, Frank O'Shaughnessy, recently made a millionaire by his 592-page novel, *Wet Dreams*, condescended to tell Amos as, in the sumptuous ground-floor lavatory of the hotel, he adjusted the zip of his Stuart tartan trousers, while Amos himself still continued to urinate in the nervous spurts which always afflicted him when not alone at this task.

Later, the most taciturn of the innumerable taciturn Japanese novelists attending the Congress came up to Amos at a reception while he was wolfing a jumbo prawn, gave a deep bow, drew in a breath and then, expelling it on a sigh, told him: 'You are diplomat, Amos-san. England is the land of diplomats.'

'And Japan is the land of jumbo prawns.'

The Japanese looked puzzled, as he wandered off.

'What a silly thing to say!' Laura reproved Amos. 'What *will* he think?'

'The truth often sounds silly. There are more jumbo prawns in Japan than there are diplomats in England.'

The next day there was a ferocious row during the assembly of delegates. In later years Amos would often say that each WAA Congress was like an old-fashioned three-act play. The first act was one of leisurely preparation, in which characters and themes were introduced; the second throbbed with conflict, recrimination and passion; the third brought harmony and peace. Laura put it differently. A WAA Congress, she would tell people, was like a bout of love-making. There was the tentative, sometimes embarrassed foreplay; there was the self-forgetting, wild, even savage act itself; and then, finally, there was the aftermath of sad repletion – *omne animal post coitum triste est*, she would quote, remembering the sentence from a far-from-satisfactory lover who had taught classics at Eton before entering first a monastery and then a merchant bank.

14

On this occasion the row had been between, on the one hand, the excitable French novelist who was the President of WAA and, on the other, a female publisher's reader who was one of the lesser American delegates. The American delegate had wanted to propose a resolution demanding the instant release of Nelson Mandela. The French novelist had objected that, since Nelson Mandela was not a writer, he was no concern of WAA. The American delegate had maintained that Nelson Mandela was a writer and that anyone indifferent to his fate could only be a racist.

'You call me a racist, madame?' the Frenchman demanded. 'You call *me* a racist? America is the most racist country of the world. America *invented* racism! My wife's brother has married a *quatronne* of Martinique! This year my wife's brother and my wife's brother's wife have made the New Year at us! I have many records of Josephine Bak-err! Once I take James Baldwin to Biarritz, Barbizon and *La Rocambole* all in one week. You call *me* a racist?'

'I call anyone who objects to this resolution a racist. I demand that it be put to the vote!'

'Madame, you have no right to demand anything in this assembly. You are not even a writer yourself. You are an *éditrice*, madame!'

'I am *what*? I refuse to be insulted.'

There were shouts of 'Withdraw! Withdraw!' from the other, numerous members of the American delegation, followed by answering shouts of *'Taisez!'* *'Assez!'* and *'Mais non!'* from the Francophone delegates. When Amos rose, waved a copy of *The Times*, three days old, in the air and bleated, 'I should like to propose a formula', for once no one paid him any attention. The time for formulae had passed.

*'Bien! Je m'en fout! Je veux me démettre! Je résigne la Présidence! Oui! Oui! Mais oui*! Yes! *J'en ai assez*! I have it up to here! I resign!' As the President stepped down

from the platform, various distinguished writers, Vice-Presidents of WAA, who had been somnolently perched up there beside him, attempted to restrain him. But he petulantly pushed them away. Then, catching the pointed toe of his glacé-kid shoe on a briefcase propped against a table-leg, he tripped, clutched at one of the people whom he had previously been repelling, and thumped to the floor. Papers shot out of his hand and cascaded in all directions.

*'Monsieur le Président! Monsieur le Président!'* The horrified French delegates crowded around him, some stooping to pick up the scattered papers. One of them, a Prix Goncourt winner with the looks of an ageing bruiser, glared at the American delegate who had precipitated the rumpus. *'Voyez donc, madame! Voyez!'* He might have been accusing her of assault or even of murder.

Having reassumed possession of his papers, rubbed at a shin and tossed back a lock of thinning hair, suspiciously auburn for one of his age, the President staggered out of the hall, the French delegates pressing close around him, as though in protection. Amos later likened the event to the moment when the heroine of a well-made play flounces out of the drawing-room, slamming the door behind her. Laura later likened it to an orgasm.

The chairman gone, what was now to be done? Had he truly resigned? Should someone be sent to coax him back? Everyone began shouting at someone – or everyone – else. Soon the English-speaking delegates, who did not like or admire the President, were in furious argument with the French-speaking ones, who did. 'He's resigned! So that's that. We elect someone else,' an Australian author of historical text-books, dressed in gaudy T-shirt and soiled sneakers, shouted from the platform on to which he had leapt. *'Ja, ja!* That is right!' The Germans, both West and East, were for once in agreement. But a diminutive Cambodian writer, living in penurious exile in a cubby-hole in Neuilly and working as a taxi-driver, remembered the occasions when the French novelist had graciously either slipped him a note or stood him a meal or drink, and demanded, in a shrill falsetto, that the novelist should receive an apology from the American delegate and be asked to reconsider his decision. 'Apology! *Apology*! You can bet your little ass I make no apologies! That shit owes *me* an apology. Get that into your head!' The Cambodian quailed in dainty horror as the brawny American, huge ear-rings pulling down outsize ear-lobes, lowered above him. '*Quelle vache!*' an elegant, ivory-coloured *griot* from the Côte d'Ivoire muttered of this American to a darker female compatriot in multi-coloured robes and a towering headdress of African feathers and Hong Kong rayon. A gaunt young Dane appeared to be squaring up to a fat elderly French Canadian leaning on a zimmer.

It was then that Amos, pushed up on to the platform by Laura in the manner of a mother propelling her timid child forward to sing a song or recite a poem, once again made his suggestion. 'May I – ?' The pandemonium continued. He said it a little louder: 'May I – ? . . . Ladies and gentlemen . . . Please . . .' He raised his hands in appeal. But no one heeded him.

Laura leapt on to the platform and stood there, legs wide apart and arms akimbo. She bawled: 'Quiet please! Quiet! Quiet!' Miraculously, at the third 'Quiet!' everyone fell silent. 'My husband wishes to come up with a little formula. Amos! Tell them!'

Amos cleared his throat, as he tried to think of some little formula. 'Let us be calm. Let us be rational. Let us be tolerant each of the other's viewpoint.' Heads nodded below him. 'What does WAA' – as always, he felt an inward squirming as he brought out the blurred acronym – 'what does this precious organization of ours stand for if it does not stand for calm, rationality and tolerance?' Again he cleared his throat. 'This is what I suggest.' What did he suggest? He had no idea. But he began to extemporize, hoping that he would discover. 'Our President has resigned. That we know for sure. We must elect a new President if our deliberations here – our most important deliberations – are to continue. I therefore suggest that we now adjourn.'

'Until when?' an Italian voice shouted from the crowd.

Until when? Amos hesitated. Then he said boldly: 'Until tomorrow. Then, first thing tomorrow morning, we shall hold our election. Our present President will – I'm sure we all hope – agree to stand again. But, of course, anyone else may stand. I suggest that, for that election, Señor Gabriel Lopez Martinez' – he named the doyen of the Vice-Presidents, a nonagenarian Chilean novelist whose sole, fallacious claim to eminence was that, in the Paris of the 'Twenties, he had simul-taneously been the lover of Cocteau and Colette – 'should take the chair for us. Agreed? Agreed?'

Laura, standing behind and above him, stared down at the upraised faces. 'Yes, that's agreed, Amos,' she said, although no one had voiced agreement. At that, at first sporadic and then gathering in volume, clapping broke out. Laura put out an arm and hugged Amos to her. Into his ear she whispered, 'You've done it again.'

Released from the air-conditioned hall in which they had been incarcerated for almost four hours, the dele-gates dispersed, some to go shopping, some to take siestas and some to concoct the fiercely peremptory resolutions (eventually to be forwarded to heads of states who rarely, if ever, read them, much less acted on them) which each such Congress spawned in such abundance. Laura and Amos settled down to writing postcards to their numerous relations. Some of the postcards, depicting the swimming-pool, the gardens or the restaurants of the hotel, had come from a folder on the desk of their sitting-room. Other, similar ones

Laura had filched from a trolley abandoned outside the suite that morning by their Filipino cleaning woman.

Having already discovered that their Japanese hosts were paying only for their bed and breakfast and uncertain whether the English Centre of WAA would reimburse them for their other meals, Laura and Amos debated whether to take the hotel bus – it was, after all, free – into what they had heard the American delegates call 'the downtown area', or whether to order the cheapest dish on the room-service menu and then to supplement it with the fruit, so waxen as to look unreal, which, on their arrival, they had found in a basket to which was attached an envelope containing a card of 'friendliest greetings and the wish that you will have a truly joyful stay, From Mr Fukushima Kazuo (manager).' The cheapest dish seemed to be *sushi*.

'What on earth do you suppose that is?' Laura asked.

'Search me.'

'I do wish you were a more *sophisticated* traveller.'

'I might wish the same of you.'

A waiter, even more diminutive than the bellboy who had shown them up to the room, arrived with two red-and-black lacquered trays on which the *sushi* had been laid out with elaborate artistry.

'It *looks* stunning,' Laura said, as the boy put down one of the trays and then the other. 'Like a still-life by some Dutch Old Master.'

'The question, of course, is whether one would want to *eat* a still-life by a Dutch Old Master.'

The waiter was hovering around them, fidgeting now with the chopsticks and now with the paper napkins, printed with a design of bamboos, which he had set down before them. 'Iptay,' Laura hissed in what she regarded, often mistakenly, as their secret language.

'Iptay? Owhay uchmay?'

'Ootay undredhay.'

'Gosh, that's far too much!'

'Ootay undredhay.'

Amos produced ootay undredhay in crumpled notes of small denomination from his trouser pocket. Impassively the waiter accepted them, murmuring 'Thank you, sir.'

'I honestly don't think one is expected to tip.'

'I honestly think one is.'

Using not the chopsticks but his fingers, Amos popped a piece of the *sushi* into his mouth. 'Um.'

'Um.' Laura had popped a piece into hers.

'I'm sure that this ought to be hot, not cold.'

'Perhaps we should ring to have it microwaved.'

'It would mean another iptay.'

'Would it? Then better not.'

The *sushi* had the unexpected effect on Amos of making him feel, as he put it, 'horny'. It did not have the same effect on Laura, who really wanted to get on with washing out some smalls. But eventually she gave into him and they retreated into the bedroom.

'Darling, you do smell awfully strongly of fish.'

'Well, so do you.' Amos sucked, a contented child, on one of her nipples. 'You *are* beautiful,' he mumbled.

'Nice of you to say so. I wish I could say the same for you. But you have character. And that's just as appealing to a woman.'

As Amos went on nuzzling at her nipple, Laura began to think of the teacher of classics at Eton, who had proved to be such an unsatisfactory lover. Having nuzzled at a nipple precisely as Amos was doing now, he had raised his head to subject her whole body to a careful scrutiny. Then he had pronounced: 'The Ancient Greeks would have hated you, you know.'

'No, I don't know. What do you mean?'

'μηδὲν ἄγαν.'

'What's that?' It sounded unpleasant.

'"Nothing in excess." Oh, I do wish you weren't quite so uneducated. If only your parents had sent you to Roedean or Cheltenham Ladies' College instead of to that progressive school.' Again he surveyed her body.

'You see, there's just too bloody much of you. It's magnificent, I grant you. But, well, it all has the effect of one of those outsize, polychrome hybrids in a municipal rose garden.'

'Thanks a lot.' That was the moment when she realized that he was never going to do for her.

It was as Amos, burping sea-bass from the *sushi*, was about to climb on top of her ample body, that the telephone rang out.

'Don't answer it.'

But Laura could never leave a telephone unanswered, any more than she could leave a letter – even one addressed to Amos – unopened.

'Yes? . . . Yes . . . It's for you, darling.'

Amos recognized the voice, resonant and with a strong American accent, as belonging to one of the Taiwanese delegates, who taught Chinese at some women's college of which no one had ever heard, in a Middle West town of which no one had ever heard either. The Taiwanese and the Japanese delegations had something urgent to discuss with Amos. No, it was not something that could be discussed over the telephone. He and a representative of the Japanese delegation would like to come up. Or, of course, Amos-san could come down.

'Oh . . . er . . . well, come up then . . . But in about ten minutes.' Amos put down the telephone. 'Hell!'

Secretly Laura was thinking 'Thank God!' She could now get on with washing out those smalls.

The Taiwanese delegate, who was surprisingly large, loud-voiced and expansive for a Chinese, entered the room first, followed by a young Japanese woman, in an elaborately patterned kimono, whom, glimpsed across the assembly room, Amos had already decided to be, as he would put it, 'BW' (bed-worthy). The Taiwanese was Mr Tong and the Japanese woman Miss Shimada.

'Your lady wife is not with you?' Mr Tong enquired.

'She's washing out her smalls. In there.'

21

'Smalls?' Clearly Miss Shimada had never heard the word before. Amos found himself speculating about what kind of smalls Miss Shimada might be wearing under that elaborately patterned silk kimono, with its embroidered dragon writhing over one of her dainty thighs.

'Can I offer you anything?' Amos crossed over to the minibar. Had he then known that the 'drinkies' were not courtesy the management, he might not have done so.

Mr Tong opted for bourbon on ice, obliging Amos to go into the bathroom in order to get the ice out of its tray by running warm water over it.

'What's it all about?' Laura hissed.

'No idea. Come and join us.'

'In a mo.'

But Amos rather hoped that she wouldn't join them. He wanted to have Miss Shimada to himself – or, at least, to himself and Mr Tong.

'Lovely suite,' Mr Tong said, after he had raised his glass first to Amos and then to Miss Shimada, who had opted for 7-Up. 'VIP suite. As befits a writer of your distinction. I have only one room. But I am well satisfied.' He did not sound as if he were.

'We're delighted with it. In fact, it's the first time that my wife and I have ever had a suite at our disposal. Or indeed have stayed in a hotel of this class.'

Mr Tong threw back his head and laughed, and Miss Shimada raised a hand to her mouth and tittered behind it. Clearly they thought that Amos must be joking.

Mr Tong turned to Miss Shimada. 'Do you wish me to speak or do you wish to speak yourself, Miss Shimada?'

'You.' The monosyllable, delivered as the faintest of squeaks, affected Amos as though he had been brushed momentarily with the petal of a camellia.

'Very well. But this idea originates with Miss Shimada. She's a great fan of your work. She thinks a hell of a lot of it.'

Amos looked across at Miss Shimada, who nodded her head vigorously. 'Great fan. Yes.'

Amos wondered which of his books she had read. Perhaps she had read all of them, including the privately printed volume of undergraduate poetry and the history of a grocery chain which had gone into liquidation almost as soon as the book had been published. That was what a true fan would have done.

'Tomorrow we must have our election. Frankly, my delegation is not sold on the – er – present or, rather, recent holder of the office. He tends to lose his cool – as he did today – and, in any case, whatever his fame in France, who's ever heard of him anywhere else? He's just not Nobel Prize material.'

Amos nodded, while peering obliquely at Miss Shimada's ankles below the hemline of her kimono.

'I'll come directly to the point. That's something I've learned to do in the States. Right?'

'Right.'

'We wish you to stand.'

'*Me*?'

Her head tilted to one side, Miss Shimada was smiling at him, her eyes glistening with what he hoped was admiration not merely for his books but also for his person.

'Yes, you. Why not?'

'Yes, why not?' Laura had appeared, a bundle of what must have been the largest smalls in Japan dripping from a hand.

Amos made the introductions.

'I'll have to hang these by that air-conditioning duct over there. The bathroom has a hair-dryer, a telephone and a bidet but it has nowhere to hang one's washing. Perhaps I'm the first person ever to have washed clothes in this suite.'

The smalls, suspended from two coat-hangers attached to the air-conditioning duct, began to drip on to the parquet floor.

'Darling – don't you think it might be a good idea to put a towel or something underneath that lot?'

'Later.' Laura seated herself, crossing one shapely leg high over the other, in a chair opposite to Mr Tong's. She leaned towards him. 'My husband's always far too modest. And diffident. Of course he must accept.'

'Well, I'm glad we're in agreement on that.' Mr Tong was sucking on a cube of ice which he had fished out of his glass with forefinger and thumb. It made his face look as though he were suffering from a toothache. 'As I see it, International Presidents of WAA usually fall into one of two categories. On the one hand are the first-rate writers, known all over the world, Nobel Prize material. On the other hand, there are the people who are well versed in the arts of diplomacy, of administration, of chairing a committee. The unique advantage of your husband – what would make him the ideal choice for the job – is that he combines both of these attributes. I can't say that I've read any of his books myself, since his – er – field of – er – operation is so far removed from my own. But Miss Shimada tells me . . .'

Once more, eyes glistening and head tilted to one side, Miss Shimada was smiling at Amos. Then she gave a little nod. 'Amos-san – you must stand for the Presidency. You can win. I know that you can win.'

'Of course you can win, Amos,' Laura said. It was not an opinion but a command. 'You can have it, if you're prepared to put out your hands for it.'

'Well . . .'

'You don't owe this only to yourself, you owe it to WAA.' Mr Tong spat the cube of ice back into his glass. 'I've been making my soundings. As your wife says, if you just put out your hands for it . . .'

Amos extended his hands before him, as if he were indeed now about to assume the proffered crown. He flexed the fingers vigorously. He looked at Laura, who gave him a nod. He looked at Miss Shimada, who gave him another nod. It was Miss Shimada's nod which

24

decided him. 'All right! Why not? Yes, all right. Let's give it a whirl.'

'A *whirl*, Amos-san?'

'A try,' Laura said.

Soon after that Mr Tong got up to go. With obvious reluctance, Miss Shimada also got up, her eyes fixed on Amos.

'I am so happy to meet you. My favourite author. I must congratulate, Amos-san.' She gave him a deep farewell bow, small hands on knees which he was sure must be dimpled, and murmured a single word as she did so. What was it? Book? Bookie? Bookman?

Mr Tong punched the air. 'We're going to go right out there tomorrow and win you that Presidency.'

'Well. Er. Yes. Thanks.'

Miss Shimada had clicked open her bag and was taking something out. Her card. 'Please.' She handed it to Amos.

'I wish I could give you mine. But, in the rush of packing, I forgot to bring any,' Amos lied, as he had already done to others. In fact, he had no cards.

He was sure that Miss Shimada's card would smell of the same fragrance, piquant and lemony, which emanated from her exquisite person.

When Miss Shimada and Mr Tong had gone, Amos examined the card. '*Shimada Keiko*,' it read, and then, underneath her name, '*Poet and playwright*'. Laura was now peering over his shoulder. He could hear the water still dripping off the smalls on to the parquet.

He was puzzled. 'I thought that Mr Tong introduced her as Miss Shimada. But here her surname seems to be Keiko.'

'Don't be silly! Japanese put the surname first, the given name second.'

Suddenly Amos Kingsley realized who it was that Miss Shimada imagined him to be. That word which she had said when bowing to him, small hands on, yes, they *must* be dimpled knees, could only have been 'Booker'.

'Wasn't that marvellous?'

'Marvellous!'

Laura was laughing so vigorously that some fat off the piece of chicken she had just raised to her mouth splashed on to the front of her blouse. Naylor was also laughing, mouth open so that Amos could see a large pea and some half-masticated potato on his tongue. Then Naylor began to choke. 'Oh, Christ!' He gulped at some water. 'Now see what you've done to me.'

Amos glared at Laura. However often she told the story, she always succumbed to this idiotic laughing.

'Don't look so hurt, darling. You've made an absolutely first-rate President.' She turned to Naylor, who was still red in the face from his choking fit. 'Far better than Kingsley Amis would have done. He'd have been no good at all. No tact, no finesse, no patience. You've shown all those things.'

'But what . . . what . . .?' Naylor succumbed to another fit of wheezing laughter. 'What happened when everyone discovered?'

'Nothing,' Laura said. 'Precisely nothing. Miss Shimada would have lost face if she had revealed her mistake. And she would have also caused Amos to lose face. People who'd voted for him didn't wish to confess to their ignorance. And neither, for the matter of that, did people who hadn't voted for him.' She put a hand over Amos's. 'Anyway, darling, though you may not be nearly as famous and though your books sell far less copies, *I* think that you're every bit as good a writer as Kingsley Amis.'

Amos's scowl began to relax. But then Naylor had to go and spoil it all. 'When we heard about the Congress and that you were President of this WAA thing, we none of us could imagine how you'd come to be elected.

In fact, H.E. was sure that there'd been some mistake of some kind. Unless someone was trying to play a practical joke on us of course. Well, well, well! So, all because of that Japanese bird, here am I entertaining you both to lunch, when I might have been playing golf.' He turned round in his chair to bawl: 'Semba!'

'Yas*sir*!'

'Clear away the debris! We've finished! Double quick!'

# 2

Suffering from indigestion from Semba's half-cooked chicken and sweating in the damp afternoon heat, Amos and Laura eventually found the courtesy bus which would take them back to the hotel. 'I suppose I ought really to drive you back,' Naylor had said. 'But I had a pretty rough night with the Burns Society, and I'm desperate for a zizz.' The courtesy bus was crammed with people – foreign students, elderly peasant women, a middle-aged man with a white rat in a wicker cage – who were presumably only there because out of courtesy the driver did not evict them. Standing, Laura had to bend forward, a hand on Amos's shoulder, so that her head should not graze the roof. As, with a screaming of tyres, the bus swivelled round one hairpin bend after another, Amos began to feel queasy. This queasiness made him also feel bad-tempered.

'I wish you hadn't told that story yet again.'

'Which story?' During their time with Naylor, Laura had trotted out a number of her favourite stories, including the one about the former teacher of classics at Eton and the one about how she and Amos had come to get married.

'About my becoming International President of WAA.'

'I thought it would amuse him. As it did. As it amuses everyone.'

'It's so – humiliating.'

'I don't see why. After all, you've made a great success of the job.'

'You know that isn't true.'

'Of course it's true. Every International President has his enemies and you have yours. You may even have more than most of your predecessors. But you have a damned sight fewer than Kingsley Amis would have had.'

'Kingsley Amis would have been far too fly to have accepted the job in the first place.'

'You should be thanking your lucky stars that you ever got it. I'm certainly thanking mine. All this free travel. The best accommodation in the best hotels. Being someone who matters after years and years of not mattering at all. Any day now they'll give you an OBE.'

'Rubbish!'

'Well, an MBE then.'

'You've no idea of all the work involved.'

In fact, since Laura typed Amos's Presidential letters, she had a very good idea. But at that moment she was too much distracted by an elderly woman who was pushing her way past her to point this out. 'Would you mind! That's the second time you've trodden on my toes!'

'Quick! That man's getting out. Sit down there!'

But Laura was too late. A teenage boy had slipped into the seat of the man with the white rat. 'Clearly this isn't a courtesy but a *dis*courtesy bus,' Laura remarked sourly.

For a time Laura and Amos swayed against each other, her knees digging him in the thighs. Then dreamily she said: 'He's really rather attractive.'

Amos thought that she meant the teenage boy who had grabbed the seat. 'He looks as if he were mentally deficient,' he objected, although the boy's alacrity in forestalling Laura had provided no evidence for this.

'I don't mean *him*. I mean Bob Naylor.'

'Oh, you can't!'

'I certainly can. There's something very attractive about men who have hair sprouting out from the tops of their shirts.'

Amos, who had always been conscious that even his pubic hair was scanty, felt even more bad-tempered than previously. 'He's such a bore – and so *crude*.'

'Not at all. Neither of those things. In fact, I thought him, well, fascinating.'

Amos now began to fear the worst. Was Laura about to embark on another of her temporary fugues from reality and their marriage?

'I wonder if he'll give us a ring as he said he would.'

'If not, no doubt you'll give him one.'

'Oh, I do believe you're jealous! You're jealous, darling!'

'Easeplay! Anyone ancay earhay ouyay on isthay usbay!'

'Allsbay!'


Because of the fear that terrorists from across the border might make some attempt to disrupt the Congress, there was the strictest security at the entrance to the hotel. Invariably Amos had no trouble at all, even when the coins and keys in his pockets set off the metal detector. But no less invariably Laura became an object of suspicion.

On this occasion, as soon as she and Amos had followed the perennial American delegate, Frank O'Shaughnessy, in his Stuart tartan trousers, through the metal detector, she was at once beckoned to one side by a stocky little woman security guard, who first turned out the contents of her bag, revealing another Cartier and another two Rolex watches (for whom were *they* intended? Amos wondered darkly), and then slapped her briskly all over as though dusting down a sofa.

'Why do they always pick on me?'

'I've a theory about that.' O'Shaughnessy had turned round.

'Yes?'

'You're big even for a Western woman. No Eastern woman can ever have been your size. So I guess that they must suspect you of being a man. In drag, of course.'

'They must be the first people who've ever suspected that.'

'I hope my observation hasn't caused any offence?'

'No. Oh, no.' But as the American moved off, whistling 'Tea for Two' under his breath, Laura exploded: 'Ghastly poof!'

'Oh, I hardly think . . . He has that huge moustache. And he's constantly chatting up the waitresses. And his best-known novel is called *Wet Dreams* and it's all about call-girls and massage-parlours and – '

'All those things prove it.'

A tiny Malindian, whose face suggested a dart both in its long, pointed nose and in its intentness of purpose, stood on tiptoe in order to touch Amos on the shoulder. 'Excuse me, Mr Amos, sir.'

'Yes?'

'May I please speak to you, sir?'

'Well – er – I'm afraid it's not very convenient just now. I have something extremely important to do.' In fact, all that Amos had to do was to take some Alka-Seltzer or BiSoDol in an attempt to get rid of the heartburn created by Semba's ill-cooked and ill-digested chicken.

'But this is very important, sir. I shall keep you only a moment.'

'Well, what is it?'

'In private please, sir. Maybe we can go up to your suite? 727,' he added, having clearly done his homework at reception.

'Oh, all right! Come along then,' Laura said. She was

constantly telling Amos that an International President of WAA must always be accessible to the rank and file.

In the lift Amos said: 'You speak good English.' What he really meant was that the little man spoke better English than most of the Malindians whom they had so far met.

'I am a ship's officer, sir. Second engineer. I have travelled to England. Liverpool, Southampton, Bristol, Har-wich.'

'Harwich.' But the little man paid no attention to Laura's correction.

'Then you're not a writer?'

The little man gave a rueful shake of the head. 'Sorry. I regret.'

'I'm not a writer,' Laura said. 'But I don't regret. Far from it.'

'And you're not part of the Congress?'

'Sorry.' The little man drew a card out of the breast pocket of his orange aertex shirt and handed it to Amos. 'Nu,' he said. 'My name is Nu.'

After his election to the Presidency, Amos had at last had some cards printed. *'Mr Amos Kingsley,'* they read, *'President, International WAA'*. He always hoped that the home address in Tooting SW17 would not strike foreigners as unworthy of a holder of the office. One of these cards Amos now handed to Mr Nu, who first looked at it, as he scuttled after Amos and Laura down the corridor, and then placed it in the breast pocket of his shirt, along with his own cards. Might he not eventually give it in error to someone else, Amos wondered.

Once in the suite, Amos was so eager to get to the important business of the Alka-Seltzer or the BiSoDol that it was with unusual peremptoriness that he said to Mr Nu: 'Well, what exactly was it that you wanted?'

'You are an important man, Mr Amos. I think that you can help me.'

'Can I?'

'Sure. May I sit?'

'Please.'

All three of them sat, Mr Nu with his feet dangling about six inches from the floor. Beside Laura he looked like a child.

'I think that a man in your position meets many queens, Mr Amos?'

Amos was taken aback. What confession would now follow? 'Well . . . yes. I suppose that in WAA we have our fair – or some might perhaps say unfair – share of queens.' (Could Laura have been right about O'Shaughnessy?) 'The literary temperament perhaps? Yes, certainly.'

Mr Nu frowned in puzzlement. 'In WAA?' Then he slipped off the chair and hurried over to the window. Standing with his back to it, he faced them, hands clasped before him. 'Please, Mr Amos, listen. Mrs Amos.'

Amos and Laura listened.

Mr Nu began to recite: 'We shall not flag or fail. We shall fight in France, we shall fight on the seas and oceans, we shall fight with growing confidence and strength . . .'

If Mr Nu had been an Englishman, no one would have thought the imitation, of a kind that might have been given over a dinner-table, in any way remarkable. But coming from a Malindian, it astonished both Amos and Laura. There was the right kind of gruffness, there was the right kind of sibilance. Mr Nu's face even seemed to transform itself into Churchill's, the sharpness of its features dissolving, the jaws strengthening, the brows beetling, the flesh sagging beneath the chin.

Having concluded, Mr Nu added in his own light, slightly nasal voice: 'House of Commons. June 4th 1940. You like?'

Laura began to clap. 'Yes, I like. Jolly good. Is that your usual party piece?'

'Please?'

'Oh, never mind. The important thing is, I like, I like. We both like. Don't we, darling?'

Amos nodded. When he had accepted the Presidency of WAA, he had never supposed that his duties would include hearing a Malindian naval officer give an imitation of Churchill in a suite of the most expensive hotel in Batu.

Mr Nu stepped forward, as decisively as if he were stepping out of his adopted persona. 'Mr Amos, sir, now you must help me. I have dream. You must help me to make dream true.'

'What is this dream?' It was Laura and not Amos who put the question.

'I can speak all the famous speeches of Sir Churchill. I have studied from books, from records, from tapes. Many years, so many years. Now I have my dream. I wish to visit Buckingham Palace and speak these speeches for your Queen.' As he came out with this last sentence, he beamed in triumph – a conjurer whisking a rabbit out of a hat – first at Laura and then at Amos.

'For our Queen?'

Mr Nu nodded. 'Right, sir. For Her Majesty Queen Elizabeth II. Soon my ship will again go to England. I will travel to London – no problem. But I wish you to arrange for me to see Her Majesty.'

'*Me*?' Amos squeaked, as though he were himself that rabbit just whisked out of the hat.

'As head of international organization like WAA, you must know Her Majesty. I think so. You will help me? You will tell Her Majesty of me? You will arrange appointment?'

'But I've never met the Queen.' Nor would he, Amos thought, unless Laura's hopes for that OBE – or at least MBE – were ever to be realized.

'But I cannot believe – '

'We just don't move in that sort of set,' Laura said. 'Never have done.'

'Mr Amos, sir, why do you not wish to help me? Is it because I am not writer?'

'That has nothing to do with it. If I did know the Queen, then I'd be only too happy . . .' But would he really be only too happy to inflict on anyone, let alone the Queen, a Malindian imitation of Winston Churchill? Unlike Laura, Amos always had difficulty in telling a lie. Having started to tell this one, he broke off and felt the blood mounting first to his cheeks and then to his forehead.

'When I saw your picture in the paper, I thought, "Mr Amos will help me." But now – big, big disappointment.' Head hanging and knees close together, Mr Nu looked like a small boy on the verge of tears.

'I wish I *could* help you.'

'I thought you to be sincere man,' Mr Nu murmured in obvious reproach.

'My husband *is* a sincere man. No one has ever – or could ever – call him insincere. But, like everyone else, he can only operate within the parameters of what is possible to him in any given situation.' Laura was now quoting from a speech which she had recently helped Amos compose on cooperation with the Soviet Union, so far unrepresented in WAA.

'Please see what you can do, Mr Amos. Please, sir!'

Even more eager to get to the Alka-Seltzer or BiSoDol, Amos conceded dubiously: 'Well, I'll *see*, yes. But I really cannot make any promises.'

Mr Nu's face was illuminated by a sudden joy. 'You will see!'

'My husband and I will see.'

'You have my card?'

'My husband and I have your card.'

'You will be in touch?'

'My husband and I will be in touch. Now my husband and I would like to take a little siesta.'

Clearly Mr Nu did not realize that, in speaking these sentences, Laura was unconsciously imitating the monarch with whom he so much wanted an audience.

# 3

>:> <:<

As a precaution, even though, the school holidays not yet over, it had meant dumping the Sealyhams on Laura's mother for more than a severely stipulated week, Amos had insisted that the two of them must arrive in Batu at least four days before the Congress started. One had to see the lie of the land, he had explained. One had to make sure that all the arrangements were in order. One had, above all, to decide what action to take about the three writers still languishing in prison despite numerous attempts by WAA to secure their release.

Many Centres, notably the Scandinavian, had criticized the holding of a WAA Congress in a country in which writers, if not sufficiently circumspect, could still be banned or gaoled. But Amos had taken the line, although far from sure if in fact it was the right one, that if the Congress were to be held, then the Malindians would, as he put it, 'clean up their act' by freeing the writers. So far the writers had not been freed. If they were not freed, then Amos was likely to incur even more odium than he had done by repeatedly insisting that the Congress should take place. Odium was something which Amos wore with as much pleasure as a renegade monk a hair-shirt.

Amos cared about the prisoners. He also sometimes shared Laura's suspicion that the Scandinavians and their allies cared about them only in order to get at him for having, as they now saw it, tricked his way into the

Presidency. Often he would confide in people that he was 'absolutely no use at the literary chat side of WAA'; but he did like to think that he was good at its task of battling against censorship and securing the release of writers. *'On behalf of International WAA I am writing to protest in the strongest possible terms . . .'* 'Yes, yes, I know what you want to say,' Laura would tell him wearily as, with two forefingers, she jabbed at the keys of an ancient typewriter. Sometimes she would add: 'If you'd only agree to having a word-processor, I shouldn't have to type the same letter over and over again for you.' One of the problems of WAA was that, although many individual Centres were rich, the International office survived on what Amos, with his knack of hitting on a cliché, called 'the proverbial shoestring'.

Because of the generosity of the Malindian Centre, Amos and Laura had travelled out first class. Unable to resist either the ceaseless offers of champagne or one lavish meal after another at times when they would normally have been asleep, they had both been in such a bemused condition on their arrival in Batu that, as they had staggered down the gangway, they had been unaware that, at the bottom, a girl in Malindian Airlines uniform was chanting Amos's name. Beside her stood three men in elegant dark silk suits and white shirts.

As Amos tottered and almost fell on the last step of the gangway, one of the men stepped forward and grabbed his arm. 'Mr Kingsley! I am the President of the Malindian Centre. Mr Tu. We have corresponded. My card, please.' He held it out.

'Oh, how nice! How very nice – and how very unexpected – of you to have come to meet us. This is my wife, Laura.' Amos was frantically searching in his wallet for a card of his own. Blast! They must all be in his briefcase.

Laura's bottle of duty-free Scotch would have shattered if Mr Tu had not caught it as it slipped from her shaky grasp.

'You had a good journey?' Mr Tu asked after he had introduced both his colleagues, and they had also presented Amos with their cards.

'Yes, a good one. But a long one.'

'A very, very long one,' Laura corroborated.

'Please give me your baggage check. And your passports. Mr Mu will see to all procedures for you. You must hurry to the press conference. Unfortunately, your plane has been late.'

Photographs in the press the next day would show Amos looking as though he himself had just been released from prison. Tufts of his sparse hair stood on end, there were bruise-like shadows under each of his eyes, his collar was soiled and creased, and the small, tight knot of his tie rested on his diaphragm. Laura herself looked as if she had just been released, beyond all redemption, from a centre for alcoholic vagrants.

The first question, delivered by an attractive Malindian girl, had been flattering: Was Mr Amos about to publish another of the books which had given so much pleasure to so many people in all parts of the world? Amos replied that, yes, in seven weeks' time his publishers would be bringing out, to catch the Christmas trade, an anthology – he hoped an entertaining anthology – entitled *Let Dogs Delight*. No, no, he replied hurriedly to a second question from another, no less attractive Malindian girl, the anthology had nothing to do with dogs in the, er, kitchen, absolutely nothing at all.

The third question, from an elderly Malindian man, had been merely foolish: What did Amos think of Malindi? 'Well, it's a little premature to venture an answer to that. But I'm sure, from everything that I've read and been told, that I'm going to enjoy my visit very much indeed.' Despite the fierce air-conditioning, he could feel the sweat breaking out on his forehead and his palms. The lights for the television cameras not merely made him feel headachy and nauseated, but also obliged him constantly to shield his eyes to identify his interrogators. Laura's own eyes were shut. Could she – horrors! – have fallen asleep? Yes, clearly she had.

'Mr Kingsley.' The American voice, rasping in its scarcely disguised hostility, might have emanated from some District Attorney in an American television drama. 'I have a question.' Again Amos raised a hand to his eyes, to make out a young Caucasian in a seersucker jacket and open-necked shirt, his long legs stretched out ahead of him, his hands deep in his trouser pockets and his head tilted backwards.

'Yes.'

'Am I right in thinking that there are three Malindian writers at present in prison?'

'That is correct. At least we think that that is correct from the information available to us.'

From Laura beside Amos there came a muffled snore.

'But you thought that, despite this, it was right to hold a Congress in this country?'

Suddenly Amos had an image of a darkened room, a glass with Alka-Seltzer fizzing in it, a bed with clean, cool sheets. But he put the image from him, at the same time tightening his grip on the overstuffed briefcase which he had laid across his knees. Invariably there was never any room for his spare pyjamas in his suitcase, already crammed with an overflow from Laura's.

'In deciding to come here – by a democratic vote of our assembly of delegates, I must add – we had to consider what action was most likely to secure the release of those prisoners. Had we decided not to come, we should have made a fine moral gesture, for which no doubt we should have received publicity all over the world. But would the prisoners have been released? Somehow I doubt it. It seemed to me that by coming here we stood a much better chance of achieving our objective.'

'But here you are, Mr Kingsley, and the writers are still in prison. Am I right?'

'Yes, regrettably, they are still in prison.' Amos drew one foot backwards and sideways and gave Laura a sharp kick on the ankle. The snoring was interrupted by a hiccough. Then she jerked herself upright.

'Now that you *are* here, Mr Kingsley, what steps are you proposing to take to secure the release of these men?'

'That is something which I shall be discussing with my colleagues of the Malindian Centre – Mr, er, Tu' – Amos looked over in Mr Tu's direction, to receive a nod and a smile – 'and, er, the other officers of that Centre.'

'You really feel that the Malindian Centre is exerting itself in this matter?'

'Most certainly. Yes. Yes, I do. Their task is by no means easy, of course. But yes, I have the fullest confidence in their, er, efforts both to date and in the future.' The sweat was trickling down Amos's backbone. Now he had another tantalizing image: of the nozzle of a shower, his face upturned to it as its icy needles descended.

'You know of course that many Malindian writers do not belong to the Centre?'

'The freedom not to join an organization is as important as the freedom to join it. Neither of those freedoms exists in many of the countries behind the Iron Curtain.'

At that Mr Tu nodded and smiled. So did his two colleagues. So did many of the Malindian journalists.

But one of these Malindian journalists, a middle-aged woman with an untidy sweep of hair across a broad, lined forehead, now raised her hand.

'Yes?'

'Mr Amos – people say that you are a right-wing writer. Correct, please?'

In putting this question, did she know who he was or did she imagine him to be Kingsley Amis? 'As

40

President of WAA, I try to be above all politics. WAA is not a political organization. It is totally apolitical.'

'But you have personal convictions, Mr Amos?'

'If I have personal convictions, I keep them out of my work for WAA.'

Suddenly Laura tottered to her feet, stooped and picked up her duty-free bag. 'Well, for the moment, I think that'll have to do. My husband needs some rest. Sorry, folks.'

Amos expected everyone to share his shock at her intervention. But there was good-natured laughter from most of the people present, and even a smile from Amos's previously scornful DA interrogator.

Laura looked at Amos. 'Astlygay. Erfectlypay astly-gay. Come!'


In the black, air-conditioned Mercedes, Mr Mu, the smallest and clearly least important of the officers of the Malindian Centre of WAA, sat beside the driver, while Mr Tu and Mr Chu, so like each other in their athletic good looks that they might have been brothers, perched on the tip-up seats opposite Amos and Laura.

'You handled that very well, Mr Kingsley,' Mr Tu told him.

'Very well,' Mr Chu corroborated. 'When I saw that American reporter, I guessed there would be trouble.'

'Maybe he is a Communist sympathizer,' Mr Tu said.

'Or maybe only stupid,' Mr Chu added.

'The Americans in the Far East are like children,' Mr Tu said. 'Not bad, but like children.'

It was a judgement that was to be expressed to Amos many times during his stay in Malindi.

Mr Chu leant forward, clasping his beautifully mani-cured hands – they made Amos dismally conscious of his own grubby finger-nails – almost in Amos's lap. 'We must discuss strategy as soon as is possible.'

'Strategy?'

'About the prisoners. I see big trouble ahead.'

'Big trouble?'

'Mrs Svenson.'

Margaretta Svenson, a Swedish novelist, always suggested to Amos, in both her compact, rotund figure and in her menacing resilience, an outsize rubber ball. As a small child, he had always been terrified of rubber balls after one, carelessly thrown by a woman for her dog, had hit him in the face by the Round Pond. Margaretta had frequently attacked him, with cheery contempt, for advocating that the Congress in Batu should go ahead despite the continuing detention of the three writers. She had also attacked him on other issues – notably for his inertia (as she saw it) in persuading the countries of Africa to open WAA Centres, and for his failure to ensure that existing Centres had more women on their executive committees. In vain did he bleat first that the African countries could not afford Centres and in many cases would not be allowed by their governments to have them even if they could afford them; and second that he could not really be expected to *force* Centres to elect women as committee members. Whenever Amos thus expostulated, Margaretta would merely gaze at him with mocking pity, shrug her shoulders as if to say, 'God, what can one do with him?', and then burst into derisive laughter.

'What exactly is Mrs Svenson up to?'

'Is there a *Mr* Svenson?' Not for the first time Laura put the question; and not for the first time no one could vouchsafe her an answer.

Mr Tu now leant forward, clasping his equally well-manicured hands almost in Laura's lap. 'Mrs Svenson will arrive on Friday. As you know, other delegates will arrive on Monday.'

'Why should she be arriving so early?'

'To make trouble, big trouble,' Mr Tu said.

'That woman never makes anything other than trouble, big trouble,' Laura said.

'Trouble? What kind of trouble?' The huge ball was bouncing towards Amos. At any moment it would strike him in the face, perhaps even knock him sprawling.

'About the prisoners,' Mr Chu took up. 'Already she has sent her American friend ahead of her. Mr O'Shaughnessy. You know Mr O'Shaughnessy?'

'We know Mr O'Shaughnessy,' Laura confirmed with a sigh.

'Mr O'Shaughnessy has already been getting in touch with certain anti-social elements in Malindi,' Mr Tu said. For anti-social read anti-government, Amos privately told himself. 'Such people claim that they are writers but they are really political journalists and agitators. Riff-raff. You know the sort, Mr Kingsley.'

Amos knew the sort, since about such people there was so often contention in WAA. Should they be accepted for membership or not? They were writers in the sense that they wrote and were even (if they escaped banning) published. But they were hardly writers in the sense that Margaretta Svenson, Frank O'Shaughnessy, Amos's French predecessor or Amos himself was a writer.

'Things in the East are done differently than in the West,' Mr Chu said.

Mr Tu nodded his head in vigorous agreement. 'There is the importance of face. You know about face, Mr Kingsley?'

Amos, who had again been thinking about that glass fizzing with Alka-Seltzer and that shower-nozzle, said: 'Yes, of course. Of course. If only one could persuade some other people of its importance.'

'In the East, if you want something, you do not walk up to the person from whom you want it and say in a loud voice, so that everyone can hear, "I must have this." That is not our custom.' Now Mr Chu shook his head in agreement with Mr Tu as vigorously as Mr Tu had previously nodded his. 'Instead, you must find a close friend of the person from whom you want something, you must go to that friend in private, you must speak to him so that no one else can hear. That way, often you get what you want.'

'But Mrs Svenson does not understand this,' Mr Chu said.

Laura was running a comb through her tangled blond hair. 'You can say that again! That woman has absolutely no idea that foreigners might just occasionally be different from Swedes.'

'Maybe you can persuade Mrs Svenson to change her attitude,' Mr Chu said.

'I doubt it,' Amos answered on a sigh.

'My husband has never persuaded Mrs Svenson of anything of which she did not wish to be persuaded.'

'Is Mrs Svenson a big writer?' Mr Tu asked.

'Do you mean in size? She's about as big as I am, kilo for kilo, but far more compact,' Laura answered. 'Or do you mean in talent? In that case unfortunately the answer must be that yes, she's also big. Nobel Prize material, as one of our colleagues from Taiwan would put it.'

'She'd just love to be President of WAA,' Amos said. 'The first woman President.'

'And that's the real reason why she always tries to make things as difficult as possible for my husband. She's jealous of him.'

'I wouldn't say that, darling.'

'Well, I would. It's obvious.'

They had now begun to enter the city. Amos gazed out of the window at the wide, winding river, with its green banks on either side. 'I'd never imagined that Batu would be so beautiful.'

'We are proud of our city,' Mr Tu said. 'Forty years ago it was only a large, muddy village.'

'Beautiful, beautiful,' Amos said, still looking out of the window.

'Now I must tell you of what we have achieved,' Mr Chu said. 'The President has agreed to see you in private.'

'*Me*?' Amos squeaked.

Mr Tu nodded. 'He will come to open the Congress. But that is not the proper occasion to talk to him. He will give a party for the delegates. But that is not the proper occasion to talk to him either. After these two occasions, he will receive you at the Palace.'

'Gosh! Golliwogs!'

The two Malindians looked at Laura in bewilderment.

'Amos – my husband – has met *loads* of mayors and ministers of culture and even one or two governors. But this will be the first time that he'll have actually met a *President*. He's never even met Mrs T., you know.'

'Mrs Thatcher,' Amos explained.

'When you meet the President, you must of course speak of the prisoners. But you must be very polite, Mr Kingsley.'

'Mr Kingsley is always very polite,' Mr Chu said. 'Always very polite, always very diplomatic. Real English gentleman.'

'You will tell the President, Mr Kingsley,' Mr Tu went on, 'of the concern of all the members of WAA for the prisoners. You will tell him that the whole world is watching Malindi as it moves towards becoming a true democracy. You will tell him that three writers in prison is bad, very bad for the image of Malindi.'

'Yes, I think I've got all that.'

'We are hopeful of the outcome,' Mr Chu said.

'Very hopeful,' Mr Tu confirmed. 'We have a great trust in you, Mr Kingsley.'

'We have great trust in the power of English diplomacy.'

There was a silence, as everyone pondered on the fateful meeting ahead.

Then Mr Tu sighed and said: 'Already we have the trouble of many expenses with Mrs Svenson.'

'Is she very poor?' Mr Chu asked.

'Poor! She's certainly not poor,' Laura answered, remembering a mink coat carelessly thrown over the back of a chair, so that part of it trailed in the dust of the pavement outside a Via Veneto café.

'Why do you ask?'

'Well, Mr Kingsley, as you know we must pay her fare. From Stockholm to Batu. That is our obligation. We accept that. So we send her economy class ticket. She then writes to say that she expects first-class ticket, she always travels first-class. So we send her business-class ticket. Then she sends us a fax that she wishes to bring her daughter and will require not one but two tickets. So we send her business-class ticket for her daughter.'

'Well, I suppose you did right,' said Amos, supposing nothing of the kind.

'I imagine she couldn't get anyone to look after the brat,' Laura said, thinking of the Sealyhams. 'Perhaps there's no Mr Svenson. And no grandparents either.'

'She could well afford to pay for her daughter's ticket,' Amos said. 'Or she could hire a nurse. But we don't want to give her yet another grievance or make her even more difficult to handle.'

'We think that, if we agree to pay for all these things, maybe Mrs Svenson will be more cooperative,' Mr Tu confessed.

'Obligation is very important in the East,' Mr Chu said. 'One obligation creates another, reciprocal obligation.'

'I doubt if an obligation will do anything of the kind for Margaretta Svenson,' Amos said gloomily.

He could hear that rubber ball bouncing nearer and nearer to him.

# 4

>:> <:<

That first night in Batu was one of nightmares for
Amos, as though in prefiguration of all the nightmares
to be suffered in the days ahead.

'You never know how to say no,' Laura told him
when, at long last, they had reached their hotel suite
after an interminable meal in a private room of what
their hosts of the Malindian WAA Centre had been at
pains to tell them was the most exclusive and expensive
restaurant in Batu.

'What do you mean that *I* don't know how to say no?
I didn't see you saying no whenever a bottle went
round.'

'You should have said no to an evening out, in the
first place. Then you should have said no to that awful
*botni* stuff. And then you should have said no to drinks
afterwards.'

'As President of WAA, I have to do my duty.'

'Well, your immediate duty now is to swallow this.'

'What is it?'

'Vitamin B. And after that's gone down, I'm going to
mix you some Alka-Seltzer.'

As he waited for the Alka-Seltzer to stop fizzing,
Amos asked: 'What do you suppose goes into that
awful *botni*?'

'Mr Nu – or was it Mu? – told me. It's absolutely
gruesome. Beetroot. Chillis. Garlic. Then it's all put in
a huge urn and buried for months and months on end.
So that it can really ferment.'

'Oh, no! No!'

'And you told them how much you liked it.'

'I always tell foreigners how much I like their national dish.'

'You're so insincere!'

Laura herself, as always, slept deeply, only stirring from time to time to emit a loud fart. Clearly it was she who ought to have said no to the *botni*. Amos now tossed, turned and groaned, and now started up, heart beating, mouth gaping and eyes wide.

The nightmares were sometimes of the Sealyhams, to which, in moments of annoyance with both Laura and them, he would refer as 'those beastly dogs of yours'. In these dreams he would be chasing, increasingly breathless and with a stitch in his side, after the Sealyhams across Tooting Common; or one of them, suddenly afflicted with elephantiasis, would be lowering over him, a canine King Kong; or he would be walking them past Tooting Bec Station and there, precisely in the entrance crowded with commuters, each would squat and, after repeated straining, would deposit a gigantic turd.

The nightmares were sometimes of Margaretta Svenson. He would be seated up on the platform flanked by the Vice-Presidents of WAA, most of them dozing, and she would be standing in the auditorium below, rapping out at him a succession of questions – how many writers were now in prison in South Korea? had Amos written a letter of protest to the President of the Soviet Union of Writers? under which subhead of the accounts was she to find the figures for his expenses? – to which he was totally unable to give answers. Or she would be swaying along ahead of him in tightly tailored trousers, O'Shaughnessy beside her, when inadvertently Amos would tread on the mink coat trailing from her plump, bejewelled hand, splitting it up a seam. Or, worst of all, he was tied up to some railings and she, hugging a large rubber ball, was standing before him, prepared to use him as her Aunt Sally. 'Did you really think it a good idea to hold a Congress in Batu?' she would demand, beginning to bounce the ball with increasing rapidity before her. And then, even more menacingly: 'Did you really think it a good idea to get yourself elected as President under the pretence of being Kingsley Amis?'

But worse than any of these nightmares was the nightmare of what he and Laura had come to call *l'affaire Fluck*. At one moment, indeed, he had started up gasping, 'Fluck! Fluck! Fluck!' so loudly that Laura, whom usually it was impossible to rouse from her sleep, had also started up, a trembling hand to her forehead as the room reeled about her, and had then told him, 'Fuck Fluck! I want to sleep, for God's sake.'

Amos often had nightmares of *l'affaire Fluck*, just as he imagined that Zola must often have had nightmares of *l'affaire Dreyfus*. Like Zola from *l'affaire Dreyfus*, so he from *l'affaire Fluck* had learned the full extent of human intolerance, vengefulness and malevolence. And it had all really been the fault of those bloody Sealyham bitches – although Laura would never acknowledge that, preferring to blame the overdue proofs of *Let Dogs Delight* ('As if any dog ever delighted you,' she would say. 'You're the quintessential pussy man.').

The proofs, the two Sealyhams' litters and the letter from Fluck's schoolmaster son had, by a singular mischance, all arrived on the same day. After four months spent in deciding whether after all to go ahead with the anthology commissioned by someone already sacked from the firm, Amos's publishers now insisted on having the proofs back by the end of the week if they were to hold out any hope of achieving publication before Christmas. The litters of puppies – 'There must be a pill for bitches,' Amos had wailed, when hearing that both of them were pregnant – meant that Laura, acting as their midwife, kept issuing Amos with peremptory instructions about such tasks as the disposal of the afterbirths. It was, indeed, with one of the afterbirths in a tissue clasped in his hand, that Amos had confronted the postman with the registered letter from Hans Joachim Fluck. 'Just let me put this down somewhere,' he had stammered, before depositing it on the hall chair and then signing the receipt.

*'As you will know, my father, Moritz Fluck, was one of the greatest of German twentieth-century novelists, the peer of Hermann Hesse and Thomas Mann . . .'* Amos did not know. He also doubted if anyone else in England knew. ('Hands up those who have ever heard of Moritz Fluck,' he imagined himself rising to demand at one of the quarterly dinners of the English Centre of WAA. Not a single hand.) But then, of course, the English were notoriously provincial about cultural matters. Hans Joachim Fluck was preparing a *Festschrift* on the anniversary of his father's birth (he listed all the eminent scholars, not one of them known to Amos, who, from places as remote from each other as Buenos Aires and Tokyo, Toronto and Manila, Gothenburg and Harare, would be the contributors); and since his father had been a founder member of WAA, had been such a staunch internationalist, and had devoted so much of his life to fostering intellectual cooperation and exchange between writers around the world, he wondered if, as President of WAA, Amos would be prepared to contribute a few lines by way of preface. Unfortunately, if the *Festschift* was to appear before the centenary was over, it was essential that the preface should be received before the end of that month.

As so often in the case of such requests in the past, there was absolutely no mention of payment.

'The trouble with you is that you can never say no.' In this case at least, Laura had been right. Amos put aside the proofs. He ignored Laura's cries of, 'Oh, Amos, do come and help me clear up all this mess!' He took down his *Encyclopaedia of Modern Literature*. Fluck seemed to have been as versatile as Amos himself, producing not merely novels but volumes of poetry, biographies, travel books, memoirs, a work of philosophy and a history of the Seven Years War. Clearly he had also been far more successful at his profession than Amos: admittedly never having been elected to the International Presidency of WAA, but having won the Goethe Prize, the Schiller Prize and the Hölderlin Prize all within a single decade, the 'Thirties. From the account of Fluck's novels, with their 'creation of a world of magic and marvels', Amos formed an impression of a kind of Teutonic C. S. Lewis; and it was therefore this parallel that he imaginatively pursued when ('All right, all right, Laura! I'll ring the vet just as soon as I've got this bit of writing out of the way') he had stabbed out a rough draft of the preface on Laura's ancient typewriter (no use asking *her* to type it, those bloody dogs always came first).

As President of International WAA, [he began] I am happy to introduce this collection of essays in commemoration of the hundredth anniversary of the birth of Moritz Fluck, since the ideals for which WAA has always fought since its inception – internationalism, reconciliation between nations and people, freedom of speech and movement about the world – were ones which he shared so wholeheartedly, and since he played so important a role in the German Centre of WAA before the Nazi persecution of writers and burning of books resulted in its expulsion

In the loftiness of his spirit and the range of his genius, he had much in common with Goethe. But any English reader and admirer (and there are many) of his *oeuvre* must at once be struck with the uncanny parallels with C. S. Lewis, scholar, poet and creator of the haunting 'Narnia' stories . . .

When, finally free of her duties as midwife, Laura settled down to retyping the preface – 'Why, why, why does your little finger always hit an S when it ought to hit an A?' – she burst into scornful laughter. 'Oh, you really are a fibber! You know how much you've always loathed those "Narnia" stories. You used to try to persuade the children not to read them.'

'That was precisely why I settled for "haunting". The *mot juste*, my dear. I'm still haunted by the tedium of them.'

'I honestly cannot see why you have to fall in with each and every request of this nature.'

'Neither can I,' Amos sighed. But, at heart, he knew the answer. Vanity. It afforded him immense gratification that, after so many years as a little-known journeyman of letters, contributions of his, admittedly often unpaid, now appeared all over the world with the superscription or subscription that they were by 'Amos Kingsley, International President of WAA'.

'I must say that you've become awfully clever at bluffing your way. No one would guess from this that you'd never read a single word of this Fluck.'

'Nor do I ever want to. A Teutonic C. S. Lewis – can you think of anything less appealing?'

Some three months later the scandal broke.

From the West German Centre of WAA – with which he had been on uneasy terms ever since he had inadvertently mistaken their dinner-jacketed President for a waiter at a Congress in Bogotá – a letter arrived by express, registered mail. Since at the time of its delivery Amos was busy on an article about the Notting Hill Carnival for the Jamaica Airlines magazine, he threw it on one side, and it was therefore Laura who opened it.

'Oh, gosh! Oh, golliwogs!'

'What is it?'

'You've made the boob to end all boobs. Oh, Amos, I always had a feeling that that Fluck character was going to fuck you up! I felt it in my bones!'

Dear Mr Kingsley,
We trust that you will appreciate our request that you respond to a highly serious matter immediately on receipt of this letter.

On September 3, one of our most influential newspapers, the *Göttingener Allgemeine Zeitung* (commonly known as 'GAZ') reported in extremely unfavourable terms on a preface which you, in your capacity as International President of WAA, are alleged to have written for a *Festschrift* in commemoration of the centenary of the birth of Moritz Fluck.

There are no serious doubts among historians on the fatal role which Fluck played as a highly decorated propagandist of the Nazis. We are therefore both amazed and shocked that you could have written such a preface in his honour. It is essential that we should have your explanation as speedily as possible, so that we can communicate it to the readers of GAZ . . .

Amos felt that he was going to be sick. Nothing worse had happened since, seven weeks before, the smaller and tetchier of the two Sealyhams had bitten an elderly, female Jehovah's Witness on the calf and she had then threatened to sue.

'You'll just have to eat humble pie,' was Laura's advice. 'Make yourself less than the dust. Grovel. Germans like people to do that. Abject admission of ignorance about Fluck's career. Even more abject apology.'

Amos did as she advised. But before he could hear again from the Germans, he heard from Margaretta Svenson:

Dear Amos
I was profoundly shocked when I heard from Herr Gamringer of the West German Centre (he was writing to me about a wholly different matter) that

you had contributed a laudatory preface to a *Festschrift* for – of all people! – Moritz Fluck. I can only assume that it was out of that sweet unworldliness of yours that you were persuaded to do such a thing.

In spite of – or, rather, because of – my strong feelings of friendship for you and, of course, dear Laura, I must make it absolutely clear that in my eyes you have committed an appalling blunder, with no less appalling consequences for WAA. The *Dagens Nyheter's* correspondent in Bonn has already been on to me for my reaction. Of course I did all I could to minimize your action, but I'm afraid that WAA is in for a rough ride not merely in Germany and Sweden but all over the world.

To me, the only daughter of a newspaper proprietor who was always in the forefront of the struggle against the Nazis, Fluck is a writer whose very name makes my blood run cold. He was the most vulgar, opportunistic, anti-intellectual writer you could think of – a real monster.

I've absolutely no wish to join a witch-hunt and so to add my voice to what I fear will be an inevitable clamour for your resignation. I merely leave it to your own good judgement to decide how most effectively and most honourably to remedy and atone for what, I am sure you will agree, was a truly grievous error . . .

Amos's and Laura's reactions to this letter – and to others like it, from other Centres hostile to him – were totally different. Amos, who always accepted the simplest explanation for any event, was fully prepared to assume that Margaretta's letter said no more than it seemed to be saying. It was really rather decent of her to write in so friendly and sympathetic a manner. *Au fond* she was not a bad sort. One couldn't help liking and respecting her.

Laura, on the other hand, was one of those people

who always prefer an abstruse to a simple explanation. 'Balls! This is all part of a plot,' she protested. 'How do you suppose that a newspaper as important as that GAZ thingummy got hold of that miserable *Festschrift*? A print-run of a book like that is about one thousand, and the publisher counts himself lucky if he manages to sell five hundred. Don't be so naive, darling! It should be obvious to anyone! Your enemies have seen in that wretched preface a perfect opportunity to get you to resign. You just wait and see.'

Amos waited and saw. As so often, Laura was right. The Danes, the Dutch and the Americans joined the Swedes and the Germans in producing a resolution of censure of Amos, to come up at the Batu Congress.

Meanwhile Laura had failed to improve the situation by writing five letters on his behalf but without his knowledge. For years now she had been able to produce a passable version of his signature.

To the Germans she wrote:

. . . The implication of both your first letter and its predecessor [by now Amos had heard again from the Germans, in terms even more peremptory than before] can only be that I am some kind of neo-Nazi. I am prepared to be called a neo-Nazi, however unfairly, by your Dutch, Danish and even American colleagues, but not by you Germans. Let me remind you that Nazism, in all its incalculable evil, was a specifically German invention . . .

To Margaretta Svenson she wrote:

. . . The very name of Fluck may indeed make your blood cold. My own blood runs cold at childhood memories of the Nazi bombs which your country so adroitly managed to avoid – admittedly at some slight inconvenience to your neighbours . . .

To the Presidents of the American, Danish and Dutch Centres she wrote identical letters:

> In this extremely unfortunate matter some people have behaved better than I should have expected and some people have behaved worse. You have behaved exactly as I should have expected.

'Oh, Laura, you shouldn't, shouldn't, shouldn't have written like that!' Amos wailed when she showed him not the letters (she had already posted those) but the carbons.

'Why not? One has to stand up for oneself. That's always been the trouble with you. You take everything lying down.'

'Perhaps I *ought* to resign.'

'Certainly not! You'll resign when you've had enough of the job. You're not going to be forced into resigning – not by that crowd!'

'Oh, Laura!' Amos was torn between admiration for her pugnacity and strength, and fury that she could never, as he put it, *leave things alone*.

Now, on the morning after their arrival in Batu, mouth sour and head throbbing, Amos yet again repeated 'Perhaps I *ought* to resign.' Such was his stress that he then nicked himself for the second time with his razor.

Angrily, Laura yet again countered, as she had done so often in the past during his moods of self-doubt and despair: 'You'll resign when you've had enough of the job. You're not going to be forced into resigning – not by that crowd!'

'But I *have* had enough of the job! Don't you understand! Ouch!' Again he had nicked himself, so badly this time that blood had begun to trickle down his chin. 'I've lost all desire to be famous a moment longer. I want to be obscure. Oh, let me be obscure, Laura. Please! Please!'

'That's enough of that! Now pull yourself together.'

It was fortunate that Amos found himself somehow able to obey this command, since at that moment the telephone began to ring. It was Bob Naylor, with his invitation to luncheon.

Naylor began by explaining: 'I'm afraid that H.E.'s so busy with some bigwigs who arrived on the same plane as yours that he's deputed me to offer you some kind of official entertainment. On these occasions it's usually the poor old British Council which has to carry the can.'

As he replaced the receiver, Amos wished that he had had the pride and courage to refuse so ungracious a summons. Oh, he was feeble, feeble, feeble!

# 5

After their luncheon with Naylor and their encounter with Mr Nu, Amos and Laura threw themselves on their beds and at once plunged into a sleep so profound that he suffered not a single nightmare and she emitted not a single fart.

They awoke to an argument. Should they go out to the airport with the Malindians to meet Margaretta Svenson?

'You can't be planning to meet every delegate, can you? You've never done it before.'

'No. But it might be rather nice.'

'Nice for her, nice for you, or nice for both of you? It certainly won't be nice for me.'

'Nice for both of us.'

'You just want to placate her. But it won't work, it just won't work. You don't placate bullies by being nice to them. Why have you never learned that lesson?'

'She's not all bad.'

'I daresay one could have said the same about Lucrezia Borgia. Oh, well, if you're really set on going, I'll go with you. You're less likely to make a fool of yourself if I'm around.'

As they wandered about the airport – their three Malindian companions, not those who had met them the evening before but three less important members of the Centre, had opted to drink in the bar – Amos and Laura ran into Frank O'Shaughnessy. Now clad not in Stuart tartan trousers but in Stuart tartan Bermuda shorts, he was drinking out of a Coca Cola can, which he waved in the air as greeting as soon as he saw them.

'Hi, there!'

'Hi!' Amos returned.

'Are you meeting someone?' Laura asked, knowing perfectly well whom he was meeting.

'Yah.' He gulped from the can, leaving drops of Coca Cola to glisten along his drooping moustache. 'Margaretta Svenson.'

'Oh. We're also here to meet her.'

'Is that so?' For all the nonchalance of his tone, he was clearly disconcerted.

'With three Malindians from the Centre.'

'I don't think that Margaretta expects to be met. By the Malindians, I mean. Or by you. I guess she'll feel honoured.' He had begun to look shifty.

'Well, we thought . . .' Amos began. What precisely had *they* thought? It was he who had thought it. 'We thought it would be nice.'

'And it will be nice.'

'One wonders what her daughter will find to do,' Laura said. 'Presumably someone will have to take charge of her during meetings. Margaretta can hardly bring her along. I suppose I ought to offer – seeing that I'm not really a member of WAA.'

'That would certainly be kind of you.' O'Shaughnessy looked even shiftier than before. 'It's been good to have met you both. We'll see each other again – just as soon as that plane touches down. I've got to do some shopping now.' He gave a valedictory wave of the can.

When Laura and Amos told the three Malindians of the encounter, their leader, another Mr Tu, looked troubled. 'I find no explanation.'

'No explanation of what?' Amos asked.

'Why Mr O'Shaughnessy arrive so early in Batu. Even before you. We offer him a lady to take him shopping and a gentleman to take him sightseeing as part of our hospitality programme. But he say that he

59

has plenty to do. Very strange. He hire car, he leave hotel every morning early.' This Mr Tu's English was inferior to that of the other Mr Tu.

'Perhaps he has friends at the Embassy.'

Mr Tu shook his head. 'Embassy worried, I think.' He did not elaborate, even when Amos said: 'Worried? I wonder why they should be worried.' Instead, he merely drew deeply on yet another of the crumpled Malindian cigarettes which had stained his forefinger and middle finger an unattractive shade of orange.

Margaretta Svenson seemed as disconcerted as O'Shaughnessy had been to find not merely the three Malindians but also Amos and Laura awaiting her at the bottom of the gangway. 'Darlings! How lovely of you to meet me! So unexpected!' She hugged both of them, innumerable bracelets making a jangling noise against Amos's ear as her right arm went up and around him. Then she embraced O'Shaughnessy, with a cry of 'Frank!' in unconvincingly simulated surprise, before she turned to the three Malindians to shake them by the hands.

'Where's your little girl?' Laura asked, looking around for a child.

'My little girl? Oh, you mean Helga! Here she is.'

Amos and Laura had noticed a plump young woman, her blond hair extremely short in a pudding-basin cut about her spherical face, hovering around them in what they had supposed to be no more than the curiosity of a passenger awaiting the arrival of a bus to take her to the airport building. She now shuffled forward. 'I'm Helga,' she said. She extended a hand to Laura, her prematurely sagging jowls shaking with the movement. Then she drew a sweet out of the top pocket of her denim jacket, unwrapped it and popped it into her mouth.

'Helga is also a writer,' Margaretta explained. 'Or should I say a journalist? Amos is always insisting on that distinction, whenever some poor son-of-a-bitch lands up in the clink. So far only a few pieces published here and there. But she has great promise, everyone agrees. Takes after her mother,' she added with a laugh. 'Not her father, who was – and still is – a near-illiterate bastard.'

'If you would like to give me your passports and baggage checks . . .?' one of the Malindians suggested.

'Am I going to get VIP treatment?'

'Of course, Mrs Svenson.'

'Oh, lovely! . . . Helga, give him the passports and baggage checks.' As Helga began to fumble in the leather bag slung across her shoulder, Margaretta turned to O'Shaughnessy to ask, in a voice so low that Amos could only just hear what she was saying: 'Are all the arrangments OK?'

'Yup. Fine. We must just . . .' His small, hooded eyes indicated first the three Malindians and then took in Amos and Laura.

'I'll leave that to you.'

Outside the airport, O'Shaughnessy said: 'I can take Mrs Svenson and her daughter back to the hotel. I've hired a car.'

'Are you sure?' Mr Tu asked. 'We have another car here.'

'We've things to discuss.' Margaretta put a hand on the Malindian's arm, smiling up at him with roguish allure. 'It was so sweet of you all to meet me, Mr Tu. It *is* Mr Tu, isn't it? I don't want to waste any more of your time.' She turned to Laura and Amos. 'We'll meet soon, my pets. For the moment, all I want is a bath and a long, long sleep. But tomorrow – let's try to have breakfast or lunch together. Then we can have a really good talk.'

In the huge Mercedes, with two of the Malindians facing them and one seated in front – the other, smaller Mercedes had been dismissed – Laura said: 'She's up to something.'

'With O'Shaughnessy you mean?'

'Yes, of course.'

'You don't mean that you think they're having an affair?'

'Of course I don't. But they're *hatching* something.'

From the way she spoke, Amos had a vision of a giant egg out of which some monster, terrifying in its hairy obscenity, was about to emerge, to crunch them in its jaws.

'And of course little Miss Svenson will also be involved.'

'Little Miss Svenson?'

'Helga. And to think that you were thinking that I might offer my services as baby-sitter.'

What Margaretta had been up to became apparent that night, as Amos and Laura were preparing for bed.

'Sideways, sideways, sideways, sideways! Up, down! Up, down!' Amos was muttering to himself as, dressed only in pyjama trousers (oh, if only he had a few hairs on his chest!) he plied a toothbrush so worn that each time he used it he told himself that he really must buy a new one. Then he heard Laura's excited screech from the bedroom, where she was half-seated, half-lying on the bed, while alternately painting her toenails and gazing at the outsize television set. 'Amos! *Amos!* Come here! Quickly!'

It was a recording of Margaretta giving a press conference, presumably immediately after they had said goodbye to her. On one side of her, Frank O'Shaughnessy leaned back in his chair, from time to time chewing on his moustache or biting at a thumb-nail. On the other side, Helga leaned forward in her chair, from time to time picking at her short, upturned nose ('a really piggy nose to go with her piggy charac-ter,' Laura was later to comment) or rummaging, seem-ingly unsuccessfully, in the leather bag slung across her shoulder.

'I demand . . .'

Precisely what Margaretta was demanding it was impossible to know, since each time that she said the two words a voice-over, at a pitch comically far higher than hers, immediately superimposed itself. But it was clear, from the constant repetition, that she was either demanding a lot of things or one thing with monotonous vehemence. With each 'I demand' she banged with a fist on the table before her, the bracelets jangling on her wrist and the carafe of water set down before her juddering from side to side. At the final 'I demand' both Frank and Helga turned towards her, beaming their congratulation. Frank raised his hands (Amos noticed enviously that their backs were covered with hair) and began to clap. Helga extended a plump arm and gave her mother a hug.

'What do you suppose that she was demanding?' Amos asked fearfully. The image of Margaretta, flanked by her two supporters, had now been succeeded on the television screen by one of a tall, gaunt Malindian – the President, whom Amos was due so shortly to meet? a weather forecaster? – pointing to various areas on a map of Asia.

'Your resignation, I should guess.'

'Or the release of the prisoners?'

'Hm. Could be. Or the release of Nelson Mandela?'

'Or the repeal of Clause 28?'

'Or condemnation by WAA of the Iranians?'

'Or of the South Africans?'

'Or of the South Koreans?'

'Or of the North Koreans?'

'Or of the Turks?'

'Or of Pinochet?'

'Or of Castro?'

In a sad world, the sad possibilities were infinite.

*

What Margaretta had been demanding became clear next morning. An English-language newspaper had been pushed under the door of Amos's and Laura's suite at an hour so early that they had heard nothing of its arrival. Amos tucked it under his arm without looking at it, when they quit the suite for breakfast. They had already had their usual argument. In a hotel, Amos always wanted breakfast brought up, whereas Laura always wanted to go down. Eventually they always, as now, went down.

Margaretta was already seated in one corner of the dining-room, with O'Shaughnessy opposite to her. The bracelets jangled as she waved a hand negligently at Laura and Amos; but, despite what she had said the previous evening, there was no invitation to join her. 'Hi there!' O'Shaughnessy called out in a voice which Laura was later to describe as 'cocky'. He had just raised a coffee-pot and now jiggled it from side to side in an apology of a wave.

'It's clear we're not wanted *there*,' Laura said, as the head-waiter drew back a chair for her at the other end of the dining-room.

'Well, you're clearly wanted here. Those five Japanese men can't keep their eyes off you.'

'Probably out of amazement.' But Laura had already become delightedly aware that her size – however much it might have repelled the ancient Greeks, according to that former teacher of classics at Eton – acted as a potent aphrodisiac on male orientals.

Amos unfolded the newspaper and then gave a little squeak. There, on its front page, far more prominently displayed than his own photograph the day before, was a photograph of Margaretta leaning forward in her chair as her fist was about to thump the table. 'I demand . . .' What was it she demanded? 'Swedish President of WAA demands immediate release of prisoners', he read. But she was not Swedish President of WAA! She was President of Swedish WAA. A totally different thing. 'Just look at this!' He held out the paper to Laura, who attempted to take it from him. Each of them tugged, with Amos for once finally the victor. He then began to read out passages, oblivious of the scrambled egg and bacon, the coffee and the toast which their waiter was now setting down on the table. '. . . There are certain elements in WAA who, regarding the Congress as merely a pleasant social occasion, are determined to obscure the issue of the prisoners . . . *I demand*, in the name of all that WAA has stood for in the past, that the prisoners be released . . . If they remain in prison, then this Congress will be a mockery . . . *I demand*, in a spirit of fellowship with these unfortunates now being persecuted for nothing worse than writing what they think, that the President of this country take action at once . . . *I demand* not an amnesty, not a pardon, but a frank acknowledgement that a grievous error has been made . . . *I demand* . . .'

'You would think she was President of WAA,' Amos lowered the paper to say.

'I shouldn't think it for a moment. But she clearly does.'

'And the paper clearly does too. She's got *far* more space here than I did.'

'It must be an opposition paper.'

Amos went on reading. 'Unfortunately, within WAA there are now highly influential people who, for all their literary abilities, belong to the extreme right-wing. That three left-wing writers should at present be languishing in gaol in this country clearly does not concern them as much as it concerns certain other members of WAA . . .' He broke off. 'Oh, the unfairness of it! The unfairness! I care far more about those three prisoners than she does.'

'Of course you do. The night before last you said the name of one of them when talking in your sleep. I heard it distinctly. It was Tu. Or was it Nu? Or Chu?

She just wants to milk the whole affair for publicity. She's publicity crazy.'

'She wants the Presidency,' Amos said gloomingly, as he at last began on his congealed scrambled eggs. 'She wants me out and herself in.'

'How did you both sleep?'

Suddenly Margaretta was standing beside their table, with O'Shaughnessy behind her. Both of them were smiling.

'Very well, thank you.' Amos wished that he was not smiling back at her and that his voice did not sound so ingratiating. Laura was right: he *was* feeble. 'And you?'

'Well, I never need much sleep. Just three or four hours. I regard that as one of the good God's many gifts to me. That's why I can get so much done. But poor dear Helga – she needs nine or ten hours.'

'There's a lot about you in the newspaper,' Laura said darkly.

Margaretta gave a clear, jolly laugh. 'Isn't it an awful photograph? Frank was saying that it makes me look like an overweight Nancy Reagan. Usually I'm rather photogenic. Well, we'll be seeing each other.'

She and O'Shaughnessy moved off.

'I wonder what she'll get up to next,' Laura said.

'Nothing good,' Amos said. Then he burst out: 'Oh, I do wish I'd never taken on this Presidency!'

'Now, Amos! Stop that! That's enough of that! You *are* President – and you're going to remain President!'


Three of the Malindians ahead of them and four behind, Laura and Amos progressed through the deserted basement of the hotel. They passed a chemist's shop, with a white-coated elderly man asleep in a chair; another shop, with 'Savile Row Tailors' inscribed with elaborate curlicues on a window beyond which a large, muscular tourist (German? Swedish? American?) was stripping to his exiguous underwear for a small, spindly Malindian

66

with a measuring tape draped about his neck; a Japanese restaurant called Cherry Blossom, a French restaurant called Le Tour d'Eiffel, and an Italian restaurant called Ponte Vecchio; two lavatories, one with a pair of high-heel shoes and another with a pair of cowboy boots depicted on a plate on its door; and a jeweller's and a florist's. They then passed a door open on to a large room in which innumerable people were stuffing leather folders with the programmes, brochures, maps and tickets for the Congress, and another door open on to a small room in which two melancholy-looking men faced each other in silence across a table with a single telephone on it.

Finally they actually entered a room, garishly lit by a neon tube running down its centre. One of the two Mr Tus present placed a hand on a photocopying machine. 'Photocopier,' he said, as though Laura and Amos had never seen one. The other Mr Tu waved his hand in the direction of some desks set out as though for a class, each with a brand-new electronic typewriter on it. 'For press,' he said. 'Sister.'

'Sister?' Amos asked, bewildered.

'Sister typewriters. Made in Malindi. Maybe we give you one after Congress.'

Thinking of Laura stabbing at her dilapidated portable as she typed yet another of those letters beginning 'As President of International WAA, I write to protest in the strongest possible terms . . .', Amos all but said: 'Perhaps you could make that a word-processor.'

Eventually they reached their final destination, a small, windowless, air-conditioned room with two uncomfortable sofas and a number of equally uncomfortable chairs all upholstered in a leather of the same unappealing orange shade as that of the chain-smoking Mr Tu's index and middle finger.

'Please,' one of the three Mr Mus said, pointing at the nearest sofa.

'Please,' one of the two Mr Chus said simultaneously, pointing at a chair.

Laura placed herself on the sofa, Amos on the chair. At the same moment, through a door opposite to the one by which they had entered, a beautiful girl – she could not be more than seventeen, Amos decided in excitement – arrived with a vast tray set out with cups of coffee. Amos at once jumped up to help her. But what with his attempting to take a grip on one end of the tray and her attempting, for some inexplicable reason, to retreat from him, two cups slid off it and splashed his trousers as they crashed to the floor.

'Ouch!' The coffee was hot. Then seeing that the girl looked as if she were about to burst into tears, he said: 'Not to worry! Not to worry!'

But everyone was worrying, with two Mr Tus mopping at Amos's trousers with a handkerchief, two Mr Chus picking up the fragments of broken china, and one Mr Mu taking the tray away from the girl and placing it on a table.

'God, how clumsy you are!'

'I've been *scalded*!'

'Serves you bloody right. Frigging around with that waitress.'

Amos wished that Laura would not use words like bloody, and even worse, in public. It was so crude and unladylike. One never knew how much foreigners understood.

When, at long last, they were all once more settled with their cups of coffee, a Mr Mu opened his briefcase and took out a sheaf of Malindian newspaper cuttings. 'You have seen these already, Mr Kingsley?'

'Not those. But we've seen the English-language paper.'

'This is most unfortunate,' another Mr Mu said.

'I know, I know!'

'Mr O'Shaughnessy arrange this press-conference. We know nothing.' It was one of the Mr Chus.

'It's so terribly rude to arrange a press conference without consulting you,' Laura told the Malindians. 'Or my poor husband, for the matter of that.'

The Malindians all drew down the corners of their mouths and shrugged their shoulders. The implication was that such rudeness from foreigners, though regrettable, was not unexpected.

'And why should that daughter of hers be present?' Laura demanded.

'We pay her ticket. Business class,' one of the three Mr Mus said.

'I don't mean that. I mean, why should she be part of the press conference? She's not even a member of WAA.' Laura had clearly forgotten that she herself had been part of Amos's press conference, even though she was no more a member of WAA than Helga was.

'Frankly I'm scared.' This was the Mr Tu, President of the Centre, who spoke almost impeccable English with an American accent. 'What are they going to get up to next? That's what I ask myself.'

'That's what I ask myself too,' Amos said dolefully.

'Worse is still to come,' a Mr Chu surmised.

All the Malindians nodded their agreement.

At that moment an elderly Malindian woman entered the room, a large, buff-coloured envelope in her hand. She gave a series of low bows to everyone, before holding it out to the Mr Tu who was President of the Centre.

Thoughtfully he examined a seal on the back of the envelope. 'This is from the President,' he said. He seemed reluctant to open it, as though it might contain his death-sentence.

'What does it say?'

Mr Tu handed the letter to a Mr Mu, who handed it to a Mr Chu. This Mr Chu opened it and read it. Then he handed it back to the same Mr Mu, who also read it, before handing it back to the same Mr Tu.

Mr Tu began to read. 'This is bad. Very bad.'

'What is it?'

'The President will not be coming to the opening ceremony of the Congress. *"In view of the tone of the demands made by the President of WAA for the release of three criminals who – "'*

'The President of WAA! That woman isn't President of WAA! My husband is.'

Once again all the Malindians drew down the corners of their mouths and shrugged.

'This is what I feared,' said the Mr Tu who was President of the Malindian Centre.

'This is what we all fear,' the other Mr Tu said in gloomy confirmation.

'How will it end?' a Mr Chu asked, as the door again opened, this time to admit a young Malindian man, a large, buff-coloured envelope in his hand. He, like the elderly Malindian woman, also gave a series of low bows to everyone, before holding the envelope out to the Mr Tu who was President of the Malindian Centre. This time Mr Tu did not hand the envelope on but tore it open with such speed that he severed the letter inside it. Fitting the two pieces together, he shook his head repeatedly as he perused them.

'Bad, bad, bad.'

'What does he say now?' Amos asked, with a quaver in his voice.

'Bad, bad, bad. He says that after such an insult from the President of WAA, he must cancel his reception.'

'But *she's* not President of WAA. *I'm* President of WAA. Can't we get at least that straight?'

The corners of mouths were once again drawn down. Shoulders were once again shrugged.

'This is disaster.'

'Complete disaster.'

'What will our sponsors say?'

'What will newspapers say?'

'What will happen to prestige of WAA?'

'What will happen to prestige of Malindi?'

70

There followed a silence. To these questions no one had an answer.

'Oh, that bitch, that fucking bitch!' Laura exclaimed.


'You're giving a coming-out ball.'

'Oh, lordy!'

'I really don't know why you have to go on wearing those droopy drawers. What happened to that slip I bought you in the Marks and Spencer sale?'

'Harry borrowed it.' Harry was their son. 'Which means he pinched it.'

'Why do you have such a down on the boy?'

'Why does he have to keep pinching my clothes?'

Laura and Amos were stretched out on chairs beside the open-air swimming-pool of the hotel. Although the temperature was so high, they had been told that this was the last day when the pool would be open. Apparently every open-air pool in Malindi closed on September the first.

Suddenly Laura let out a squeal, sat up and pointed across the water. 'Look!'

'Yes?'

'Isn't that Bob?'

'Bob?'

'Bob Naylor. The British Council man.'

Now Amos also sat up. 'Yes, it looks like him.' Perched on the highest of the three diving-boards, Naylor looked like a yak in his squat hirsuteness. Or so Amos thought. Laura, Amos knew, would think differently.

Naylor dived.

'He certainly knows how to dive.'

'Not very gracefully.' Amos, with his terror of heights, never ventured on to a diving-board.

'What do you mean? That was a perfect dive.'

Laura got to her feet, tugging at her bathing-costume

where it bit into her ample thighs. 'Look after those for me.' She held out her dark-glasses.

'Why?'

'Because I'm going in again.'

'But I thought you said we were going to have lunch?'

'In a moment.'

Laura sauntered off.

Amos decided not to watch what happened next. He crossed his hands over his naked, slightly protuberant stomach, used a forefinger to excavate for some lint in his navel, and then closed his eyes. But it was no good. Less than a minute later he had reopened them.

It was exactly as he had expected. At the far, deep end of the pool, Naylor and Laura, holding on to the rail, were chatting animatedly to each other. If only he could hear what they were saying! No, on second thoughts it was probably better that he couldn't.

Naylor ought to be working at this hour. But of course, yes, it was Saturday, he remembered. Suddenly Naylor disappeared. Then he reappeared under Laura, lifting her up into the air before, with a huge splash, she toppled over into the water beside him. Amos could hear her delighted squeal. No, he mustn't watch and he mustn't listen. Once again he used a forefinger to excavate for that lint. Once again he closed his eyes.

His eyes were still closed when, several minutes later, he heard a voice saying: 'You're going to look like a lobster tomorrow. The sun can be deceptively strong on a day of haze like this.'

Amos squinted up at Naylor. Then his eyes shifted over to Laura. He always knew when she was excited. She was excited now, her lips slightly parted and glistening, her eyes wide open and also glistening, and her large breasts pushed out ahead of her, their nipples erect. The awful thing was that it was at such moments that she looked her most attractive.

'You must have the whitest body here,' Laura said cruelly.

'One hadn't much chance to sunbathe this summer in England, had one?'

'Bob suggests we have some lunch together. It's our turn to treat him after that lovely lunch two days ago.'

The insincerity of it made Amos furious. After that lunch Laura had continually complained about the heartburn given to her by the undercooked, over-greasy chicken prepared by Semba.

'I've not much appetite.' What Amos really meant was that he could not bear to sit watching the two of them flirt together. 'And this glare is giving me a headache. You two have lunch together. I'll go up to the room and have a sandwich and some beer sent up to me there.'

'Please yourself.' Laura turned away. She didn't care, she just didn't care!

'Well, see you, Mr President!' There was something snide in the way in which Naylor said the words. 'Forgive my mentioning this but, er, you're showing rather more than you probably mean to be showing.' He pointed downwards.

'Oh, lordy!'

Laura turned back. 'Oh, Amos, why *do* you have to wear those droopy drawers?'

# 6

On the next day, one of the two Mr Chus approached Laura and Amos as they were dithering between buying a copy of the *Independent* four days old or one of the *Guardian* three days old at the bookstall in the hotel foyer.

'Good morning, Mr Kingsley, sir! Good morning, madam!' Mr Chu looked natty in his ivory-coloured silk suit, white silk shirt and plum-coloured tie, open-work white shoes and panama hat. 'I trust you are both well?' This Mr Chu, a professor of linguistics at one of the lesser of the numerous universities in Batu, had studied briefly at the Institute of Education of London. Having been presented by him with a totally incomprehensible (because in Malindian) textbook, fulsomely inscribed *'To Mr Amos Kingsley, Great Novelist, from a humble scholar'*, Amos had wondered what precisely had been his qualifications to become a member of WAA.

'Yes, we are both well, thank you,' said Amos, in a voice that suggested that they weren't. After his brief spell in the pool the previous day, his sinuses were blocked and, worse, he had fulfilled Naylor's prediction that he would look like a boiled lobster from sunburn.

'Very well indeed,' Laura said with a joyful enthusiasm which had on Amos's already apprehensive spirits the effect on a pilot of the faltering engine of a light plane suddenly conking out altogether. 'It's such a beautiful day, isn't it?'

'Very hot.'

'Oh, but I love the heat. I feel at my best in the heat. Sadly, heat always makes my poor husband droop. He has the greatest difficulty in functioning.'

Could she be referring to some strenuous but far from satisfactory love-making – at one point, in the middle of it, she had even begun to suck an orange left over from breakfast – the night before? Since the suite was air-conditioned, the heat had had nothing to do with the fiasco. But his sunburn, making him feel as if he were running a low-grade fever, might have done.

'I came to ask if you wish to attend morning service.'

'Morning service?' Amos had forgotten that it was Sunday.

'I am a Christian convert. C of E. Each Sunday I go to the Anglican Church in the Embassy compound. I can take you there in my car.'

'Well, we're not really church-goers,' Amos said. 'Not that we've anything against the Church of England. Or any other church for the matter of that. As such.'

'Speak for yourself!' Amos was astonished and hurt by Laura's tone. 'I'd love to come with you, Mr Mu.'

'Chu.'

'Sorry?'

'Mr Chu.'

'Chu, Chu, Chu! Oh, it's all so confusing.'

After Laura and Mr Chu had vanished through the revolving doors of the hotel into a world of sunshine, heat and (yes, Amos was miserably sure of it) imminent betrayal, he sat himself down on a chair in the foyer and morosely watched the crowds passing through the security checks. A middle-aged, busty Englishwoman, looking even more like a boiled lobster than he, made a raucous scene when the squat, muscular woman security guard started dusting her down with rapid, vigorous pats, as she was accustomed to dust down Laura. An unruly child kept dashing back and forth through the metal detector. A Malindian sauntered through, dressed in a scarlet tracksuit, with a Sony Walkman earphone plugged in one ear.

Then, with a mingling of relief and apprehension (it was good to see someone whom he knew, but he wished that it were someone whom he not merely knew but also liked) Amos glimpsed Heinz ('Heinz comes in only two varieties – high-minded and self-seeking,' Laura had once remarked) de Kuhlenkampf, one of the Netherlands delegates, making his way through the revolving doors, an attaché case in one hand and a briefcase in the other. Certainly, if past form were anything to go by, he had also brought other suitcases. But what did they contain? At idle moments, fellow members of WAA discussed the matter of Heinz's landslides of luggage. His wardrobe was so limited that he was capable of attending a Presidential reception in tweed jacket, grey flannels and open-necked shirt. Perhaps, as an inveterate hypochondriac, he carried around with him a vast pharmacopoeia? Perhaps, as an inveterate reader of detective stories, he carried around with him the collected works of the Dutch equivalent of Agatha Christie?

On this occasion Heinz was wearing baggy dark-blue serge trousers, a short, matching dark-blue serge cape fastened at the collar with a gold buckle, and a gold-braided dark-blue pill-box cap with a peak. He looked like a comic gendarme out of a French operetta. But amazingly, despite a temperature in the upper eighties, he showed no sign of being in the least bit overheated.

Amos jumped up from his chair. 'Heinz!'

'Ah, Amos.' Heinz was far more restrained in his response than Amos in his greeting. 'You are here.' He removed his cap, revealing an incision-like red line across his bulging forehead.

'Laura and I arrived two days ago. To make sure that everything was in order. I didn't expect you until tomorrow.'

'I found a wonderfully cheap way to travel.' Heinz was adept at finding wonderfully cheap ways of doing most things in life. 'It meant two stop-offs, one in Dubai and one in Singapore, and starting out two days before the KLM flight from Amsterdam. But I am satisfied.' In his discreet, sombre way, Heinz usually was satisfied with any course of action which he took.

By now a bell-boy had appeared with a trolley loaded with three large suitcases. Patiently he waited, looking now at one of the two foreigners and now at the other.

'I nearly did not come,' Heinz said.

'Oh, really? Oh, why?'

'You ask that! It is clear, surely, Amos. Three innocent men are in prison. These men are writers like ourselves. We are guests of the government which has put them in prison.'

'Oh, we're not guests of the government. Not at all. We're guests of the Malindian Centre of WAA.'

'And from where does the Malindian Centre of WAA get its money?'

'From sponsors, of course.'

'Ah, Amos, you are so innocent! . . . Well, I must now go to register. But later I wish to have a talk with you.'

'Yes, of course. What, er, about?'

'About our strategy for this week ahead of us.'

'Oh. Good. Any time.'

Naturally pacific, Amos found himself wishing that people like Margaretta, Heinz and even Laura would not constantly talk as if they were members of a General Staff planning a campaign.

Once again Amos seated himself in the same chair, with its view of the entrance to the foyer.

Then he heard Heinz's angry voice from the reception desk. 'No, no, I cannot accept this!' (How often during WAA assemblies had Amos heard Heinz shout out, in exactly that same tone of hectoring vehemence, that he could not accept this or that punishment, deprivation or humiliation inflicted on this or that writer.) 'I write a letter! I write! Look at my letter to you! My room must overlook the garden! It must be on the top floor! I must have a bath and not a shower! I am Honorary Treasurer of the Dutch Centre of WAA! Look! Here is my card!'

Like many otherwise unworldly people, Heinz worried a great deal about his creature comforts.

At quarter past one Amos was once again seated in the same chair in the foyer, as tides of noisy tourists swept in and out, leaving behind them a detritus of fag-ends, used tickets and unwanted receipts, which two boys in vigilant attendance with brooms and trolleys then patiently swept up. Amos, his shirt glued to his back by sweat, had forlornly wandered round first the now drained and deserted pool and then gardens in which he from time to time came on some young Malindian couple strolling decorously, hand linked in hand. He had gone up to the suite but had at once left it when he found two cleaners at work. He had strolled through the basement, where the elderly white-coated man was once again asleep in the pharmacy, and where Savile Row Tailors was now shut. A youth, barefoot and wearing nothing but some ragged khaki shorts, was hauling a net full of live crabs behind him into the Cherry Blossom restaurant.

What on earth could Laura be doing? Eleven o'clock Matins could not possibly have gone on as late as this. And why should she, so aggressive in her agnosticism – she had absolutely refused a church wedding much to the distress of his widowed father and her own widowed mother – have opted to go to church? It was unlikely that she would remember any of the responses. In fact, she might even have forgotten the Lord's Prayer.

It was possible, of course, that she was curious about an Anglican Church in a predominantly infidel Far East city. Or she might have simply wanted to meet the members of the English community, who would be more likely to turn out for Matins in their isolation abroad than in some such cosy environment as Guildford, Worthing or, yes, Tooting. Or, of course, she might have been suddenly attracted by Mr Chu, so dapper in his ivory-coloured silk suit and open-work shoes. But no. It was no use fooling himself, even though he had a talent for doing so – as Laura often pointed out to him. It was obvious. She had set off for church because she had surmised that Naylor, as second-in-command of the British Council (his boss, he had told them, had returned to England to conclude a nervous breakdown), would probably be there out of a sense of duty, if not out of religious conviction. *It'll all pass, it'll all pass* Amos told himself, as he had told himself so often before. But until it all passed, it was all so agonizing. On their first night in Batu, during that interminable meal in the restaurant, one of the Mr Tus had told him that there was a Malindian prayer to Bantra which went, 'Teach me to care and not to care.' If only that wish could be granted to him. If only he could care for Laura and yet not care what she got up to.

He looked at his watch. As he did so, Margaretta and Frank O'Shaughnessy strolled past. Either they had not seen him or they had pretended not to see him. Amos heard Margaretta laugh, and then Frank laugh with her. Yes, they had pretended not to see him. It was he who was the cause of their laughter. At that moment, Amos was in the mood to give way to the vague paranoia which tended to afflict him with the same frequency and discomfort as heartburn.

Heinz was again at the reception desk. 'That room is a disgrace. There is a crack in the ceiling. And the air-conditioning makes so much noise that I do not know how I can sleep there. You must give me a reduction. I have told you – I am Honorary Treasurer of the Dutch

Centre of WAA. Look at my card, look at my card!' He had taken off the cape but, oddly, was still wearing the gendarme's cap. Amos found himself speculating, not for the first time, how a man so correct and humourless could be the author of sexy farces.

'Oh, *there* you are!'

Laura had whirled through the revolving doors, her face flushed and her eyes unnaturally bright. As she was being dusted down by the midget football-player of a woman security guard, she pointed at Amos and cried out, so loud that everyone in the foyer must have heard her: 'What's the matter with you? You look like a little boy who's just wet himself!'

'Nothing's the matter with me.' By now Laura had passed literally through the hands of the guard and was swaying towards him. 'But there's something the matter with you. You're drunk.'

'Not drunk, darling. Merely tipsy – in the most genteel fashion.'

'And where did you manage to get drunk – or tipsy, if you prefer it?'

'It's a ritual after church in these out-of-the-way communities. To have a drink all together, I mean. Not to get drunk.'

'And where did you have a drink all together?'

'Well, it wasn't *all* of us. Let me be truthful. But six or seven of us went back to Bob's house.'

'Oh, so you went back to Naylor's house!' Amos refused to speak or even think of him as Bob. 'I thought so!'

'Six or seven of us. And Semba looked after us. By the smell, she'd been having her Sunday drink before we'd arrived for ours.'

Amos felt an overwhelming despair, followed by a fatalistic inertia. *Que sarà sarà* . . . Many years ago, cheek to cheek, he and Laura had danced in a country hotel near Perth to Doris Day singing those words, while in one of the hotel garages his exhausted donkey,

Pepita, slept. Perhaps he should never have abandoned Pepita, now in a donkey sanctuary in the New Forest, for Laura and all the heartaches and anxieties that she caused him. 'Oh, let's eat!' he said.

'Good idea. And after that I'm going to have a kip. That's what I need. Food, lots of lovely food, and then a long, long kip.'


As Laura had her long, long kip, Amos lay on the bed beside her, chewing on a thumb-nail until it began to bleed. He would write a novel, he suddenly decided, and, yes, he would call it *Possession*. About a love, unreasoning and all-consuming, which binds a man to a woman totally unworthy of him. Time after time the man takes the woman back, after yet another bastard has exploited, ill-treated and finally abandoned her. On the final occasion, she is desperately ill. Or the bastard has somehow disfigured her. Or . . . Or . . .

At that moment the telephone began to ring. Laura grunted, shifted, but remained still asleep. Amos leaned across for the receiver.

'Hello.'

'Mr Amos?'

'Yes.'

'I would say to the House, as I said to those who have joined this Government, "I have nothing to offer but blood, toil, tears and sweat."'

'Well, offer them to someone else! Now just bugger off!'


Later that afternoon the Mr Tu who was President of the Malindian Centre of WAA leaned forward in his chair in the sitting-room of the suite, while next door, in the bedroom, Laura remained insensible in what Amos described to himself as swinish slumber.

'She has done it again,' Mr Tu said.

'She?' In his present state Amos had for a moment assumed that Mr Tu must be referring to Laura.

'Mrs Svenson. She has given an interview on radio.'

'Oh dear! What did she say?'

Mr Tu shook his head and pursed his lips, as though in a refusal to divulge anything so unpleasant.

'Please tell me, Mr Tu. I must know the worst.' Yes, he must know the worst, not merely about the interview but about Laura and Naylor.

'She made an attack on the Malindian Centre. She said that we were, quote, creatures of the Government, unquote. She even referred to the fact that Mrs Tu – my wife – is a cousin of the wife of the President. How did she come by such information? And what is its relevance? Clearly she is being well briefed by dissident elements.' He adjusted cuffs held together by huge diamond links (could diamonds of such a size be real? Amos wondered, staring at them) and then gave a small smile. 'The Malindian Centre is used to such denigration. What has angered us is what she said about you.'

'About me?' (Oh, lordy, lordy! At that moment, Amos did not feel strong enough to endure any criticism, however mild.)

'I do not wish to repeat what she said verbatim,' Mr Tu said, as though he had intuited Amos's feelings. 'Suffice it to summarize. The, er, gist was that you are an, er, innocent abroad. A decent enough guy but, er, one totally without the strength of character or the diplomatic skills to function effectively as President.'

'And of course she herself has that strength of character and the diplomatic skills!'

'That was indeed the, er, implication.'

'It is *she* who's the innocent abroad. And all her allies are innocents abroad. They think that you can go about things in the same way in the Far East as in America or Western Europe.'

'I entirely agree with you.' Since Amos was merely repeating what he had heard Mr Tu and his Malindian colleagues say, this agreement was hardly surprising. 'Mrs Svenson and her friends are jeopardizing two things at one and the same time. The first is the eventual release of the prisoners. The second is the success of this Congress.'

From the next-door room Amos suddenly heard Laura on the telephone. Since the telephone had not rung, it must have been she who had initiated the call. To whom could she be talking? There was only one possibility.

Amos went over to the minibar. 'Would you like a drink, Mr Tu?'

'No thank you. It's too early for me. I believe it used to be a rule of the British in tropical or sub-tropical climes not to drink alcohol until the sun was setting. Hence the word "sundowner". I think the rule a good one.'

'Well, I'm going to break it.'


Laura and Amos were in the middle of the *prix fixe* dinner at Le Tour d'Eiffel when Heinz de Kuhlenkampf, his cape draped around him but without his cap, walked in, indicated a table which happened already to have been booked for a party of four, ignored the protests of the head waiter, and sat down at it. Then he saw Laura and Amos and got up again. Under an arm he was carrying a guidebook.

'Ah, how lucky! May I sit for a moment?'

'Yes, of course. Please.' But Amos was determined that on this occasion Heinz was not going to repeat his usual exploit of cadging a dinner off them. In fact, he was not even going to offer the Dutchman a drink.

Heinz pulled back the chair between Amos and Laura and then, having thrown the cape back over a shoulder to reveal that he was wearing a grubby T-shirt under it, seated himself.

'I have been looking at the programme,' he announced. 'So many parties!'

'Yes, isn't it wonderful? I've never been to a Congress when there were so many parties. Sometimes three in a single day. Although', Amos went on, 'the most important party of all has unfortunately been cancelled. The President's.'

Heinz was so absorbed in pouring some wine into a tumbler that he had not taken in this last sentence. He sipped and pulled a face. 'Not good this wine.' Clearly his opinion of Amos had sunk even lower.

'Oh, I'm sorry.' (Why the hell should he be sorry if this old bore did not like the wine to which, uninvited, he had helped himself? For God's sake, Amos, show some guts!)

'These parties are obscene.'

Although Amos was used to members of WAA describing anything which they did not like as obscene, he was nonetheless surprised. 'Obscene?'

'How can we go to parties, to drink, eat and be gay, when three writers are in prison? How? How?'

Laura picked up her roll in her hand. Was she about to throw it at the Dutchman? 'If we didn't go to parties to drink, eat and be, er, gay, would it help to procure the prisoners' release?'

Heinz did not answer her question. 'Such parties are obscene. I shall not attend them. I think that many participants will not attend them.'

'But that would be terribly rude to our hosts!'

'In matters of principle courtesy is irrelevant.'

There was a silence. Then the waiter set down before Amos and Laura the *raie au beurre noisette* which formed the second course of the *table d'hôte*. The silence continued as they began to dismember their fish.

Heinz got up. 'I will leave you.' He picked up the tumbler, raised it and, throwing back his head, drained it to the dregs. Again he pulled a face, partly of disgust at its taste and partly of pity for their lack of connoisseurship. Soon they heard him ordering at his own table. 'I wish to start with *les escargots à la bourguignonne*. Then I shall have *la croustade de bécassines aux truffes* . . . And for wine . . . Let me see . . . Yes, I shall have a bottle of Bordeaux. The – the '81 Gruard-Larose.' When the waiter had left him, he shouted across: 'Amos! Amos!'

'Yes?'

'I am right to assume that the Malindian Centre will pay for our meals?'

'Oh, no, I don't think so. The custom is for a host centre to pay only for a delegate's room and breakfast.'

'Waiter! Waiter! Forget the Gruard-Larose! I wish to try some of your Malindian beer. And – and let me see the *prix fixe* menu!'

## 7

'*Ah! Voilà! Monsieur le Président!*'
  'Herr Kingsley!'
  'Hi there, Amos!'
  'Well, it's good to see you again, Kingsley.'
  '*Signor* Kingsley! *Ciao! Tutto va bene?*'
  'Amos-san! How do you do? I am very well, thank you.'
  'Good morning, sir. I bring you respectful greetings from the nine hundred and seventy-two members of the Indian Centre and from our President, Begum Ghosht.'

For most of the day Amos stood in the lobby of the hotel, with Laura sometimes beside him but more often not, as buses and taxis eructated the innumerable delegates to the Congress. This was something which his predecessor, the excitable French novelist, had always scorned to do. But Amos had long since convinced himself that, however violently the élite of WAA might be opposed to his continuing Presidency, he enjoyed the support of what he called 'the grass roots'. ('If there are any grass roots, they don't go down very far,' was Laura's cynical comment.) The best way to foster those grass roots, he had decided, was by constantly feeding them with the artificial manure of his attention.

But there was another reason for his presence in the foyer. He was hoping against hope that suddenly, through the revolving doors, Miss Shimada would appear. Constricted by her kimono, her knees would brush teasingly against each other as she walked up to greet him. Her slim body would be tilted slightly forwards and sideways, the eyes downcast except when she ventured a shy, appealing glance.

'Is Miss Shimada in your party?'

'Please?' This Japanese, in a jockey-cap too small for the football of his head, had no less than three cameras strung around his swelling embonpoint.

'Miss Shimada. You know. She's one of your, er, most prominent members. Very active in the Japanese Centre. Always comes to Congresses.'

'Please? *Wakarimasen.*'

Suddenly Amos realized that this Japanese was not a member of WAA but a tourist, seen slurping glutinous rice, a bowl held close under his chin and chopsticks busy, in the Cherry Blossom restaurant the night before.

'Sorry. That's all right. A mistake. *A mistake!*' he repeated, as the Japanese continued to gaze at him with a mixture of bewilderment and fascination. Amos waved a hand in the air, in a gesture of goodbye. With a roguish grin, football-head tilted sideways, the Japanese waved back.

'Oh, poor Amos! How hard you do work for the Presidency!' It was Margaretta, her blond hair hanging in damp tendrils and a rolled towel under an arm. Amos wondered how to take her remark and then decided that it was certainly two-edged. 'The outdoor pool is closed, so we had to go to the indoor one.'

Beside Margaretta, Helga suddenly blew out a bubble of gum towards him and then snapped it back. Amos, however mistakenly, at once took the gesture as one of hostility and derision; she might as well have stuck out her tongue. She was wearing baggy light-blue denim shorts reaching to her dimpled knees and what appeared to be a bra extemporized out of a bolt of dark-blue Thai silk.

Suddenly, behind Margaretta and Helga and through the glass doors, Amos glimpsed a kimono-clad figure, a cartwheel of straw almost wholly concealing her face, struggling to get out of a taxi. First her small feet, encased in white *tabe*, touched the ground. Then she gave herself one heave, another, and yet another, hand clutching the door.

'See you,' Margaretta said, realizing that she had lost his attention.

'See you,' Amos echoed. Mouth open and heart thumping against his breastbone, he then continued to stare out into the sunlight. Thank God Laura had taken herself off for yet another cup of coffee.

The little figure outside the glass doors was directing a couple of bell-boys as they pulled out three suitcases jammed together in the boot. She herself was carrying two carrier bags, one of which, Amos suddenly noticed, had 'Harrods' written on it. Did this mean that, without getting in touch, Miss Shimada had been in London? Or were such bags on sale in Japan? He remembered from his visit to Japan that souvenirs from the remotest parts of the country were on sale in the airports and stations of every major city, so that no traveller had to encumber himself with presents until he returned home. Perhaps it was the same with presents purporting to have been brought back from holidays abroad?

Amos stepped forward, as the doors revolved. Then he recoiled. The diminutive figure tripping towards him, her carrier bags swinging back and forth and her round, middle-aged face transformed by a peculiarly Japanese combination of joy and respect, was not, was certainly not Miss Shimada.

'Amos-san! How do you do?'

'How, er, do you do, Miss Kawai? No, it's Miss Iwai, isn't it? I thought for a moment . . .' No, better not to say what he had thought.

'Your wife?'

'Having a cup of coffee.' But could he be sure that

that was what she was doing? His ravenous longing to see Miss Shimada was briefly superseded by his acute unease over Laura and Naylor.

'Cohee?'

'Yes. Coffee. She drinks far too much coffee.'

'Amos-san.' Miss Kawai had rested one of her carrier bags against her legs – it was odd that the knock-kneed stance, so irresistible in Miss Shimada, should be so unappealing in her – and had begun to scrabble in the other bag. Eventually she extracted a scroll, encircled by a rubber band. Deftly she removed the band and unrolled the scroll. 'For you,' she said. 'I have written poem for you.' By now Amos had learned that, whereas western writers presented him with unwanted copies of their books, oriental ones presented him with unwanted poems, personally inscribed for him.

'Oh, how kind, Miss Kawai! I mean, Miss Iwai.'

'Please! Look!'

Amos looked. In beautiful calligraphy there were three vertical lines of Japanese *kanji*. Beneath them, in childish handwriting, there were three horizontal lines of poetry in English. He read the English.


AUTUMN IN TOKYO

An avenue of tainted leaves
A leaf falls
A sorrow falls from my heart.


Miss Iwai was gazing intently up into his face, her wide forehead now creased by a frown, as though she were willing him to be both moved and impressed. 'Tainted'? An all too justified reference to the pollution of the city perhaps? Or had she really meant 'tinted'? He did not dare to ask. 'Beautiful.'

'You think so, Amos-san?'

'Yes. Beautiful.'

Miss Iwai simpered and then gave a giggle which she

attempted to stifle by putting a hand over her mouth. 'I am so happy. That the International President of WAA like my poem. Very, very happy!'

It struck Amos as typically Japanese that she should have so much respect for the office of President, as distinct from its occupant. Were he not President, he was sure that there would have been no presentation of the poem to him; and if he had nonetheless passed judgement on it, he was equally sure that the judgement would then have been regarded as of absolutely no consequence whatever.

'You have a rare and, er, glowing talent.' Was he overdoing it? Well, what did it matter if he was? He wanted to be sure of the Japanese vote when the ballot for renewal of his term of office came up.

Soon after – by then Laura had rejoined him – Mr Tong appeared, accompanied by a small, stooped, grey-haired woman in a black, mannish coat and skirt. A fellow delegate, Amos decided.

Mr Tong shook first Laura's hand and then Amos's, with the brisk vigour which he brought to every action. 'I don't think you've met my wife.' Until then Amos and Laura had always assumed him to be a bachelor.

Mrs Tong gave a curt nod to each of them and then moved two or three feet away. She scowled towards the reception desk.

'Well, it looks as if you're in for a rough ride, Amos, if I'm to believe everything I hear on the grapevine.' Mr Tong and the grapevine were as inseparable as he and whatever girl he managed to pick up in the course of a conference.

'Oh, do you think so?' Amos wished that his voice would not quaver.

'I certainly do.' Mr Tong was cheerful.

'Oh, gosh! Oh, golly! Lordy, lordy!'

At that moment a voice tinkled out behind Amos's left shoulder.

'Amos-san! How do you do?'

Amos's heart, previously somewhere in the region of his navel, now seemed to leapfrog over his Adam's apple. But again it was not Miss Shimada, although the voice was so like hers.

'Amos-san, I have a little present for you. A poem which I have written. Please.'

Amos unrolled the scroll. 'SPRING IN TOKYO' he read.

'Oh, how kind of you, Miss Kawai! How very kind!'

'Your disappointment was quite pathetic,' Laura said.

'Disappointment? What disappointment?'

'Over finding that it was another Japanese woman and not that smirking little doll of yours.'

Smirking little doll! Well, yes, Miss Shimada was certainly a doll, but for God's sake, that was a shy, coaxing, modest smile, not a smirk. Emphatically not.

Laura and Amos were having drinks in the bar before dinner, while waiting for Max da Costa. Max, the twenty-six-year-old *wunderkind* who had recently been appointed the International Secretary of WAA, had only just arrived, since he had been obliged to attend the first Communion of some distant relative back in his native Goa. He was, they both guessed, still upstairs washing and blow-drying the long and luxuriant black hair which provided so dramatic a frame for his ivory-coloured, broodingly ascetic face. Things often had to wait for Max to finish washing and blow-drying his hair.

Behind them, Amos could hear Margaretta's voice, as she held forth loudly to the little coterie, all allies of hers and enemies of his, gathered around her. He strained to listen. 'I was such a precocious little girl. I must have seemed just horrid to any grown-up who came into contact with me. I know my parents couldn't stand me, and neither could my two brothers and my sister. When I had my eighth birthday, an aunt of mine gave me this children's book, all about ponies. And I was reading Proust! Yes, truly. Proust. My parents, my aunt and my two brothers and sister had never read Proust, but I was reading him.' Someone said something inaudible and she went on: 'Yes, in French, of course. By then I'd taught myself French by listening to the radio and reading the copies of *Le Monde* which my father – he was a famous journalist, you know – left lying round the house.' Someone else said something inaudible. 'How did I get the volumes of Proust? I got them from the public library. My mother used to leave me in the children's section while she got the kind of trashy biographies she liked to read and, hey presto, I'd be in the foreign section, standing on tiptoe to get down my Proust – or my Henri de Montherlant or my Sartre. Now my dear little Helga has none of that precocity. So when I say that she takes after me and not that shit of an ex of mine, I don't mean in *every* way . . .'

'Whatever criticism one can make of Margaretta's books, one can't say that she isn't an accomplished story-teller.' Laura had also been listening to the conversation.

At that moment, tall, slender and elegant in a grey silk suit nipped in at the waist and flared around the buttocks, Max da Costa made his serpentine way between the tables towards them.

'Max darling!'

Max stooped and gave Margaretta a kiss first on one cheek and then on the other. He went on to greet the people gathered round her.

'The opposition,' he said, seating himself between Amos and Laura. 'What are they up to?'

'No good,' Amos said.

'Certainly no good.'

If a stranger had come into the bar and been told to pick out a single writer, he would at once have pointed to Max. But in fact Max was totally uninterested in writing, and had only been appointed International Secretary of WAA because of his success as coordinator of an international charity, the World Save the Armadillo Fund.

Amos began to brief him about Margaretta's press conference. But, as so often, Max seemed, mysteriously, already to know everything that Amos knew, and even things which Amos did not know.

'You've heard about the boycott?' Max said.

'Boycott?'

'Of all social events. It was de Kuhlenkampf's idea, but now the Scandinavians, the Germans and the Americans are all in favour of it. They're trying to persuade everyone else.'

'But most people only come to these Congresses because of the social events,' Amos protested.

'And the screwing,' Laura put in.

Amos frowned at her. Max looked pained.

'It'll be a terrible loss of face for the Malindians if no one turns up at their banquets and cocktail parties.'

'And a terrible waste of food and drink,' Laura said.

'I can see a dreadful rift,' Max said.

'Between the party-goers and the non-party-goers?'

'Well, in effect, yes. Between those who think that we can procure the release of the prisoners by being nice to the Malindian government and those who think that we can procure the release of the prisoners by being nasty.'

'I doubt if anything we say or do either way will have any influence,' Laura said, making Amos wish that she would keep out of things.

'There you're wrong, my dear,' Max said. 'Even the most reactionary governments – and the government here isn't *all* that reactionary – pay attention to WAA.'

Laura looked unconvinced.

'I want to arrange a private meeting for this evening. After dinner.'

'What about?'

Max for a moment allowed his irritation with Amos – so unworldly, so innocent, so unskilled in the arts of diplomacy – to manifest itself. Then he smiled, running long fingers through the back of his hair. 'We don't want a public rift, now do we? We don't want it to appear that WAA is divided.'

'But WAA *is* divided!'

'Laura, please!' Amos turned back to Max. 'Yes, I see what you mean. But don't you think that, in a democratic organization, it's better to bring, er, disagreements out into the open?'

Head tilted to one side, Max once again smiled and once again ran long fingers through the back of his hair, fluffing it outwards. 'WAA is effective only as long as it speaks – at least publicly – with a single voice.' Three years ago he would have been saying that the World Save the Armadillo Fund was effective only so long as it spoke – at least publicly – with a single voice. 'Surely that's obvious? A lot of bickering and recrimination is the last thing we want at the assembly of delegates.'

'But what is the point of an assembly of delegates if no one is supposed to disagree?' Laura demanded.

'In any case,' Amos took up, 'the delegates *enjoy* bickering and recrimination. That's what they've come here for – in addition to the party-going.'

'And the screwing,' Laura added.

Max sighed and gave the understanding, indulgent smile of a parent faced with the inability of two sweet but not all that bright children of his to understand what he was telling them. 'I'll have a word with Margaretta,' he said, preparing to get up.

'What about?'

'What I propose is that she – and Heinz – and Frank O'Shaughnessy, of course – and one or two others should convene after dinner in your suite. Just a dozen or so of the more important and influential people, no more. Two or three of the Malindians, of course. In short, the chosen few. We can then have a thorough and amicable discussion and reach some agreement. A joint strategy.'

Oh, God, that word strategy again! 'If you think it'll work,' Amos said feebly.

'It's worth a try. I have a great faith in the ability of reasonable people to reach reasonable compromises. I always have had.'

Laura gulped from her glass. 'Reasonable people! How many reasonable people are there in WAA?'

As, after dinner, Amos awaited the reasonable people who would reach reasonable compromises, he could just see Laura, through the half-open door between sitting-room and bedroom, making up her face. That she was taking so much care over this operation struck him as ominous. Her usual approach to making up was that of a *tachiste* painter. He yawned and yawned again. Nervousness always made him yawn, and confrontations of the kind ahead of him always made him nervous.

Was Laura taking so much care for Max's 'chosen few'? And why had she put on that sheath-like, shiny, gunmetal-grey dress – it reminded him of a gigantic cigar tube – for which she had forced him to queue with her in heavy rain at the last Harvey Nichols sale? The dress, she had said when packing it on the top of his suitcase, so that there was no room for his pyjamas, was for 'very special occasions'. Could she have some very special occasion in mind?

Tentatively licking her lips, diamanté handbag in hand, Laura came through the door. 'I think I'll be on my way.'

'On your way? What do you mean?'

'Smoke-filled rooms are not really my cup of tea. As you know, I've never cared for Lapsang. So – as Frank O'Shaughnessy would say – I'm going to take a powder.'

'Take a powder?'

'Beat it. Scram. Vamoose.'

'But where are you going to, er, vamoose?'

'Bob said he'd show me the town. I want to see the nightlife. We're not going to get any chance to do that once this bloody Congress has started. Now are we?'

'I had thought . . .'

'Yes?'

'That I'd show you the town.'

'You'd thought nothing of the kind. You thought that only now.' She came over to him, where he sat perched unhappily on the edge of the sofa, stooped and kissed him on the forehead. 'Don't worry, darling. He's just going to show me the town. Nothing else.'

'You might have told me before.'

'I didn't think it all that important.'

'And when did you arrange all this?'

Laura gave her loud, clear laugh. 'Now you're being silly. 'Bye, darling.' The diamanté bag glittered at him as she waved it in the air. 'Be good.'

'The same to you!' But he doubted if she heard him, so rapidly did she march out of the room.

Amos went to the minibar and poured one miniature of gin into a glass. He deliberated for a moment, and then added another. He gulped.


As so often in WAA, the chosen few had become the unchosen many. Every delegation had somehow heard of the private meeting, and every delegation had then been determined to turn it into a public one. In between ringing down again and again for drinks (would the Malindians foot the bill?), Amos kept ringing down again and again for chairs, until eventually the sitting-room of the suite had been transformed into what looked like a television viewing theatre.

'What's yours, Margaretta?'

'A Margarita, please.'

'Helga?'

'A Pina Colada.'

'Frank?'

'A Manhattan.'

'Mr Tong?'

'A Tom Collins.'

'Max?'

'A White Lady.'

Amos had never heard of some of these drinks and had never drunk any of them. He certainly could not remember who wanted what, and was about to jot orders down on a piece of paper snatched off the table. But no, no, that was Miss Iwai's – or was it Miss Kawai's? – poem. He hurried over to the desk for the note-pad provided by the management.

Eventually he found himself sitting uncomfortably on the floor, in a position which, had he so wished, would have enabled him to look up the skirt of the sturdy delegate from Finland. He did not so wish. His mouth felt dry and his head was throbbing. He knew already that a third double gin had been a mistake. Did it matter to no one that the President of WAA had no chair on which to sit? Apparently it didn't. Trust Max to have grabbed the largest and most comfortable of the three armchairs.

Still more people kept knocking at the door and then squeezing in. Amos was determined to order no more chairs and no more drinks. 'Since my wife and I have to sleep in here tonight, perhaps I might ask you all to refrain from smoking?' As though in deliberate flouting of this request, one of the three paunchy and grizzled Lithuanian Writers in Exile at once set about lighting a meerschaum pipe. *Since my wife and I have to sleep in here tonight* . . . But would Laura be there that night? And if she were not there, what likelihood was there of his being able to sleep?

Max clapped his hands for silence. 'Shall we get started?' he said.

At that Helga rose from the sofa on which she had

been lolling between her mother and Frank O'Shaughnessy, crossed over to the minibar and opened it. Without saying a word to Amos, she rummaged around, removed a packet of salted almonds and returned to her seat, where she began contemplatively to gnaw on one.

'Yes, let us get started,' the Finnish delegate said, pulling down her skirt and looking skittishly at Amos. 'Some of us have jet-lag.'

Since she had not been invited to attend the meeting, there had been no reason for her not to recover from her jet-lag in bed.

'I thought – your President and I thought – that it would be useful if we could have a preliminary discussion in private, before the assembly of delegates. We all, I think, have the same objective in view – to procure the release of those unfortunate three men who, despite our protests, are still in prison. What we differ about is the strategy to be adopted.' Max looked around him, as though expecting to be contradicted. But no one spoke. 'Right,' he said. Then he leant forward and down to Amos, who had now cradled his head on the arms which he had thrown around his knees. 'Mr President – perhaps you would like to, er, kick off?'

Amos raised his head. How could he kick off when, after all those double gins, he already felt legless? And why the hell should he, the President of this fucking organization, have to address all these comfortably seated people from the floor? Drink always made him, usually so docile, aggressive and quarrelsome. 'Well,' he said. 'Yes. At our last Congress in, er, Bogotá, we agreed by a democratic vote that we should come to this Congress here. Didn't we? I'm not saying anything that anyone here would dispute, now am I? We agreed by a democratic vote. And since we are a democratic organization, we should all abide by a democratic vote. Yes? Agreed? But, despite that, certain individuals, certain people prominent in WAA, continued to campaign for us not to come here. And now that we have come here, they are deliberately attempting to make a, er, shambles of the whole show.'

'Shambles? Shambles? Shambles?' Delegates turned enquiringly to each other.

'A mess,' Max said. Then he again leaned forwards and down, this time patting Amos's shoulder, as though he were patting a previously friendly dog which, for no apparent reason, had suddenly begun to bare its teeth and snarl. If anyone was making a shambles of the whole show, it was Amos. 'I wonder if you're not, er, rather over-emphasizing the differences between us, Mr President? Such differences exist of course, but WAA has always been an organization in which there has been agreement in disagreement and, er, disagreement in agreement.' This was a formula which Max often produced when it became clear to him that there was no chance of any agreement whatever. 'Margaretta – Mrs Svenson? Have you anything you wish to say on this matter?'

'Nothing that I haven't said already.' She picked reflectively at the arm of the sofa. 'Obviously the President's somewhat, er, intemperate remarks were intended for me. Yes, I did think that it was obscene for us to hold a Congress in this country when there are still three writers in prison. And yes, I do think it obscene that we should now all be here. But I felt that I had to come, so that, through the, er, complacency – or indeed callousness – of others, the opposite case should not fail to be made. My object in coming here was to speak out about the prisoners. I have already done so at a press conference – better attended, I may add, than that given by our President. And I will continue to do so,' she added, glaring defiantly across at Amos.

At that moment Helga threw the empty salted almond bag on the floor, extricated herself from her position of being squeezed between her mother and

Frank, and once more crossed to the minibar. With mounting fury, Amos watched her. She opened the door, rummaged about inside, and eventually removed a Hershey bar. She peeled back its wrapper, examined it briefly and then bit into it, as she returned to her place.

By now Frank was speaking. 'I'd like to make an observation about all this business of a democratic organization and a democratic decision. I'm a democrat, I come from one of the great democracies of the world. But there are certain things which are obscene – morally obscene – and no democratic decision taken by a democratic organization is going to make me accept them. Never!' He pulled a cushion out from behind him, punched it and then put it back.

'Do you think I might have that cushion?' Amos said. 'It might make things a little less uncomfortable for me down here on the floor.'

But Frank either did not hear the request or decided to ignore it.

'Well, thank you,' Max said. 'Thank you for speaking your mind.' That people should speak their minds was something which he rarely welcomed. He certainly did not welcome it now. 'Perhaps we should now ask one of our Malindian friends for their view of this matter? Mr Tu?'

With a Mr Mu on one side of him and a Mr Chu on the other, the Mr Tu who was President of the Malindian Centre was perched on a window ledge. Handsome and muscular, he now rose to his feet and gave one deep, dignified bow to the people on his left, another to those on his right, and yet another to those immediately before him. 'I wish to express my thanks and the thanks of the Malindian Centre to all of you who have come here to Batu – many of you travelling for many, many hours – to attend our Congress. We hope you will enjoy yourselves here. We hope you will

100

be happy. If there is any problem, please tell us.' He held out his arms. 'I welcome you!' Then he sat down.

Was he being extraordinarily subtle, as orientals had the popular reputation of being? Or was he totally unaware of the bitter division in WAA? Amos could not be sure. But in his present mood of half-drunken truculence, he wanted to shout: 'Oh, cut all that out! Just tell the Svenson woman and her friends to go to hell!'

Mr Tong held up his hand, like a child at school.

'Yes, Mr Tong?' Max called.

'As I've often remarked before, we in the East attach a great importance to face. Maybe this seems strange or even comic to you from the West. But face is important to us. Frankly I don't think that the manner in which certain people are proceeding is the right manner. In fact, such a way of proceeding can only harm the cause of the prisoners. I must ask those certain people – '

Cheeks scarlet, Margaretta leapt to her feet. 'Who are these "certain people", Mr Tong? Do you mean me and those who agree with me?'

Staring down at the floor, Mr Tong volunteered no answer.

'If the cap fits . . .' Amos mumbled. In a surge of gratitude his heart had swept out to Mr Tong. Then he said so loudly that everyone could hear: 'It's no use behaving in Batu as though you were in Stockholm.'

Helga had again risen from her place and was again making her way over to the minibar. As Amos's eyes followed her across the room, he heard Heinz's voice from the far end of the room, by the door. 'I have reached a decision. As I have already said, it seems to me obscene that we should be attending parties – eating expensive food, drinking expensive drinks – when three fellow writers are being almost starved in prison.'

At this Mr Chu made an attempt to protest. 'Not almost starved, Mr de Kuhlenkampf. I promise you.

The prison diet here in Malindi is wholly adequate. Not very tasty, I admit, but wholly adequate.'

But, ignoring him, Heinz swept on. 'I have decided to absent myself from all these social occasions. I cannot be party to such an obscenity. And others here' – he looked around him – 'have joined me in that decision, I know.' There was a murmur of assent.

Mr Tu had risen to his feet in consternation. 'But these parties are very important. Our sponsors are giving these parties. The Mayor, the Minister of Culture, the Director of the Museum of Fine Art . . .'

Margaretta gave a little smile, as she stared at the plump hands crossed in her lap. Beside her, Helga was now burrowing her way through a packet of Marie biscuits. Then she said: 'That's too bad. But there it is. No release of prisoners, no attendance at parties. It's as simple as that.'

Partly as a result of what she had said, but more as a result of the sight of Helga munching those biscuits, it was then that Amos lost his temper. He jumped up, feeling as though his surging blood had suffered a hammer-lock in his temples, turned towards Margaretta and began to shout at her: 'It's bloody well not as simple as that! It bloody well isn't! It's bloody rude to our hosts to behave as you're doing!'

'Amos! Amos!' Max was pulling at his jacket. But Amos jerked free.

Margaretta now also rose. 'Where principles are concerned, courtesy is irrelevant. I'm sorry but not surprised that you're incapable of seeing that.'

'You have a cheek, you really have a cheek!'

'Amos! Amos!' Again Amos heard Max's anguished voice. Again he paid no attention to it.

'You come here. You demand a first-class ticket for yourself, although every other delegate is content to have an economy one. You then demand a ticket for your daughter, who isn't even a member of WAA. You accept a bedroom for yourself in this luxury hotel and you accept another bedroom for her. And then you deliberately set about doing precisely the opposite of what your hosts ask you to do. You and your friends are like – like a pack of stray dogs who leave their visiting cards on the doorstep of the family kind enough to take them in and feed them.'

Few of the delegates could understand the simile. They looked at each other in bewildered interrogation. 'Visiting cards? Visiting cards?'

During this tirade Margaretta's face had grown even more red and congested. 'I find all this talk of tickets and hotel rooms and – and visiting cards extremely vulgar,' she said.

'Well, for the Malindian Centre your behaviour is extremely vulgar. And tickets and hotel rooms, I might remind you, are extremely expensive. If your object in coming here was to defy the Malindian Centre, would it not have been better to have done so out of your own ample pocket?'

Helga had just thrown the biscuit wrapping on the floor in front of her. Once more she was lumbering up, once more she was swaying across the room.

'Leave that minibar alone! Leave it alone!'

It was then that the meeting of reasonable people reaching reasonable compromises broke up.

Helga's hand lay frozen on the door of the minibar, her mouth sagging open.

Margaretta snatched her bag off the floor. 'Come, Helga. We don't want to stay here to be insulted any further.'

Mr Tong shrugged, smiled ruefully at Amos and made for the door.

'Good-night, Kingsley.' Frank, who usually called Amos by his given name, was curt.

Miss Kawai put a hand to her mouth. 'Amos-san – you are very fierce!' She giggled behind the hand. Well, at least he had won her approval. He had also, surprisingly, won the approval of the sturdy Finnish delegate, who was almost the last to leave. She patted him on the shoulder. 'Swedes! Swedes!' she exclaimed. She barked with contemptuous laughter.

Finally Max and Amos were alone in a room full of chairs and glasses, and stinking of pipe, cigarette and cigar smoke.

Max sank on to the sofa, and put his long hands to either side of his face. 'Oh, Amos, Amos, Amos! What have you done? What *have* you done?'

But at that moment Amos was thinking: What is Laura doing?

# 8

'Golliwogs! What *has* been going on here?'

'You know what's been going on here. What I want to know is what's been going on elsewhere.' Amos lay outstretched on the sofa in underclothes and socks with a half-finished glass of neat gin beside him.

'What are all these chairs doing?'

'People sat on them.'

'And all these glasses?'

'People drank from them.'

'You're stinking, absolutely stinking.'

'Well, it was a stinking thing to go off like that.' Amos trailed an arm in search of his glass, found it and raised it. But as it was about to touch his lips, Laura snatched it from him.

'That's enough of that.'

'And that's enough of all this – this hanky-panky.'

'What do you mean?'

'You know what I mean.'

Laura sat down in the armchair opposite the sofa. Dreamily she played with a tendril of her hair. Dreamily she said: 'It was a really fun evening.'

'Oh, don't, Laura, don't. I have more than enough to contend with without having . . .' Amos burst into loud, choking sobs.

Laura stared at him for a few seconds. Then, with a sigh, she got up. 'Now come along! Silly baby!' She eased herself on to the sofa beside him and began to tickle the sole of one of his feet. 'Mother's silly little baby!'

Amos closed his eyes. The sobs became giggles. Then he opened his eyes, jerked upwards, and pulled his foot away. 'What the hell were you doing? Do you realize' – he glanced at his fake Rolex watch – 'that it's twenty-two minutes past *three*? I don't think we've ever been up so late. Except on an aeroplane. Tell me, Laura! What the hell were you fucking doing?'

'Well, I can assure you that one thing we weren't doing was fucking – as you elegantly put it.' She got off the sofa. 'But we had a fun evening. Yes, definitely. A fun evening.'

'Doing *what* for God's sake?'

'We drank a little. Walked a little. Talked a little. Danced a little. There's quite a nightlife in this city. And Bob's a super guide to it. Knows everywhere and everyone.'

'I bet! Oh, Laura, how can you do this to·me? How can you? If you only knew what I had to go through this evening!'

'Like what?'

'She crunched up a packet of almonds. She wolfed a Hershey bar. She devoured a dozen Marie biscuits.'

'Who did?'

'Oh, never mind, never mind!' Amos rolled over on the sofa and buried his face in the cushion which Frank O'Shaughnessy had punched.


'Did that go all right?'

Amos and Max were drinking coffee together in the interval after the first session of the assembly of delegates. Amos felt as if his head had become a leaden bucket against which an invisible and malevolent goblin, standing on his shoulders, kept kicking and kicking. If he opened his mouth before a mirror, he knew that he would find that his tongue had turned into an antiquated razor-strop and his teeth into orange-pips.

Max considered the question. 'Well . . .' he said at last.

'Be truthful with me. For God's sake be truthful with me. Always be truthful with me.'

Max put down his cup on the window-sill against which he was leaning. 'This coffee's just terrible.'

'Be truthful with me, Max!'

'Well . . .'

'Well, what?'

'Well, I thought that you lacked some of your usual, er, incisiveness. When that Swiss delegate – you know, what's-her-name – raised her third point of order. When the Pakistanis wanted to propose their in-session resolution about that Salman what's-his-name's novel. When it was a question whether we should send a letter or a telegram of protest to what's-his-name in South Africa. Frankly, Amos, you just didn't seem to have your usual grasp of things. You weren't on the ball. If you want me to be really brutal, you seemed, well, all at sea.'

'I was! I was! Oh, God, if only this goblin . . .' He put a hand to the back of his head and left it there. But the goblin went on kicking. 'And if only this razor-strop . . . and these orange-pips . . .'

'Are you all right?'

'No. Not really. In fact, far from all right.'

Mr Tu, athletic and purposeful, was striding towards them. He stopped and, head on one side, extended both arms in greeting. Amos felt that he and Max were expected to race forward and jump up at him like dogs. Who had originated the ridiculous idea that orientals were more introverted than westerners? 'Gentlemen!' he cried out. 'Everything all right?' He had not himself been present at the assembly of delegates, having explained that he would be busy in the Congress office.

'Oh, fine, fine! Yes, everything went most smoothly.'

'I hear that Mr de Kuhlenkampf is going to propose a resolution about not attending cocktail parties and banquets.'

'I myself heard something to that effect. But let's hope that better counsels will prevail. The wonderful thing about WAA is that they usually do.' Although a devout Roman Catholic, Max practised a kind of Christian Science where WAA was concerned.

'I have some good news.' Bouncing on the balls of his feet, Mr Tu beamed first at Amos and then at Max. 'Some very good news.'

Suddenly, as though by a miracle, the goblin had ceased to kick at the leaden bucket. Very good news could mean only one thing. 'The prisoners have been released!' Amos cried out in joy and relief.

Mr Tu looked rueful. 'No. I'm sorry. The news is not quite as good as that. But we are permitted to visit them!'

'Oh. Well. How wonderful.'

'This was something refused to any ambassador. Refused to Amnesty. And to the Red Cross. We are very lucky. Very privileged. This shows how highly the Government regards WAA.'

'That's marvellous!' Max threw an arm about Mr Tu's shoulder. 'When does the visit take place?'

'Tomorrow afternoon. But only four people may go. And nothing must be said about the visit until it is over. For reasons of security.'

'Quite, quite. But who are to be the four?'

'Well, firstly, our President of course.'

'I really don't mind *not* going if other people are absolutely desperate – '

'Oh, no, Amos, you *must* go! Your enemies are already saying that you're not interested in what happens to the prisoners. If you were not one of the party . . .'

'Well, yes. Yes. I suppose you're right.'

'And I shall have to go,' Max went on. 'Or they'll say

the same things about me. And of course Mr Tu must come, to be our interpreter. That leaves the fourth.'

The three men looked at each other, none of them prepared to commit himself.

'There'll be a hell of a row if Margaretta Svenson finds herself left out,' Max said at last.

'Oh, no, no!' Amos cried out, thinking of himself confined for hours on end with Margaretta in the huge black Mercedes.

'Mr O'Shaughnessy?' Mr Tu suggested. 'She can't complain if we ask him. They're allies.'

'Oh, no, no!' Max cried out, thinking of O'Shaughnessy's conversation about call-girls and massage-parlours, and the enormous royalties which he had earned by writing about them.

'That leaves Heinz,' Amos said.

'That leaves Heinz,' Max agreed.

'Well, I suppose he's the best of the three,' Mr Tu said.

'Or, at any rate, the least awful,' Amos concurred.


'I can see absolutely no point in bumping along for the best part of an hour in a stifling bus in order to plant a tree, when you've done absolutely nothing for the best part of a year about replacing that camellia beside the outside loo. No, I'm not coming. Absolutely not.'

'But darling . . . *Please!*' It was not so much that Amos wanted Laura to accompany him on the trip to the People's Park as that he did not want her to rush off to meet Naylor.

'Absolutely not.'

'Then what do you plan to do?'

'I plan to continue to lie here.'

'But you've been lying there most of the day.'

'Delayed jet-lag. And not getting to bed until four o'clock. And your waking me so early with all that knocking over of chairs on your way down to breakfast.'

'Only one chair. Well, two. Oh, *please*, petal!'

'Why on earth should I come? The Duke of Edinburgh doesn't always accompany the Queen. Princess Di doesn't always accompany Prince Charles. Even Fergie doesn't always accompany Andrew. I'm a person in my own right, you know. I'm not just your consort.'

'Yes, yes, I know, I know. But . . .' For a few seconds Amos leaned over the bed, staring down at Laura, who was wearing nothing but knickers and bra. Could that – could that – be a love-bite on the side of her neck? Or was it merely a shadow? He almost asked her, and then decided not to. Her soft, creamy flesh always bruised so easily. Like a ripe peach. Oh, how beautiful she looked, and how ghastly if that shit had been . . . Amos turned away. 'All right, darling. Have it your own way.' Laura usually did have it her own way.

'Don't forget your sunhat!' Laura raised herself on an elbow to call after him. Yes, thank God, it *had* only been a shadow on the side of her neck.

'I look awful in it. It's far too small for me. It shrank that time you put it in the washing-machine. Don't you remember?'

'Never mind. It's better to look awful than to feel awful from sunstroke. Take it, Amos!'

Amos took it. It moved him that Laura should display this solicitude.


In the still-empty bus – he was always too early for everything – Amos began to imagine what, at this very moment, might be happening high up above him in the suite. As soon as he had closed the door behind him, Laura would have jumped off the bed and hurried into the bathroom to have a quick shower. She would be smiling to herself in the mirror, in gleeful anticipation, as, no longer the *tachiste* painter of the past, she carefully applied one delicate layer of paint after another to her face. That done she would forage, still in nothing but knickers and bra, for the diaphragm in her suitcase . . .

Or there was another scenario. She would put out her hand to the telephone and ring down to the bar. Or to one of the restaurants. Or to his office. 'He's gone . . . To plant a tree. Yes, to plant a tree. . . . No, I've no idea what kind of tree, but it's to celebrate the Congress . . . They say it's almost an hour's drive each way. That's what they say, but with luck they may even have a puncture. At all events I'm free for at least the next three hours. If I know anything about Amos's tree-planting abilities, it'll take him an absolute age to get anything planted. Come on up!'

Oh, hell, hell, hell! Amos placed his head on the back of the seat in front of him and repeatedly punched his right knee with his fist, to the amazement of the driver who had just clambered aboard.

Now delegates began to troop out to the bus in twos, threes and fours. Because of the heat most of them were lightly dressed, and because of the glare most of them wore dark-glasses. They greeted Amos as they climbed on board but no one, he noticed, ventured to sit with him. Well, those in supreme authority were always lonely, he told himself. Probably Mrs T., Gorbachev and Bush had the same problem. There was no sign of Margaretta, Frank, Heinz or any other member of what he had now come to think of as the Opposition. Surely they didn't think planting a tree to be obscene? But they might have pretended to each other that it was, in order to enjoy a siesta.

When Mr Tu sat down beside him – he was wearing shorts, to reveal thighs so muscular that they might have been those of a gymnast – Amos was at first delighted. But that delight turned to despair when he saw that Miss Shimada, followed by Miss Kawai (or was it Miss Iwai? he could never remember), was

111

daintily edging her way through the huge revolving doors. Dressed not in her usual kimono but in a cotton frock with an extremely low neckline and an extremely short skirt, she revealed that her breasts were so diminutive as hardly to exist and that her legs were, on a magnified scale, those of a sturdy toddler. But Amos did not care. Breasts and legs both filled him with a longing so ravenous that it erased all thought of what Laura might be doing at this moment.

'There's Miss Shimada!'

'Miss Who?' Mr Tu did not share Amos's excitement. 'One of the Japanese ladies?'

'Yes, she's the attractive one. The very attractive one.'

Mr Tu peered. Clearly to him neither of the two Japanese was more attractive than the other.

'Miss Shimada! I was afraid you weren't coming.'

'Ah!' The exclamation was precisely the sound which Amos would have expected if a doctor had asked her to take a deep breath while sounding her chest. (Breast? Bosom? Why did chest sound so anatomical and unromantic?) 'Amos-san!' She gave a bobbing curtsey, hands to bare knees. 'I am very happy.'

'I'm very happy too.'

Miss Shimada was holding up all the delegates boarding the bus behind her. One of them, an elderly Cambridge don who in the distant past had also been a poet, now called out in his strangled, falsetto voice: 'Madam, do you think you could move along there? There are others of us who would like to get aboard.'

'Sorry! Sorry! Very sorry!'

'Come and sit here in front of us!'

Miss Shimada ducked her head and slipped into the seat which Amos had indicated. Miss Iwai (or was it Miss Kawai?) slipped in beside her. Miss Shimada turned: 'Amos-san – I have poem for you.'

'A poem! Oh, how wonderful! How kind of you!'

'Not here. In my room. I will give it to you this evening.'

'Splendid!'

'On Tower Bridge.'

'Then you *have* been to London – and you never got in touch with me! Naughty girl!'

'No, no!' She cupped a hand over her mouth and giggled into it, as though he had said something wonderfully droll. 'But I imagine. I read about Tower Bridge, I see photograph of Tower Bridge, and I imagine. For you I imagine!'

As the bus started up, Amos wanted to go on talking to her. But she clearly did not relish the discomfort of turning round in her seat and twisting her neck upwards and leftwards, and was soon in rapid conversation with Miss Iwai (or was it Miss Kawai?).

'Now I'll tell you the history of the People's Park.' The history, as recounted by Mr Tu, proved a long one.


They had hurtled down an expressway, the driver constantly hooting. They had bumped along beside paddy-fields, the driver constantly hooting. They had lurched up and around hairpin bends, the driver constantly hooting. Now, at a less frantic and importunate pace, they were traversing the Park. There were green slopes, with gigantic holes gouged out of their otherwise flat surfaces. There were stretches of tarmac with seesaws, swings and slides dotted about them, but not a soul in view. There was a kiosk, outside which some elderly men were staring silently into space, with cups and glasses set out on a table before them. There was a bench on which a young couple were seated, one at either end, as though awaiting a third party to sit between them. There were some concrete lavatories, with an elderly female attendant leaning against the wall of the one intended for men. If this was a People's Park, the People seemed strangely absent.

'Not many people,' Amos said.

'Not now. But in the evening many people come out here.'

Miss Shimada was asleep, her head on her companion's shoulder. Amos could see her chest (breast, bosom?) gently rising and falling. It struck him as almost unbearably erotic.

The bus stopped.

Amos heard the Cambridge don's strangled falsetto: 'I hope it's less hot outside than in here. You'd think they'd have an air-conditioned bus.'

'I must apologize. The air-conditioning is not working.' It was to Amos, not to the Cambridge don, that Mr Tu made his apology. Mr Tu then added: 'Madam Su will make a short speech. She is very interested in conservation matters. Then, of course, you will speak, Mr President. And then we shall perform the ceremony.'

'Ceremony?'

'The tree-planting.'

'What is it I'm to plant?'

Mr Tu drew in his breath. 'I'm afraid I don't know. I haven't seen the tree. We will ask Madam Su.'

But Madam Su, a jolly, plump matron in low-heeled, white strap-shoes, a white shift reaching almost to her ankles and a white straw-hat, had not seen the tree either.

Officials of the Park came forward to be introduced to Amos. Each handed him a card, and to each he handed a card of his own. There was a hole in the ground, around which the delegates, many of whom had already begun to show their usual propensity to stray, were told to take up their stations. Miss Shimada and Miss Kawai (Iwai?) were holding hands, as two little girls but surely not two adult women might do in the West. The bony haunches of the English don were propped on a shooting-stick. The Finnish delegate, outstretched on her Pakamac on the ground, looked

114

like a cow disgruntled at a delay in milking. Max had taken a comb out of his pocket and was running it through his hair.

Mr Tu clapped his hands for silence and then had to clap them again and yet again. Why should writers be so ill-disciplined? Amos wondered, not for the first time. Even the Germans were still chattering.

Madam Su advanced until she was on the edge of the hole. She began to speak, but in an English so idiosyncratic and in a voice so low that it was difficult to grasp anything which she was saying. Soon most of the delegates were once again chattering to each other. Max looked about him reprovingly, the comb still in his hand. 'Sh! Sh!' But no one paid any attention to him.

When, at long last, Madam Su had finished, Amos turned to Mr Tu: 'Is it me, now?'

'Just wait a minute please, Mr Kingsley.'

Two of the officials of the People's Park were hurrying towards him, one carrying a white coat, and the other a pair of white wellies and a pair of white gloves. 'Please,' one of the officials said to Amos, holding out the white coat.

'Am I supposed to wear this?'

'They do not wish you to soil yourself.' Mr Tu made it sound as if he were either a baby or the incontinent inmate of an old people's home.

'Please,' the official said.

Amos struggled into the coat, which was stiff and clammy to the touch, and far too tight for him across the chest and under the arms. It felt as if it had been ineptly tailored out of a vinyl tablecloth. The other official then knelt down and began to unlace his shoes. Amos looked over to Miss Shimada. Horrors! Her hand had covered most of her face. She was shaking with giggles. Then he heard other people giggling or even laughing aloud. Was this all some diabolic plot to make him look as silly as possible?

The official kneeling before him was now easing off

one of the shoes. Oh, if only Laura had darned that sock, as he'd repeatedly asked her to do! And after that long journey in the bus, its air-conditioning not working, might not his feet be ponging? Orientals were said to be extremely sensitive to the body odours of westerners.

If the coat had been far too small for him, the boots were far too large. But at least the gloves fitted him like, well, a glove.

'Now you can make your speech, Mr Kingsley,' Mr Tu whispered.

Constricted in coat, boots and gloves, his head throbbing in the overtight sunhat which Laura had insisted that he wear, Amos felt as though he were a pressure cooker about to explode. He cleared his throat. 'I don't want to keep you all standing out here in this extremely hot sunlight for more than a moment or two. But I feel it would be wrong not to say a few words about first the People's Park and then about the ceremony which, on your behalf, I'm about to perform. The People's Park, still in the process of construction, was the inspiration of the enlightened President of this country, who realized that, if people are to work hard, they must also have the opportunity for recreation and relaxation.'

As he paused, Amos heard a male voice from the crowd – was it one of the two immensely tall, immensely thin Norwegian delegates? – demanding: 'What kind of recreation and relaxation does this enlightened President allow prisoners of conscience to enjoy?' Oh, dear, it was so difficult to please everyone, guests as much as hosts!

Again Amos cleared his throat. He could feel his body burning in the constriction of the coat, each sweaty foot sloshing around in the overlarge carapace of its boot, each hand swelling within its glove. Well, he must just push on, summarizing what Mr Tu had told him at such wearisome length on the bus. 'Where we are now standing there is eventually to be a grove of ornamental trees and shrubs. It is to be known as the, er, Grove of International Harmony.' (He hoped he had got that right). 'So it is wholly fitting that, on your behalf, I should plant the first tree to be, er, planted in this, er, Grove. After all, WAA is still in the forefront of the struggle for International Harmony, as it has always been. We demonstrate, in a world unfortunately torn apart by dissension, that it is still possible to achieve, as our International Secretary so often and so rightly reminds us' – Amos gazed across to Max, who was engaged in pulling some hairs out of his comb and so not merely failed to return the gaze but clearly was not listening – 'agreement in disagreement and disagreement in agreement.' One of the People's Park officials had now approached with a tree. What was it? It looked like some sort of cedar. At that, Amos was suddenly inspired. 'The tree which I am going to plant is of the, er, evergreen variety. That seems to me an apt and welcome piece of symbolism. The natural beauty of this country is an evergreen one. Its literary creations are evergreen. And WAA itself is an evergreen organization, which through more than half a century has suffered no decline or, er, falling off.'

Since no one seemed to have realized that he had finished his speech, he gave a little bow. At that first Madam Su and then Mr Tu stepped forward to shake him by the hand. Disappointingly, since he had by now acquired an actor's appetite for applause, there was no clapping. He had thought it to be one of the better of his impromptu speeches, particularly in view of the attire in which he had been obliged to deliver it.

An official advanced and, with a low bow, handed him a spade. As Amos heaved the first shovelful of earth into the hole – why the hell had he let himself be persuaded by Laura to wear the sunhat, which now felt like a crown of thorns? – cameras began to click. One of the cameras belonged to Miss Shimada, who later was to give him a copy of a photograph in which he looked, so Laura derisively told him, like an overweight master butcher.

As he at long last was able to divest himself of the coat, wellies and gloves, he whispered to Mr Tu: 'Was that all right?'

Who was it who first originated the idea that orientals were more tactful than westerners? Mr Tu bit on his lower lip, shrugged his shoulders and then said: 'Usually you speak better, Mr Kingsley. But it *is* very hot here, and Englishmen are not used to heat.' He took from Amos the white jacket, by now damp with sweat, and passed it to one of the officials. 'There is one thing that I must tell you. Not that it is of any importance, of any importance at all. That tree which you planted is not an evergreen, Mr Kingsley. That is a, er, deciduous tree.'

'Why don't we split up?'

'Split up?'

'Yes, why don't you sit beside me, and your friend beside Mr Tu? Gentleman and lady, gentleman and lady.'

'Gentleman and lady!' Miss Shimada appeared to be about to giggle, her hand going up to her mouth, but then to have thought better of it. Instead, she began to blush. She lowered her gaze and clicked the fastening of her bag open and shut, before she said: 'I come with Miss Kawai, I must return with Miss Kawai.'

'But why? I don't see that at all.'

'Miss Kawai is my friend.'

'Yes, but aren't I your friend?'

'Please?'

'I really don't see why, just because – '

'I wonder whether you'd very much mind sitting down, madam, so that the rest of us can get to our places?' Once again it was the Cambridge don.

'Sorry! Sorry!'

Miss Shimada sat down. Next to Miss Kawai.


'But you *must* come to the banquet!'

'Must I? Why?'

'Well, it's being given by the Minister of Culture. And I'm the President of WAA and you're my wife, now aren't you? And if you don't come, you might give certain people – and even the press – the idea that you're joining the boycott.'

'In a sense I *am* joining the boycott. But not for their reasons. I'm just sick of these mass shindigs, with everyone making idiotic speeches for hours on end.'

'Do I make idiotic speeches?'

'Well, not always. And not for hours on end. I will say that for you, you soon run out of wind. Except when you've eaten *botni*.'

'Thank you.'

'No offence meant.'

'Oh, Laura, please do come!'

Laura shook her head. 'Nope, I'm sorry, Amos, I've made up my mind.'

'What are you going to do then?'

'I haven't decided.'

'And what did you do this afternoon?'

'Slept.'

'Is that the truth?'

'Trust me or don't trust me. Do as you please.'

Amos did not trust her.


As he hurried down, far too early, to meet the Malindi-ans who were to conduct him to the Minister of Culture's party in the huge black Mercedes, Amos found himself in the lift with Heinz de Kuhlenkampf and a group of American tourists. Heinz not merely pre-tended not to see Amos but edged into the centre of the tourists in the obvious hope that Amos would not see him. For the first time in Amos's experience, the Dutchman was wearing a dinner-jacket.

'Heinz!' As Heinz shot out ahead of him from the lift, Amos pursued him. 'Hey! Heinz!'

'Yes? . . . Oh, Amos. Were you in the lift? I never saw you. All those tall, noisy Americans . . .'

'So you're coming to the party after all?'

'The party? No, no! I couldn't possibly! No. You've seen my resolution for tomorrow? No, while those three men are in prison it seems to me – er. . .'

'Obscene?'

'Yes, obscene, to eat and drink at a party.'

'But then why are you all dressed up like this?'

Heinz hesitated, nonplussed. Then the answer to the question came from a Malindian in a pale-blue uniform and a pale-blue peaked cap.

'Mr de Kuhlenkampf please?'

'Yes. That's me.'

'I am chauffeur of Dutch ambassador. I come to take you to dinner.'

'Oh. Thank you. Oh, good.'

As Heinz walked off, Amos could not resist calling out after him: 'Now be careful not to eat and drink!'


Although so many delegates had already declared their intention of not attending any parties, there seemed to be an enormous number of them on the lawns of the Minister's residence. That, as he stood alone, surveying the animated scene, so few of all these people should be familiar to him, only demonstrated, Amos mused with a certain sorrow, the isolation to which any head of any great organization must inevitably resign himself.

Well, they were certainly enjoying themselves, despite the spoilsports in WAA, as they grabbed glasses from the trays of passing waiters, returned yet again to

120

the lavish buffet to pile their plates high, or shouted and even pushed at each other. But it was a pity that for an occasion such as this the sartorial standards of WAA should have sunk even lower than usual. Just in that group facing him, for example, there was a barefoot girl, a young man in tattered shorts and a singlet, and another two young men with Mohican hair-cuts. In contrast, the Malindians all looked so elegant and, well, clean.

The Cambridge don detached himself from a group of mostly English delegates and came over. 'All on your own?'

'For the moment.'

'You haven't got anything to eat!'

Amos shrugged. 'One hasn't all that appetite in this heat.'

'Let me get you something. We can't have our President going hungry, now can we?' Such was his paranoia at that moment that Amos at first suspected sarcasm. Then he realized that the don was merely being kind.

'Thanks.'

Soon the don returned with a high-piled plate. 'That should put some lead in your pencil.'

'Thanks. Awfully kind of you.'

'I didn't bring you any of that *botni*.'

'I'm glad of that.'

'Terrible for wind. Last night I was almost airborne after a plate of it.'

'The smell alone is enough to put one off.'

'Like a midden.'

The don then hurried off.

It was the turn of one of the Mr Chus to come over next.

'All on your own?'

'For the moment.' No doubt at parties people came up and put the same question to Mrs T., Gorbachev or Bush.

'You have no *botni*, Mr Amos.'

'Oh, I have a lot of other things to eat.' Amos held out his plate.

'I will fetch you some *botni*. You must have some *botni*. At dinner you told me how much you loved our *botni*.'

In a similar desire to ingratiate himself, Amos had also told his Japanese hosts in Tokyo how much he loved raw fish. From then on, he had been obliged to gulp down raw fish at every meal.

'Well, yes, *botni* is rather delicious.'

'I will get you some. A moment, please.'

Amos hurried away to another part of the garden, in the hope that Mr Chu would fail to find him there.

'All on your own?' This time it was Mr Tu.

'For the moment . . . I'm delighted to see that so many of the delegates have turned up.'

'Delegates?'

Amos used his plate to indicate a large and boisterous group of young people in front of them.

Mr Tu leaned forward and whispered: 'Those are not delegates, Mr Kingsley. When we realized that many delegates were not coming, we had to invite, er, other people. So that the Minister should not lose face. And so that we – and you – should not lose face.'

'But who are these people?'

'Most are what the Americans call "backtrackers".'

'Back-packers.'

'Back-packers. A few come from the universities. A few are working here. Mr Mu had a very difficult time to find them in such a hurry. He had to telephone many places. But fortunately his wife's uncle is manager of the YMCA. He was very helpful.'

'Mr Kingsley! Mr Kingsley!'

His name sounded like a war-whoop as Carmen Mendoza, millionairess leader of the Costa Rican delegation, rushed towards him, arms held high above her head and hips waggling.

'I didn't know you were here, Miss, er, Mrs Mendoza.'

'I have only just arrived. Whom do I wish to see first? I wish to see Mr Kingsley.' Her huge figure draped, like a statue about to be unveiled, in what might, for all Amos knew, be the Costa Rican flag, she grabbed each of his arms with such violence that that night he was to find purple imprints of her fingers in his flesh. 'But Mr Kingsley, you do not look good! You look troubled! Why are you troubled? Carmen must take away these troubles for you.'

'Oh, if only you could!'

'You must learn to enjoy.'

'Oh, if only I could.'

At that moment the little band, which Amos had last noticed eating plates piled with *botni* on a dais at the far end of the garden, suddenly struck up.

What was it that they were playing?

'This is for you,' Mr Tu said. 'In honour of our English President.'

'For you!' Carmen confirmed, gripping him again by the arms.

What was it, what was it? Then he realized: 'The Lambeth Walk'.

'You must open the dancing,' Mr Tu said. 'The President will open the dancing.'

'Yes, you will open the dancing with me,' Carmen cried out joyfully.

'Oh, no, no, no! My dancing days are over.' What he really meant was that his dancing days had never begun.

'Nonsense! Come!'

Carmen was irresistible, as she towered above him in her garishly voluminous tent of a dress. Again her fingers bit into his flesh, then she pulled him towards her, with a baritone grunt.

'Oh, no! No!'

But they were off, kangaroo-hopping round the lawn

to the amusement of all the people gathered about them. Oh, it was so undignified! Oh, it was so unworthy of a President! 'Good on you!' a voice, presumably belonging to some Australian back-packer, shouted from the crowd. Someone gave a wolf-whistle. Someone else began to clap in time to the music. Then, in couples or alone, the spectators themselves became participants in the dance.

Amos felt breathless, giddy, appalled. But suddenly he also experienced an extraordinary exhilaration. Carmen was like some irresistible typhoon which had swept him up and away, depriving him of all will. Faster and faster they hopped, faster and faster they gyrated.

Then, by some mischance, he caught his foot on the trestle of one of the long tables on which the elaborate food had been laid out. He let out a gasp, followed by a squeal. The table, acting like a seesaw under his weight, tipped first one way and then the other. Then it crashed to the ground. Amos slithered across it, with Carmen and a huge, upturned bowl of *botni* on top of him.


'You smell quite disgusting.'

'Well, I'd rather smell of *botni* than stink of booze and sex.'

'We didn't have any sex.'

'You certainly had booze.'

'If you call champagne booze, then, yes, we had booze.'

'Champagne!'

'It was Bob's birthday, so he took me to this wonderful little restaurant run by a Frenchman. I gave him a Rolex watch. Like the one I gave you. A joke birthday present.'

'You gave him a watch like mine?'

'Except that his tells the time all over the world. And has a light. And plays "Danny Boy" as an alarm.'

# 9

>:> <:<

'You have prepared some questions?'

Despite the heat, Heinz had dressed for the visit to the prisoners in the sort of clothes that, back in the Netherlands, a man might wear for tramping across windswept dykes, shotgun under arm: knickerbockers, brogue shoes with flaps and tweed cap. All that was missing was a Norfolk jacket. In its place he was wearing a khaki bush-shirt.

Amos wriggled in his seat beside Heinz in the back of the Mercedes. 'Er, well, no. I thought I'd play it by ear.'

'People who play it by ear usually play it out of tune,' Heinz said – whether in joke or in reproof, or in both of these things, it was impossible, from his rigid expression, to determine. 'You have prepared some questions, Max?'

'Only in my mind.'

Heinz unbuttoned one of the pockets of the bush-shirt and drew out a pad. 'I have made a short list. To assist Mr Tu with his translation, I have made it in English. May I read?'

'Yes, do,' Amos said, squinting down sideways at the notebook now open on Heinz's knee. The list began:

Accommodation
    Clean sheets?
    Numbers to cell?

Radio, television?
Lighting?
Food
Protein?
Green vegetables?
Choice?
Freshness?
?Reading matter
?Writing materials
Toilet facilities
Toilet off cell?
Flush?
Toilet paper?

Amos had got this far when, either by accident or by intention, Heinz shifted the notebook on to his other knickerbockered knee. He then continued to read out the list in the same monotonous drone, with occasional interpolations by himself or comments from Mr Tu or Max.

'That's it,' he said, with evident self-satisfaction when he had finished. 'I think that is comprehensive. Yes?'

'Yes, very comprehensive,' Max confirmed.

During the reading of the list Mr Tu had begun to look uncomfortable. 'You must not expect a Malindian prison to be similar to a prison in the West,' he now ventured.

'I do not see why not. There are certain basic requirements to be fulfilled in any prison in any civilized country of the world. No?'

'Malindi is a poor country,' Mr Tu said.

'There is no reason why a poor country should not also be a humane one. Yes?'

For a while all of them were silent, as though brooding on this proposition. Then Heinz asked: 'Who is to be our spokesman?'

'Our spokesman?' Max looked across Heinz to Amos, and Mr Tu leaned round from the front seat also to look

126

at him. Clearly both expected him to claim the privilege. But as Amos hesitated, Heinz provided his own answer:

'If you wish, I will be the spokesman. I have prepared the questions and therefore I can put them. It is good if one person puts the questions in order, not everyone haphazard. You agree?'

Heinz took the subsequent silence for agreement.


'Is there any danger of, er, snakes?' Amos had enquired on the first occasion when he had been obliged to ask for a stop.

'The danger is small,' Mr Tu had reassured him. 'Snakes are nervous creatures. If they hear a noise, they usually disappear, not attack.'

Before squatting among the bushes, Amos had coughed loudly and repeatedly, in the hope that the snakes would then take the hint to disappear. How fortunate, he thought, that he had persuaded Laura to let him bring with him the latest copy of the *Independent*, even if the *Guardian* – at the hotel kiosk that morning they had again hesitated between the two dailies – might, for once, have proved less abrasive.

After his second scramble from the car and into the bushes, everyone had begun to speculate about the cause of his upset.

'Perhaps you drank too much at the party,' Heinz suggested. 'Or ate too much.'

'No. I did neither. I probably ate and drank less than you did at the dinner at your Embassy.' The state of his guts had made Amos uncharacteristically tetchy.

'A change of climate can often cause such troubles,' Mr Tu said. 'When I arrived in England, I myself suffered. The students from India used to call the affliction "Blighty Blight". Or sometimes "British Belly". Many of us were stricken. Some of us even took to drinking bottled or boiled water. But I was convinced it was the change of climate.'

'You've been eating too much *botni*. That's what's caused it,' Max said.

'I've hardly eaten any *botni* at all!'

'But Mr Chu told me you were crazy about it.'

'Excuse me, Mr da Costa, *botni* cannot harm the stomach. *Botni* is extremely healthy. We give it to children with whooping-cough, and now leading Mal-indian doctors also say that it is good for Aids and Alzheimer's disease.'

'Do you think that we could stop again for a moment?'

When, after the usual noisy and prolonged coughing, Amos had once again squatted behind some bushes beside a paddy-field, he was appalled to see a group of small children, all of them dressed in ragged clothes and many of them barefoot, closing in silently around him. Had they come here to rob him? But, having formed a ring, they then did not move, their expressions all frozen into the same dreamy reflective-ness. Half-standing and half-kneeling, his trousers round his knees, he stared at them, and they stared back. Oh, hell! It was nothing but curiosity, he sup-posed. He'd better get on with it.

It was only as he was wiping himself with yet another piece of the *Independent* that he realized the enormity of his action. 'Now, darling, whatever you do, please, *please* bring me back that copy of the paper. You know I like to do the crossword last thing at night.' It was the crossword which now lay crumpled and soiled. How on earth was he to face Laura on his return?

As he hurried away from the bushes, the children let out squeals of delighted laughter and then, like a flock of birds, scattered in all directions, making derisive farting noises as they did so.

'Better?'

Amos was not sure how to answer Heinz's question

when once more, with a deep sigh, he squeezed himself back into the car. If he was better, it was, he feared, only for another few minutes.

'Sorry about that.'

'Not to worry.' But Max, looking at his watch, was clearly worried about the time.

None of the three Westerners had realized that, at that moment, the prison was before them, on the gentle slope of a hill. Except that it was enclosed by a high wire-mesh fence, it might have been yet another of the conglomerations of corrugated-iron huts surrounded by paddy-fields, orchards and woods, which, so Mr Tu had told them, were cooperative farms.

At the gate, the driver hooted a number of times, without anyone appearing. Eventually he got out, to return with a man, in a uniform of dingy white trousers, singlet and peaked cap, voraciously gnawing at an apple. Mr Tu produced a document, which the man unfolded and stared at, small eyes screwed together. Then he pointed up the drive with what little remained of the apple, said something in Malindian, and nodded to the driver, who got back into the car and drove on towards the largest and shiniest of the corrugated-iron huts.

'Terrible place,' Heinz muttered, gazing around him.

'Oh, it looks quite cosy to me,' Amos said.

'Would you wish to be imprisoned here?'

'I don't think I'd wish to be imprisoned anywhere.' Amos all but added that he would rather be imprisoned in the warmth and sunlight of this place than in the cold and greyness of the Netherlands.

The governor, a corpulent, bullet-headed man in the same dingy white uniform as the guard at the gate except that there were huge gold chevrons on his sloping shoulders, jovially greeted them in the entrance to the hut, shaking each of them by the hand. 'He asks you to enter,' Mr Tu translated. And then: 'He is very happy to see you.' And then: 'He wishes you to sit down.' All these things were already self-evident.

After some further politenesses – how long had they been in Malindi? was this their first visit? what kind of journey had they had? what precisely was WAA? – Mr Tu then said: 'He asks what it is you wish to know.'

'Well . . .' Max began.

'I think that . . .' Amos took up.

'We do not wish to put our questions to him. We wish to put our questions to the prisoners themselves,' Heinz snapped.

Mr Tu gazed at Heinz with a mixture of exasperation and alarm.

'Please translate.'

Mr Tu said something, in a low voice, in Malindian to the governor. Whether it was a translation of what Heinz had just said there was no way of knowing.

'The prisoners will come soon. They are working in the fields. If, until they come, you would like . . .'

'Well, yes, I think that maybe there are some questions,' Heinz said. 'Toilets, for example.'

'Toilets?'

'About toilets I wish to ask some questions.'

It was at that moment that a vague, dilatory churning in Amos's guts suddenly sharpened and quickened. 'Oh, dear! I'm afraid . . .'

Mr Tu did not have to be told of what it was that Amos was afraid. Hurriedly he leaned forward to the governor, speaking rapidly. The governor put out a hand and thumped its palm down on the bell before him. Again he thumped.

The sleepy-looking, elderly orderly who eventually appeared, conducted Amos not, as he had expected, down the corridor of the hut but out into the glare and heat. They walked round the hut, to its rear. Flies buzzed round piles of garbage, and a man in pale-blue cotton trousers and a ragged pale-blue cotton shirt worn loose was kneeling on the ground skinning and chop- ping up what looked like the haunch of a very large and very shaggy dog on a board. Was the man a prisoner? Perhaps even one of the three prisoners they were to interview? Amos did not have time to speculate further as, unfastening the buckle of his belt, he scur- ried into the lean-to at which the guard had pointed. He thought of those items on Heinz's list:

Toilet facilities
        Toilet off cell?
        Flush?
        Toilet paper?

If the governor's guests and presumably the governor himself had to use what was in effect a bucket placed under a rickety construction of wood in a malodorous shack festooned with spider-webs, what sort of 'toilet facilities' would be available to the prisoners? As for 'toilet paper', he was now reduced to using a copy of yesterday's agenda for the meeting of the delegates, discovered, by a fortunate chance, in the back pocket of his trousers.

When he had picked his way back to the governor's office, he found that two middle-aged men, in the same pale-blue cotton trousers and shirt as the man chopping the haunch of meat had been wearing, were standing close to each in one corner of the room, with a guard on either side of them. Both wore spectacles; both, unlike the man with the meat, looked clean.

'Are they not to be allowed to sit?' Heinz was demanding as Amos came through the door.

'Yes, they may sit of course,' Mr Tu said, having spoken to the governor.

'But there are no chairs.'

Again the governor's palm thumped the bell.

'Do either of them speak English?'

One of the two prisoners looked over to the governor and then said hesitantly: 'I do.'

'Good! It is better if we can speak direct. Translation always has its, er, dangers.' Heinz waited with obvious impatience – biting his lips, fidgeting with the flaps of the pockets of his bush-shirt – as the orderly carried in one chair and then another. 'Where is the other prisoner?'

After consulting the governor, Mr Tu gave his reply. 'There seems to have been some error. He was told to wait in his building and not to go to work. But nonetheless, by some oversight of the guards, he went to work. A guard has now gone to fetch him.'

'Was he forced to go to work?' Heinz was fierce.

'Oh, no. I gather that he *wished* to go to work.'

'He *wished* to go to work?'

'That is what I gather.'

'How is that possible?'

'It seems' – Mr Tu hesitated – 'he does not wish to meet us.'

'He doesn't wish to meet us! You mean – he's afraid of meeting us?'

Mr Tu shook his head. 'No. The governor tells me that he does not wish to meet us.'

'But why?'

Mr Tu shrugged. 'Perhaps he will explain.'

The two prisoners already present had now seated themselves. Each was perched on the edge of his chair and each had crossed one thin leg high over the other. Max held out his cigarette case. 'Cigarette?' They looked at the governor and then, at a nod from him, eagerly accepted. 'Cigarette, sir?' The governor impatiently shook his head.

Heinz was gazing down at his notebook.

'You are?' he said to one of the two men.

'Please?'

'Your name is?'

'Nu.'

132

'Nu?' Heinz was now scribbling in the notebook.

'Nu Lim-Tee.'

'To differentiate you from the few other Nus I imagine to be here.' No one responded with even a smile to Amos's comment.

'And you are an editor, yes?'

'Yes.'

'Charged under the National Security Law with fomenting a Communist rebellion through your publishing activities?'

The man fiddled with his glasses. 'Yes. But charge is false.'

Heinz turned to the other man. But since he spoke no English, Mr Tu had to serve as his translator. Name: Chu Hon-Fee. Poet. Charged under the National Security Law with sedition.

'Now I should like to ask some questions about living-conditions here. Yes?'

Heinz began to go through his list, jotting down the answers in his notebook with murmurs of 'Bad, bad, bad' or, occasionally, 'Terrible' or 'Shocking' or 'Tsk, Tsk'. Once he turned to Amos: 'Does this not make you disgusted?' There was a note of challenge in his voice.

The two men were extraordinarily calm, one might even have thought indifferent, until Heinz came to his question about writing materials. Then they both became excited. The one who spoke English began to shout: 'I ask for paper, pen, pencil! Nothing! I ask repeatedly! Nothing! Friend here, Mr Chu here, ask! Nothing! Terrible. Writer must write.'

Clearly to be able to function as writers was far more important to them than the clean bedding, adequate diet or 'toilet facilities' about which Heinz had been asking them in such detail.

'Yes, that seems a good point,' Heinz said, once more scribbling in his notebook.

From outside there came the sounds of raised voices. Then the door opened and two guards pushed in an extremely tall, extremely thin young man who was still shouting at them.

'This is the third prisoner,' Mr Tu told Amos.

The young man was glaring at Amos fixedly, as though it were he who was the governor of the prison or perhaps even the President of the country. His eyes were bloodshot and there was mucus encrusted round a nostril. A guard had brought another chair into the by now crowded office. There followed an argument, with the man first refusing to sit in the chair and then being pushed into it, a huge hand to his bony chest, by the beefiest of the guards. When he tried to rise again, the huge hand pushed him back.

Heinz looked pained. 'We do not like this violence. Please tell the governor.'

Mr Tu murmured a few words in Malindian, at which the governor threw back his head and laughed for several seconds on end. Soon all the guards had joined in the laughter. 'What is so funny?' But no one was prepared to answer the question.

He turned to the man: 'Do you speak English?'

The man squinted wildly at him. Then in a rapid, high-pitched, eerily venomous voice, he replied: '*Da*, *je parle* English, French, *Russe*, *Deutsch*, *Espagnol* and *Esperanto*.'

'Well . . .' Nonplussed, Heinz gazed down at his notebook. Then he looked up: 'Your name is – ?'

'Robespierre, Josef, Che, La Pasionara Kropotkin.'

Heinz looked in interrogation at the governor.

The prisoner who spoke English said quietly: 'His name is Mu Nam-ju.'

'Why do you wish to see me, Mr Englishman?' The voice was shrill and hectoring.

'I am not an Englishman. I am Dutch.'

'German?'

'Not German. Not Deutsch. Dutch. From the Netherlands.'

'You are not President of WAA?'

'No. Mr Kingsley here' – Heinz indicated Amos – 'is President.'

'Why you talk then?'

'Because I am the, er, spokesman of our little commission.'

'I have no wish to speak to spokesmans.'

'We've come here to help you.'

'I do not wish help from WAA!' His voice rose in both pitch and volume as he spoke the sentence so that WAA emerged as a screech. 'No help! No want!'

'I don't understand.' Heinz turned to Mr Tu and repeated: 'I don't understand.'

Mr Tu shrugged and turned to the governor, who also shrugged.

Max held out his cigarette case to the man, who scrabbled in it and removed four cigarettes. He stuck one, unlit, in his mouth, and put the other three in the top pocket of his soiled and tattered shirt. He pulled out the cigarette again and laughed, revealing front teeth with a large gap in them. Amos wondered if someone had knocked out some of his teeth. There had been rumours of the ill-treatment and even torture of prisoners.

'Why do you not want our help, Mr – ?'

'Kropotkin.' The man gave a yelp of laughter. Then he jabbed with a finger at his chest: 'Me – no writer! No like you! No writer!'

'But you've written some essays. I've seen them. Mr Tu, he's written some essays, hasn't he?'

'Me – revolutionary! Yes! Yes! Bomb in post office. Yes!' Again he jabbed at his narrow, skinny chest. 'You write! You, you, you!' He pointed at each of the foreign visitors in turn. 'Me – bomb! Post office bomb!' He rose to his feet, and on this occasion the guard made no attempt to push him back. 'Now – I go. Goodbye, gentlemans! Goodbye!' Mockingly, he raised a hand and, waggling the fingers as a small child might do, waved to each of them in turn. He moved towards the door, where the two guards blocked his way.

'Do you wish him to stay?' Mr Tu translated for the governor.

The three foreigners gazed at each other.

Then Amos said: 'If he doesn't want to stay, then we ought not to force him to do so.'

Heinz shrugged.

Max said to Mr Tu: 'He can go. Unless there's anything more he wants to tell us.'

The prisoner whirled round: 'Nothing, gentlemans! Nothing!' he shouted.

The governor waved a dismissive hand, and the orderlies then stood aside to let the man, by now muttering unintelligibly to himself, go out through the door which he had once more pushed open.

'I didn't like that at all,' Heinz said. He shook his head and then shook it again. Then he leaned across to the prisoner who spoke English. 'What did you make of that?'

The prisoner, scholarly-looking and dignified, gave a little smile. 'We here' – he indicated first himself, then the man beside him – 'writers. Only writers. But Mr Mu – freedom fighter!' He spoke with admiration.

'But Mr Mu is also a writer,' Heinz persisted.

The prisoner shrugged, drawing down the corners of his mouth. 'Writing unimportant to him. Freedom – important!'

Consulting his notebook, Heinz then began to summarize WAA's 'demands' – Amos hoped that, in translating them, Mr Tu would call them 'requests' – on behalf of the prisoners. The governor had already said that, for reasons of discipline and security – what precisely these were he never specified – it would not be possible for the visitors to be shown round any other areas of the prison.

'Is that everything?' Heinz asked Max and Amos at the close.

Max, who had been looking increasingly bored, nodded and then drew again on his cigarette. Amos said: 'Yes, I think so. The most important thing is the provision of writing materials.'

The prisoner who spoke English smiled and nodded vehemently.

The governor said something. 'The governor would like to offer you some food,' Mr Tu explained.

'How kind of him,' Amos said.

The food, brought in by the orderly on a plastic tray, consisted of plates piled high with *botni*.


'That was very odd.' Heinz was consulting his notebook in the back of the car. 'I am afraid that his treatment must have driven that poor man mad.'

Max gazed out of the window at some women knee-deep in the murky waters of a paddy-field. He ran long fingers through his hair. 'He didn't seem all that mad to me. Rather sane, in fact. In an impassioned way.'

Amos was recollecting the man's savage rejection of any help from WAA. There was an intellectual honesty there, so different from the semi-honesty or the dishonesty of people like Heinz, Margaretta or, yes, even himself. The man did not think of himself as a writer, and he did not wish others so to think of him. What he had written was irrelevant. What was relevant was the bomb which he had placed in a crowded post office, in protest against a regime which, whether mistakenly or not, he saw as tyrannous and corrupt. For him, a revolutionary in his defiant strength was more important than a writer in his compliant weakness. Even the other two prisoners, both essentially writers and not revolutionaries despite the unorthodox writings which had landed them in prison, seemed to share that view. It was a view disconcerting, chilling and even frightening to Western liberals like Amos himself and those most active in WAA. The bomb had been discovered before it had gone off. Had it gone off, WAA could certainly not have intervened on behalf of the man. But to the man the fact that it had not gone off, killing innumerable innocent people, could only be a matter for regret. Amos marvelled at a single-minded fanaticism, so totally alien to him.

What was heartening was, on the one hand, the indifference of the two writers to their living-conditions and, on the other, the urgency with which they had asked for paper and pens or pencils. To write remained, even in prison, the major need of their lives. In comparison, all other needs – for adequate food, for comfortable accommodation, for clean sanitation, for visits from their families – were of little importance.

'Maybe we should demand that a psychiatrist should see that man,' Heinz was saying.

'I don't think him mad. Not in the least. In fact, he struck me as, er, terrifyingly sane.'

Heinz stared at Amos. Then he said: 'What is your opinion, Max?'

'I agree with Amos. The important thing is to get all of them those writing materials.'

Heinz closed his notebook. Then he said: 'There is another matter I wish to discuss with you both. Not to do with the prisoners but with the administration of WAA. Yesterday evening I was discussing with our Ambassador at, er, our meeting.' Amos was amused that Heinz could not bring himself to say the word 'dinner-party'. 'It is the question of *per diem* allowances.'

'*Per diem* allowances?' Max said. He was suddenly wary. It was he who handled the day-to-day finances of WAA.

'On such a journey as this there are a lot of out-of-pocket expenses. Yes? I do not mind paying such expenses but nonetheless . . . If someone is on WAA business, then surely . . . I think *per diem* expenses should be paid.'

'But we haven't *had* any expenses,' Amos said. 'Not on this trip.'

'No. But it is a matter of principle. On other trips maybe there will be expenses . . .'

Neither Max nor Amos answered.

'It was an idea. Maybe we can discuss it in the assembly. You understand, it is not for myself. It is a matter of principle.'

As the lift ascended, Amos suddenly thought: My God, how am I to explain returning without the *Independent*? Then he had a brilliant idea. He would tell Laura that one of the prisoners had begged for it. She would be sympathetic to that, whereas she would not be sympathetic to the idea of its doing service for lavatory paper.

As he walked down the long passage, he experienced a sudden, overwhelming happiness. His guts seemed at last to have relaxed; but, even more important, in a few moments he would once again be with Laura, they would talk together, they would have dinner together. In one fist he was carrying the flowers, waxen and potent-smelling, which he had bought, at enormous cost, at the florist's shop in the basement of the hotel, after he had failed in his attempt to replace the *Independent* at the newspaper kiosk.

Laura was not in the room. He looked around already feeling that something was amiss but without knowing precisely what it was. Then he went into the bedroom. He saw that her pyjamas were not on the double bed beside his, and that her dressing-gown was not hanging where it had been hanging that morning, on the hook on the door. Her guidebook and the paperback of a detective story had vanished from the bedside table. Instead, on the bedside table, propped against his portable alarm clock, he saw a note. He approached it as warily as if it were the bomb left in the main post office by the prisoner. He put out a trembling hand and picked it up. The fact that Laura had left other notes in the past made this one not less but more terrifying. He read:

Sorry, darling. Won't be here when you return. Bob has to examine in Tongu and has suggested I go along with him. You don't really need me and Tongu is said to be the Florence of Malindi – a real *must*. I'll try to ring but, if that's not possible, don't worry. Washed out your vest and pants (hanging from the air-conditioning duct) and darned that sock of yours. Took the Puritabs, since you won't need them. Also camera, guidebook and the money hidden in pocket of blazer.

Take care.
Blessings
Laura

Amos sank on the bed. His quiescent innards once again began to churn. Then he jumped up and pulled open drawer after drawer, feverishly searching. Yes, of course, of course! She had taken the diaphragm . . . Again he sank on to the bed, biting on a knuckle. Well, he had only himself to blame, he thought – being someone who always blamed himself, not others. If he had not lusted after Miss Shimada, this might never have happened. But in his heart of hearts he knew that really Miss Shimada had nothing to do with it. Laura had been attracted to that disgustingly hairy brute long before Miss Shimada had arrived on the scene. Oh, if only he himself had even a few hairs round his nipples!

The telephone rang.

'Yes?' As he said the monosyllable, he felt as if he were going to blub like a child.

'Max here.'

'Oh, Max.'

'Are you all right, old chap?'

'Yes, I'm fine.'

'From your voice I thought you might have had another attack of the squitters.'

'No. That seems to be over. Mercifully.'

'Oh, good. I found a message in my pigeon-hole. From your friend Carmen. I imagine there was one in yours too.'

'I forgot to ask.'

'That's the worst of these electronic cards instead of keys. But isn't your message light on?'

Amos looked. 'Yes. Yes, it is. I hadn't noticed.'

'Are you sure you're all right?'

'Perfectly.'

'Anyway – Carmen wants us to have dinner with her. In Le Tour d'Eiffel.'

'It's terribly expensive.'

'Of course it is. That's why she's asked us. She's going to pay, of course.'

'Very well.'

'You don't sound exactly thrilled by the prospect.'

'Well, it's just . . . I feel rather tired after our expedition.'

'Of course she expects Laura too.'

'Laura's gone away.'

'Gone away?'

'Didn't you know?' Amos was always loyal to Laura. 'She planned this trip to Tongu. Ages ago.'

'Tongu?'

'The Florence of Malindi. She's always wanted to see it. So I persuaded her to go. There's really nothing we need her for here.'

'Well, Carmen will probably be relieved.'

'Doesn't she like Laura?'

'Oh, I expect she likes her all right. But the one she really likes is *you*.'

\*

'Kingsley – why are you so sad?'

Did Carmen still not realize that Kingsley was not his Christian name but his surname? There was something so eighteenth-century in being addressed like that. 'Oh, I'm not sad. Just – reflective.'

'On what do you reflect?'

'On the prisoners we visited,' Amos extemporized.

'You have such a big heart! You have done all you can for them today. Tomorrow you can try to do more for them. But tonight – let's enjoy! . . . Max, give him some more champagne.'

At the other end of the restaurant Miss Shimada was one of a group of seven Japanese, all of whose faces were flushed from what appeared to be only a single bottle of wine among the lot of them. Next to her was a young Japanese writer of thrillers, who – perhaps in a misguided attempt at Americanization – constantly chewed gum and wore a broad-brimmed hat even when, as now, he was indoors. This man kept leaning against Miss Shimada and even touching her, in a totally unJapanese manner. Amos had repeatedly tried to catch her eye, but she seemed deliberately to avoid looking at him. Had something turned her against him? Oh, lordy, lordy! Perhaps he'd been too fresh with her on the bus? Perhaps she'd somehow heard of Laura's desertion?

'You seem more interested in the other tables than in us,' Max said.

'Yes, you keep looking at those pretty young Japanese ladies,' Carmen took up. Now she grabbed the champagne bottle and filled Amos's glass to the brim. 'Chin, chin!'

'Er – chin, chin!' When Amos raised his glass, Carmen banged her own against it, splashing champagne on to the tablecloth and over his hors d'oeuvres. 'We must make Kingsley happy,' she told her other guests – all of whom, with the exception of Max, were Costa Rican delegates.

Amos resolved to be happy. It was not easy; but for the rest of the evening, as one of the Costa Rican delegates jumped up and gave his imitation of Charlie Chaplin, a second sang a Costa Rican folk-song all about a blind old man wooing a flirtatious young girl, and Carmen herself told a succession of jokes hingeing on the disparity in size between Jamaican and Costa Rican bananas, Amos did his best.

He lay on the bed, still in his clothes. If he buried his face in the pillow next to his own, he could smell the scent – what was it? it had cost so much even in the duty-free and now he could not remember its name – which he had bought Laura at three o'clock in the morning at Anchorage. Now, oh now, his anchorage was gone, and he was adrift on a sea of loneliness and longing and regret. Instead of reproaching Laura, he began to reproach himself. If a man could use his wife's crossword puzzle as lavatory paper, he deserved to lose her love. Oh, if only he could recover that copy of the *Independent* and so recover her!

He turned over on the bed and, in an attempt to comfort himself, began to think of Miss Shimada. As Carmen's party had left the restaurant, he had walked over to the table of Japanese and asked: 'Enjoyed your dinner?'

'Yes, enjoy, very much enjoy,' the writer of thrillers had answered, even though it had really been to Miss Shimada that Amos had put the question.

Amos had placed his hand on the back of Miss Shimada's chair, resisting the impulse to place it on the bare nape of her neck where her elaborately patterned kimono dipped so tantalizingly. 'What did you have to eat, Miss Shimada?'

'Prawns.'

'Ah, but the prawns here are not like the jumbo

prawns in your country. Japan is the land of jumbo prawns.' (Where and when had he last said that?)

'Please?'

No point in repeating it. 'You forgot to give me the present that you promised me.'

'Present?'

Had she drunk too much, as her flushed face indicated, or was she being deliberately obtuse?

'Your poem about Tower Bridge.'

'Ah!' It was a little wail. Then she raised her napkin to her mouth with both hands, and giggled into it.

'Don't forget it next time!'

'I gave Amos-san poem,' Miss Iwai said. 'About autumn in Tokyo.'

'Yes, indeed,' Amos said. 'And a fine poem too.'

'Kingsley! We are going!'

Carmen's voice was imperious. Amos said his hurried goodbyes.

Now, remembering that bare nape which he had so nearly touched, Amos felt increasingly uncomfortable, until he was obliged to turn over on to his back. He stared up at the ceiling. Oh, Laura! Oh, Miss Shimada! Oh, Laura! Oh, Miss Shimada! Miss Shimada! Miss Shimada! Hurriedly he pulled down the zip of his trousers . . .

Seconds, not minutes, later he was wildly groping for a Kleenex tissue from the bedside table. His hand eventually encountered what he assumed to be one. Oh, oh, oh . . .

Then he looked at the paper in his hand, now disgustingly moist.

Oh, God, those tainted leaves, those tainted leaves!


In the middle of the night, as Amos lay exhausted but still sleepless, his knees almost touching his chin and his thumb in his mouth, the telephone began to ring.

Hurriedly he reached over to it, removed the receiver

and croaked: 'Yes?' He was sure that it was Laura, guilty for her desertion of him, troubled about his welfare, perhaps even about to announce her disillusion with Naylor and the imminence of her return.

'Mr Kingsley?'

'Yes?'

'Please do not ring off. Please listen to me. This is important. I need your help, Mr Kingsley. As President of WAA only you can help me.'

Some other writer banned, harassed, perhaps even gaoled? Amos threw his legs off the bed and sat up. 'Yes? What is it?'

'Listen to me, Mr Kingsley! Listen to me!' Then the voice was transmuted. 'When I warned the French that Britain would fight on alone whatever they did, their Generals told their Prime Minister and his divided Cabinet: "In three weeks England will have her neck wrung like a chicken." Some chicken! Some – '

But by now the telephone receiver had tumbled from Amos's grasp.

# 10

Amos was by the newspaper kiosk, deliberating whether to buy the *Independent* or the *Guardian* – he would have preferred the *Guardian*, but if Laura were to return suddenly that day, he wanted to have the *Independent* crossword awaiting her – when Max and Mr Tu approached. Both looked grim.

'This is it,' Max said, without any greeting.

'It?'

'What we'd feared. The day of confrontation.'

All through his solitary breakfast – without Laura, he had for once been able to have it up in their suite – Amos had been thinking of another sort of confrontation: between himself and Naylor. 'Now look here,' he had said fiercely to Naylor in his imagination. 'Your wife may have run off with a Greek bum met in a Nigerian supermarket, but I'm not going to allow my wife to run off with an English bum met at a Malindian lunch-party. Get that into your thick head of yours!' But now he merely echoed: 'The day of confrontation?'

Max nodded. 'What I most wanted to avoid. Confrontation. So bad for the image of WAA.' He lowered his voice conspiratorially as two members of 'the Opposition', poets from Iceland, shambled past on their way to their late, liquid breakfast at the bar. 'If we can't present a united front to the world, the world will never take us seriously.'

'What, er, will the confrontation be about?'

'What do you think it will be about?' There were

146

times when Amos's cluelessness ceased to touch and appeal to Max, and instead got on his nerves. 'How to handle the issue of the prisoners.'

'The Opposition have produced an in-session resolution,' Mr Tu said. 'Condemning the Malindian Government for its handling of the prisoners. Such a resolution will be disastrous, if it's passed. It may even mean the end of the Malindian Centre.'

'How is that possible?'

Mr Tu shrugged, clearly not willing to explain how it was possible. Amos wondered if the rumours, circulated by Margaretta Svenson, Frank, Heinz and others, that the supposedly independent Centre was in fact financed by the Government, might not be true.

'It's all up to you,' Max said.

'To me?'

Max nodded.

'But as chairman . . .'

'As chairman you're in a unique position to give the assembly a lead. You must give that lead.'

'Oh, well, yes. Yes. But in what – in what direction should I lead it?'

'Away from a resolution,' Max said firmly.

'Towards a petition,' Mr Tu said.

'A petition?'

'There's nothing offensive about a petition,' Max said. 'I've already drafted one. It begs the President – respectfully, even humbly – to show, er, clemency to the prisoners. To grant them an amnesty. Or, if an amnesty is impossible, to alleviate the conditions under which they are held. An improvement in diet. Better sanitary arrangements. More frequent visits.'

'Writing materials,' Amos put in.

'Of course. Yes, those too.'

'You see,' Mr Tu took up, 'there is the question of face. In the East – '

Dreading yet another disquisition on face and its

importance, Amos said hurriedly: 'Point taken. Face must be preserved at all costs. That's obvious.'

'To give in to the demands contained in a resolution already made available to the press of all the world is something our President could not do. Out of the question. The loss of face would be colossal. But to concede graciously what WAA has requested with extreme respect and even humbleness in a petition, is something wholly different. That the President can do. That the President may very well do.'

'I see,' Amos said.

Max put a hand on Amos's shoulder. 'So, dear chap, it's all up to you. Not for the first time. I know you won't fail WAA.'


During the past two-and-a-half years, Amos had presided at many acrimonious sessions of the assembly; but none had been as acrimonious as that of that morning. It could have been predicted that the other Asians would, inevitably, side with the Malindians. After all, they understood the importance of face. It might also have been predicted that the French too would side with the Malindians, since, far back in the history of WAA, long before Amos had become a member, there had been some insult – an accusation of plagiarism, or it might have been of collaboration with the Nazis, made against a wholly blameless delegate – for which the French had never forgiven the Swedes and for which Margaretta Svenson now had to pay the price of ferocious French opposition to the resolution which her Centre proposed. Less predictable, since the reasons were not generally known, was the opposition of the Mali delegate, whose lesbian passion for Margaretta had been brusquely, even brutally rebuffed, and that of one of the German Swiss delegates, a rigid Calvinist, who had been horrified by Frank's *Wet*

148

*Dreams* when he had glanced at it at a bookstall at Zurich airport.

Margaretta had made an impassioned speech, her arms flailing and her voice so strident that the interpreters hastened to turn down the amplification through their earphones. When something as obscene as the imprisonment of innocent writers took place, she declared, it had always been the procedure in WAA to pass a resolution. The resolution was released to the press and forwarded to the head of the government concerned. What reason was there now for abandoning that procedure? People had urged the courtesy due from guests to their hosts. But when such obscenities were taking place, courtesy was irrelevant. One had to stand up and be counted, however discourteous that seemed and however unpopular it made one. Frankly, she could not understand how a President of WAA – the chief custodian, after all, of its long and honourable tradition – could take any other view than her own. But of course the present incumbent of the office was a man widely known for his right-wing – she hesitated to say reactionary – convictions, and the government of Malindi was, despite recent improvements, essentially right-wing. She had thought it obscene – and had made no pretence of not thinking it obscene – that so many delegates had been prepared to guzzle and swill and, yes, dance at parties, while three innocent fellow writers were, in effect, starving. It would be even more obscene if this resolution were not to be passed.

Heinz spoke, in a slow, solemn voice, his body tilted forward, his hands clasped before him, and his eyes half shut. He might have been pronouncing the final obsequies by a graveside. '. . . It is difficult for me, terribly difficult, to convey the conditions in which those men there must live. . . . squalor which is unspeakable . . . miserable diet . . . clearly suffering from malnutrition and the diseases which malnutrition causes . . . brutal guards . . . a governor who, I regret, obviously has no interest in the welfare of the men in his care . . .' Tears formed along his lower lids. Was he talking of things which he had actually witnessed and which through obtuseness or callousness Amos had failed to witness? Or was he talking of things which he had never actually witnessed but which he imagined that he had witnessed? Amos could not be sure; and not being sure, he felt bewildered and uneasy. That Heinz was genuinely moved, there could be no doubt. When he sat down, there was a sympathetic sough, like a wind high up in the branches of a forest, from the whole assembly.

There were other no less emotional speeches, with a succession of Asian delegates accusing the Europeans of being incapable of understanding the ways of the East, and a succession of Western delegates saying, in effect, that the ways of the East should long since have been abandoned.

Eventually Max hissed at Amos: 'Now call on Mrs Yu for the Malindians. She's the one they've chosen to speak for them.'

Amos ignored a number of other raised hands and called on Mrs Yu, a motherly-looking woman in a cotton dress patently too tight for her across bosom and thighs, her greying hair piled in an untidy bun on top of her head. 'I speak for the Malindian Centre,' she began in a small, tremulous voice. 'My name is Mrs Yu. I am poet. Many Malindian writers are poets. I am sorry, I am not very good poet.' She gave a jerky bow, and followed it with a laugh. Her plump hand went up to the untidy bun and patted it, as though in an attempt at self-reassurance. 'We have caused you much trouble. You are guests in our city of Batu and we have caused you much, much trouble over three prisoners. I am sorry, we are all sorry.' Again she gave the jerky bow, but this time without the following laugh. 'You are all very kind. I understand your feelings. We all – all

Malindian members of WAA – understand your feelings. Prisoners must be released. But I think – we think . . .' She screwed up her eyes, hand once again patting the untidy bun, in an apparent attempt to remember what she or they thought. 'Resolution is not good idea,' she said at last. 'Please forgive. Sorry. But resolution is not good idea. We must think of face. Face is difficult for Westerners to understand. But very important in Malindi, very important in the East. Sorry, but this is true, I think. We must send polite petition to our honourable President. We must ask him, Please release prisoners. Very polite. Sorry, very sorry, but think this opinion right. This is not only my opinion, it is also opinion of whole Malindian Centre. Ladies, gentlemen, please try to understand.' She smiled, staring out over the seated people before her up to Amos on the platform. 'Sorry, Mr President. I speak too much. I speak too badly. Sorry.' She sat down.

'Thank you, Mrs, er, Yu, for that very interesting and, I also think, very moving intervention. Thank you.'

Yes, it had been moving. But it had also infuriated Amos. Why did Mrs Yu, like all the Malindian members, have to sound so humble and apologetic? In reality, probably she and they were no more humble and apologetic than Margaretta, with her strident assertions that this or that was 'obscene' and her no less strident demands for 'instant' and 'unequivocal' action. But oh dear, speeches of that kind could only confirm Western critics in their belief that the Malindian Centre had something of which to be ashamed.

Max rose, ran his fingers through his long, luxuriant hair, and smiled self-deprecatingly at the people before and below him. 'I have listened to everything that has been said with the utmost interest. And with the utmost sympathy. I fully concur with the delegate from Sweden, the delegate from the Netherlands and the delegate from the United States of America – all highly respected members of WAA over a long period of years

– that it is obscene that, while we are holding a Congress of writers in this country, three innocent writers should be in prison. I also fully concur with those delegates – from Japan, Taiwan and Singapore and other countries of the Far East – that the whole conception of face is something vital in this area, and that we shall ignore considerations of face to our peril. I agree with those who say that the normal procedure in WAA is for the assembly of delegates to pass a resolution of censure. But I also agree with those who say that, in the circumstances of the moment, such a resolution might be less than productive. Let us set our eyes on the objective which we all have in common. What is that objective? The release, of course – with the utmost despatch – of the three men whom your President, Mr de Kuhlenkampf, Mr Tu and I had the sad privilege to visit yesterday on your behalf. How can we best achieve that objective? In that, I am prepared to be guided by Mr Tu, Mrs Yu and their colleagues within the Malindian Centre. They say that, if we forward a petition instead of a resolution, then the President may well grant us what we ask. If, on the other hand, we insist on a resolution, the President may well feel so insulted that the prisoners will not be released in the foreseeable future and may even be penalized. I am, as you all know, a great believer in agreement in disagreement and disagreement in agreement. Let us now try to reach that agreement in disagreement – while at the same time privately preserving that disagreement in agreement, essential if we are not to do violence to our consciences. Let us follow the course suggested by our hosts. Let us opt for a petition.'

Max sat down, to mingled cheers and boos. Then he leaned towards Amos, beside him on the rostrum, and whispered: 'Now you do your piece. Then wind things up and take a vote.'

Amos, whose thoughts had been far away in Tongu with Laura, banged with his gavel repeatedly for silence, without getting it. Since Laura was not there, it was left to Max to jump to his feet and yell: 'Ladies, gentlemen, please! *Please!*'

'Er, thank you,' Amos said, when silence was at last achieved. 'I am not, er, proposing to call any more speakers on this matter.' From the assembly in front of him there arose cries of protest from those who had wanted to speak but had not had a chance to do so. It was unlikely, Amos knew from similar past occasions, that they had anything new to say. Many of them would simply arise to declare that their Centres would be voting this way or that way – something which would be perfectly evident from the votes themselves. 'I'm sorry,' Amos said. 'I'm sorry. But we have, as you will see, a very full agenda ahead of us, and this morning we still have to discuss the whole fraught question of translations from literatures in languages of lesser currency – about which, I know, many of you wish to speak.' In fact, he knew nothing of the kind, but it was a safe supposition. Any member of WAA who wrote in a language of lesser currency was always passionately interested in translations from literatures in languages of lesser currency.

'Before we take a vote, I'd just like to put my own thoughts to you, if you will allow me. But before I do that, I should like to repudiate any suggestion – implicit in some of the things said by some of the speakers – that my views are right-wing, perhaps even, er, neo-Nazi. I have repeatedly explained the circumstances of that, er, unfortunate preface which I wrote for a *Festschrift* in honour of a German writer whom most of you would probably feel deserved only *dis*honour. I committed an error. I have freely and publicly admitted that I committed an error. I freely and publicly admit yet again to all of you here today that I committed an error. But to maintain that, because of that error, I am on the side of the, er, forces of reaction is not merely an untruth but, to speak frankly, an insult to me. As a

153

young man, at the University of Birmingham, I was treasurer of the University Labour Party. I have marched with CND – along with my wife. For many years, before the deterioration of its literary pages, I was a regular reader of the *New Statesman*. Admittedly in the last election I did not vote for Labour, but that was not because of any change in my convictions but because I could not see how Neil, er Mr, Kinnock could offer us a viable government. But I did not, let me repeat, I did not vote for Mrs Thatcher. I voted for the party then jointly led by Mr David Steel and Dr David Owen.'

People were rapidly becoming restless, shifting in their chairs, scribbling on the pads before them, even whispering to each other. The Argentine delegate, a chain-smoker, had got up and begun to stalk towards the exit, since smoking was forbidden in the hall. Max, head tilted sideways so that his long, luxuriant black hair brushed a shoulder, was gazing up at Amos. Amos knew that gaze. It said: 'Now, Amos, stop all that! Get on to the business in hand.'

'Well, I'd better leave that there. I hope that, at any rate, I have said enough to make it absolutely clear that I am not, I repeat not, a reactionary and that it is a slander to suggest that I am . . . Now, let's get back to the matter before us. A resolution or a petition? To be or not to be. That is the, er, question.' There were gratified smiles from those of the delegates who recognized the quotation, puzzled frowns from the rest. 'In this connection I'd like to say something about self-righteousness. Self-righteousness,' he repeated with more emphasis. Suddenly, he felt passionate; and he knew that, as so often in the past, passion would give him an eloquence which otherwise he lacked. 'Self-righteousness is the most agreeable of emotions. I know that from my own experience – not merely in WAA but in the whole varied arena of life from almost as long as I can remember. We all like to think that we are superior to others; and to feel that we are morally superior to others is so much easier than to feel that we are socially superior or intellectually superior, since moral superiority is so much less susceptible of proof. There is a lot of genuine compassion in WAA, and a lot of genuine indignation and anger at the way in which, in all parts of the world, writers are banned, persecuted and even imprisoned. But there is also far too much self-righteousness – and, with it, far too much sense of moral superiority and far too much moral indignation.'

Yes, they were listening to him, they really were listening to him! Even Max had stopped doodling large-breasted women in spectacles on his copy of the agenda. 'It's very nice – very comforting to one's ego – very sustaining to one's *amour propre* – to pass resolutions condemning this or that outrage and demanding this or that action. Whenever I send out some protest in your names, I have to confess that I get a kick from it. But more important than that kick – far, far more important – is the ultimate result of the protest for the person or persons on whose behalf the protest has been made. So now I beg you – put aside your own feelings of moral superiority and moral outrage and self-righteousness and just think, think solely, of the three men whom Mr da Costa, Mr de Kuhlenkampf, Mr Tu and I visited yesterday in their prison. What we feel, and the satisfactions that we can derive from our feelings, and the actions that those feelings prompt us to perform, are all equally irrelevant. All that is relevant is how to help those three men. If the members of the Malindian Centre tell us that the best way to help them is to send a petition to the President instead of passing a resolution, then I, for one, think that we should follow their advice. They are after all, nationals of this country. They have passed all their lives in it. They *know*. We, all of us visitors here, can only guess. So – I beg of you – fellow members of WAA – please, please vote for a petition!'

'You had better put the choice clearly before them,' Max hissed *sotto voce*. 'If they can possibly misunderstand something, they always do. We don't want more of those complaints that the vote wasn't fair.'

Amos nodded. 'Let me put the alternatives clearly before you. On the one hand you have the Swedish resolution, seconded by the Americans. Copies have been tabled.' Amos ignored a cry of 'Where? Where? I have no copy!' from an Omani delegate dressed in burnous, sandals and a great number of heavy gold rings. 'On the other hand you have the petition drafted by our International Secretary after consultation with the Malindian Centre and, er, myself. That has also been tabled.' Again there was a cry of 'Where? Where? I have no copy!' from the Omani delegate, and once again Amos ignored it. 'You may vote for one of these two alternatives, but not for both. Have I made myself clear? One of these two alternatives – either the resolution *or* the petition, but not for both . . . Now hands up all those who wish for the resolution . . . No, I'm sorry, we'll have to do that again. Each delegation has only one vote . . . Each delegation has only one vote. Three delegates of the Hawaiian Centre were voting, and four delegates of the Cuban Centre were voting . . . Each delegation has only one vote. All right? . . . Now – those in favour of the resolution, please. Hands up . . .'

From the back of the hall an invisible Brazilian woman delegate asked: 'Are we voting for the resolution or the petition?'

'At present I am taking the votes for the resolution.'

'But we voted for the resolution last time.'

'We are voting for it again.'

Hands were raised, and Max stood up on the dais to count them. Margaretta had also jumped to her feet, to join in the counting. 'No, please keep your hands up! Please keep them up!' Amos shouted. 'Suisse Romande! Only one vote per Centre!' How could people be intelligent enough to write books and yet so unintelligent that they could not grasp something so simple?

'Thirty-seven,' Max announced.

'Any abstentions?' Amos asked.

A hand was raised.

'You have already voted for the resolution, Oman.'

'Sorry, I did not understand.' The hand was lowered.

'So we have thirty-seven for the resolution. Now let us vote for the petition. And remember – if you've voted for the resolution, then you can't vote for the petition. It's an either/or situation. One or the other. Not, please *not*, both! Those in favour of the petition . . .'

Hands were raised. Max once again rose to count, and Margaretta once again jumped up to do so as well.

'No, Oman, you cannot vote for the petition. You have already voted for the resolution.'

'Ah! I am sorry. I did not understand.'

'Thirty-eight,' Max announced, to cheers and groans.

'Thirty-seven,' Margaretta challenged. 'I'm right, aren't I, Frank?'

'Thirty-seven it is,' Frank confirmed.

'We'd better have a recount,' Amos said.

After two recounts, it was agreed that the figure was thirty-eight.

'So we send a petition.'

As Amos announced this, the Argentine delegate rushed in, cigarette in hand. 'No one call me! No one warn me! I do not vote!'

'I'm afraid you're too late.'

'But no one tell me! My fellow delegate is not here! Why no one tell me?'

'I've already said . . .'

Amos's voice was swamped in shouts of protest from all those who had so narrowly lost the vote.

'Let him vote!' Max whispered. 'It won't matter. He's on our side.'

But Max had forgotten the Falklands factor. Since it

was clear that Amos, an Englishman, supported the petition, the Argentine had decided to support the resolution.

'Well, we seem to have an equally divided vote,' Amos said. 'Thirty-eight, thirty-eight.' He turned to Max and whispered: 'What do I do now?'

'You have the casting vote.'

'Do I?' Amos, knowing how unpopular it would make him with the losers, was reluctant to exercise it.

'Of course you do. Tell them.'

'It seems that, er, in these circumstances, I have the, er, casting vote. So I shall – I shall . . .' For a moment he felt as though his throat was closing up, refusing an exit for the fateful sentence. Then, with a gulp, he got out: 'I cast my vote in favour of a petition.'

There were cheers and clapping. There was also a baying of rage. Margaretta leapt to her feet. She pointed at him, as she screeched: 'I hope that, in the years ahead, no one will ever forget the President's part in this matter. I shall certainly not do so when it comes, at the end of this week, to a vote on a renewal of his office for a further term.'

Amos gathered up his papers with trembling hands. Should he respond? No. More dignified to ignore her. 'We shall now adjourn for a ten-minute coffee-break. Let me repeat. A *ten-minute* coffee-break. We have a crowded agenda and we need a lot of time to discuss this whole problem of translations from literatures in languages of lesser currency.'

Max put a hand on Amos's shoulder. 'Well done, Amos. You handled that very well.'

Mr Tu was hurrying up to the dais. 'Thank you, thank you, Mr Kingsley. We will never forget what you did today.'

Nor will the Opposition, Amos thought gloomily. But he put on a brave smile. 'A man's gotta do what a man's gotta do,' he told Mr Tu.

'Please?'

'Duty. One must just do one's duty.'

'If you feel it's your duty to destroy WAA, then that's what you've succeeded in doing, Kingsley.'

It was Frank, menacing him from behind, his face white and his small eyes glinting, mica-like, with fury. 'You know damn well that a petition is just something that WAA never, ever sends. WAA passes resolutions of censure. Always has done ever since it was founded. It wasn't a petition that it sent to Mussolini in 1932 or a petition that it sent to Hitler in 1933. Now was it? You bet your ass it wasn't! This is the end of WAA. And this, as far as I'm concerned, is the end of you, Kingsley!'

'Oh. I'm sorry you feel like that. But I do honestly think that you're . . .'

No good going on. Frank was striding off down the hall to where Margaretta, Heinz and the rest of his allies awaited him.

'Bad loser,' Max said.

'What a way to speak to me!'

'Don't take it personally.'

'As though there were all that difference between a resolution and petition.'

'The difference, Amos, is between getting one's own way and not getting one's own way.'

Max spoke as a precociously experienced international negotiator.


Instead of joining the delegates for lunch that day, Amos had some sandwiches and a bottle of Malindian beer sent up to his room. In between munching at a sandwich or crunching a crisp, he looked up the hotels in Tongu and, starting with the two with the most stars, telephoned them. Was Mrs Kingsley there? No? Well, then, was there a, er, Mrs Naylor there? Or a Mr Naylor, a Mr Bob Naylor? No? The fewer the stars, the more difficult the conversation. When he was down to one star, no one seemed to understand him, however much he shouted. After some hesitation, he decided not to ring the Tongu YMCA. It was clear either that Laura and Naylor had never gone to Tongu or that they were staying in some private house.

On an impulse, Amos telephoned the British Council office.

A woman's voice answered, harassed, even irritable. 'Mr Naylor? Oh, he never tells me anything . . . No, I've not a clue . . . We had the Royal Ballet arriving here last month and he was nowhere to be found and I just had to cope on my own . . . Then there was that mix-up with the Henry Moores and the muddle between the three Penelopes – Mortimer, Lively and Fitzgerald. The trouble is that Malindi is not Nigeria.'

Next, Amos rang Naylor's house.

Semba answered. 'Yah!'

'Mr Naylor, please.'

'No*sir!*'

'Isn't he there?'

'No*sir!*'

'You wouldn't happen to know where he is, would you?' A silence followed. In desperation, Amos shouted: 'Where is he?'

'No*sir!* Him gone!'

'Where? *Where?*'

'No*sir!* Sorry, sir!'

It was no good. Amos rang off. Where were they, where were they?


A little later, as Amos was staring at the telephone wondering whom next to interrogate, it began a shrill ringing. He snatched at it, imagining once again that perhaps it was Laura.

'Yes?'

A supercilious-sounding male voice announced that the caller was *The Times'* correspondent. 'I gather that there was a bit of a set-to during your meeting this morning?'

Not for the first time, Amos wondered how newspaper men managed to gather things so quickly. 'Well, I'd hardly have called it a set-to. We had a, er, lively – and, er, useful – discussion. As we often do. All quite amicable.'

'Anyway, I gather that the assembly opted for the petition idea? With your using your casting vote to break a nasty deadlock?'

'Er, yes. That's right.'

'Now what I'd really like to know, before I write my little piece, is what precisely is the difference between a petition and a resolution.'

'Well, there isn't much difference. Not really.'

'Then why did everyone get so steamed up?'

'I've no idea.'

'D'you think you're going to pull off being re-elected?'

'Um.'

'I gather there'll be a lot of opposition. You seem to have made yourself extremely unpopular with a large section of WAA.'

'I'm not sure I want to be re-elected. I'm not sure I'll stand.' Without Laura, it was so much easier to make these pronouncements.

'Really?'

'Yes. Really. To tell you the truth, I'm absolutely fed up with the whole organization.'


By the evening, Amos had persuaded himself that Semba had been lying. Laura and Naylor were holed up in Naylor's house, and all that business of a visit of inspection to Tongu was just a cover-up. It wouldn't, after all, be the first time that Laura had lied to him. There had been the occasion when she had told him that she would be spending a week with her aunt in

161

Perth, and he had then learned, through a series of fortunate (or unfortunate) chances, that in fact she was with a widower and his five children at a Butlin's camp in Skegness. There had been the other occasion when she had told him that she had an appointment with the dentist, and he had later seen her strolling along Tooting Broadway hand in hand with a young, pock-marked Tunisian waiter from the local McDonald's.

Amos ordered a taxi and set off for Naylor's house. When he got out of the taxi, nervousness had made him so breathless that he might have run all the way there . . . Oh, damn, he'd given the driver a thousand note instead of a hundred one! Oh, well, never mind. What was the loss of nine hundred thingies when compared with the loss of Laura?

From the wide-open windows of the house came a deafening cacophony:

*Yeah! Baby!*
*What a mess!*
*I want it more*
*You want it less . . .*

They were there! They were giving a party! Laura had always had this depraved love of pop music, so that often when he was looking through his records to find the Elgar Cello Concerto or the Beethoven Fifth, he would come on something like Dire Straits or The Replacements . . . Amos gave a shudder. Well, he wasn't going to stand for it. He didn't care if his irruption created a scandal. After all, the scandal would be far worse for Naylor, whom all the guests would know, than for a stranger like himself.

He rang the bell. Then, when it was not immediately answered, he rang again and at the same time thumped with the palm of his hand on the door.

Eventually a black man, in a shimmering white suit, opened the door a crack.

'Yeah?'

'Mr Naylor, please.' Could this be Semba's husband?

'Mr Naylor is not here,' the man said in an impeccable English accent, with a touch of hauteur. He now opened the door to its full extent, to reveal a host of black people, male and female, all elegantly dressed and all jerking and gyrating wildly to the music. *Yeah! Yeah! Baby! Baby!* Amos felt giddy and slightly sick. Noise, like heights, always had that effect on him. Could that be Semba in that orange, extravagantly pleated dress, with a turban of the same shade of orange on her head and the highest of high heels?

'Is that Semba?' he asked.

The man nodded. 'Do you want to come in?'

Amos hesitated, then shook his head. 'If you're sure Mr Naylor . . .'

'Mr Naylor's gone away. This is Semba's party.' Suddenly the man had lost all his hauteur; he had become affable and relaxed. 'Let me introduce myself. My name is N'Buli and I'm Head of Chancery at the Upper Volta Embassy.'

'I'm Amos Kingsley.' No, he wouldn't say that he was International President of WAA.

The two men shook hands.

'You're sure you won't come in? It's a wild party.'

'No. I really think . . . Thanks, all the same.'

'Just for a moment.'

'I've got one of my splitting headaches,' Amos extemporized. 'Noise always makes them worse.'

'Cobra venom,' the man said.

'Sorry?'

'An infallible cure. A microscopic amount rubbed into the temples. Anyway – hope you soon feel better.'

Amos walked away, hands in pockets and head bowed. How was he to find a taxi?

Finding a taxi proved as hard as it would have been to find cobra venom.

# 11

>:> <:<

By the newspaper kiosk the next morning – neither the *Guardian* nor the *Independent* had yet arrived – Margaretta passed Amos, with Helga in her wake. Margaretta, who was wearing dark glasses (a hangover, perhaps?), removed them, stared at Amos for several seconds, and then walked on. Helga, who had been nibbling on one end of a croissant, presumably left over from her breakfast, jerked her head upwards and away, her teeth bared, like a mare shying at some unfamiliar obstruction.

'Good morning!' Amos shouted after the pair of them, his first 'Good morning' having been ignored.

Margaretta paused and looked round. She said nothing.

'Aren't we friends any longer?'

'No.'

Margaretta walked on.

'You've seen this?'

'What is it?'

'The local English rag.' Max held it out.

'Funny. I've just been at the news kiosk. I never noticed it.' Only then did Amos take in the headline: '*Thoroughly fed up.*' And below it: '*President of WAA speaks his mind.*'

'I wish you hadn't agreed to an interview. We don't

want to give the impression that WAA is in any way divided.'

'But I didn't give an interview!'

'You must have spoken to *someone*. Even the most unscrupulous journalist wouldn't *invent* an interview.'

'In England he might.' Amos looked again at the headline. 'The man told me that he was *The Times'* correspondent, and so, of course, I assumed he meant the London *Times*. I didn't even know that there was a paper called *The Times of Malindi*. All we did was to have a short chat on the telephone . . . Anyway, I *am* thoroughly fed up!' Suddenly Amos felt defiant. He was not going to knuckle under to Max or anyone else any longer. 'I've had enough of WAA.'

'Now, Amos, the time to say you've had enough of WAA will surely be when your term of office has come to an end.' Max was using the same nanny voice, kindly but implacable, which Laura used to him.

Oh, Laura, Laura! If only, by some miracle, he could suddenly hear her say: 'Now pull yourself together, Amos!' or 'Amos, stop that now!' or 'Get on with it, Amos!'


'Point of order, Mr President!' Margaretta had jumped to her feet, as soon as Amos had announced the first item on the agenda for that morning.

'Yes?'

'This petition to the President.' She brought out the word 'petition' as though she were naming some peculiarly repulsive venereal disease. 'Has it been delivered?'

Amos turned to Max.

'No, it has not yet been delivered,' Max said calmly. 'It will be delivered this morning. Your President will sign it on the behalf of all of us and it will then be delivered. By hand, of course.' The truth was that, in all the uproar of the day before, no one had thought even to have the petition typed. Amos had assumed that Max or Mr Tu would be seeing to the matter, and they had made the same assumption about each other.

'By whose hand?'

'Well – by a – messenger, of course. A trustworthy messenger. Perhaps even by some member of the Malindian Centre.'

'That won't do,' Margaretta declared, amid cries of support from her allies.

'I'm sorry. I don't understand you.' Max smiled sweetly.

'A petition as important as that can't be delivered by anyone. It must be delivered by our President!'

Oh, lordy, lordy!

'Well, if you feel . . . But I am not sure if, at such notice, the President – I mean the President of Malindi – would agree to . . . He's a very busy man, needless to say.'

'It would be an insult to WAA if he refused to receive our President.'

Agreement rippled through the assembly.

'We must demand that he receive him!' Margaretta concluded.


Max sipped at his coffee. 'Would Bush agree to receive you with no notice at all?'

'Would Mrs T.?'

'Or Gorbachev?'

'Or Mitterand?

'Of course not. So why should the President of this country? Particularly after the offence he took over Margaretta's press conference.'

'He never came to the opening ceremony.'

'Cancelled his party.'

Mr Tu was hurrying over, with one of the Mr Mus and two of the Mr Chus hurrying along behind him.

'The news is bad.'

'He's refused?'

'He says that he can receive Mr Kingsley on Thursday of the week after next.'

'That means that he can't see him. Or won't see him,' Max said.

'In effect. Yes. In the East, face is very important. We do not say a definite no. Even the President does not say a definite no. But in effect . . . You see, for us orientals face is . . .'

'Yes, yes,' Max interrupted him, for once losing his international negotiator's cool.


'Mr President, that just isn't good enough!' Amos quailed visibly before Frank's onslaught. 'You and the International Secretary and the officers of the Malindian Centre may be prepared to accept that kind of dusty answer, but I am not. And my surmise would be that many other delegates are not prepared to accept it either. Such an answer can only be regarded as yet another affront to WAA. We have our corporate pride, after all. WAA is a supranational organization of immense prestige and importance. It was an insult that the President refused our request to release the three prisoners before this Congress started. It was an insult that he did not attend our opening ceremony, as had been agreed, and another that, for reasons best known to himself, he cancelled his reception. Not of course,' Frank added hurriedly, 'that many of us here would have felt ourselves able to go. Now we have yet another insult. Are we to accept it? My answer is no, no, and again no!'

Applause broke out from all over the hall, with only the Malindians sitting silent, motionless and glum.

Max raised a hand. 'Mr President – may I be allowed . . . ?'

Amos was only too delighted not to have to make any answer himself.

167

'Please.'

'On the one hand, I am in wholehearted agreement with the American delegate. For the Malindian President to refuse to receive our President when he wishes to deliver a most important petition strikes me as wholly unacceptable in a civilized country such as Malindi now prides itself on being. On the other hand, my years with the World Save the Armadillo Fund have taught me the need to be realistic. My rule then was: "Define the parameters and then work as efficiently as you can within them." That remains my rule now. What are the parameters? Clearly we must see that this petition – this most important petition – reaches the President as soon as is possible. But the President has refused to accept it personally. I therefore think that the only course left to us is to have a messenger deliver it to one of his officials. One of his high-ranking officials,' he amended. He smiled round at the assembly, a chin cupped in one of his elegantly long-fingered hands. 'Are we in agreement?'

Unlike Amos, who invariably expected the worst, Max was taken aback when from the floor there came shouts of 'No!', 'Certainly not!', 'Think again!'

'Evidently we are not in agreement.' He drew the microphone closer to him. 'What then do you propose?'

Various hands were raised, as were various voices.

Usurping Amos's role of chairman, Max called out: 'Mr de Kuhlenkampf! The delegate from the Netherlands!'

Heinz gave his answer: 'Our President must go down to the Presidential palace. He must demand to see the President. There is nothing else for it. He must present himself there. He must explain the nature of his mission to whoever it is receives him. He must refuse to go away until he sees the President.'

Oh, lordy, lordy!

'*Oui, oui! C'est ça!*' '*A ragione! Assolutaménte!*' '*Bravo!*' '*Ja, ja!*' '*So desu!*' 'Of course!'

168

'The general feeling of the assembly seems to concur with mine,' Heinz declared, looking around him with some self-satisfaction. 'Mr President – are we to assume that you will now take the necessary action?'

'Er – yes. Yes. Just as soon as the petition is, er, ready. Yes. Of course.'

Amos was awaiting Mr Tu in the lobby of the hotel, when he saw Miss Shimada, in a tartan skirt and tam o'shanter, a shopping bag in either hand. It was odd that, whereas tartan looked incongruous and therefore unappealing on Frank, it looked similarly incongruous but delightful on her.

'Miss Shimada!'

'Ah! Mr President! Amos-san!' She gave him a small, jerky bow.

'You were not at the assembly this morning.' The sense of danger which had been with him ever since the delegates had decided that he must force himself and the petition on the President now made him reckless. 'I looked for you. I – I so much wanted to see you. Naughty girl!'

She raised a hand (if only, a camellia petal, it were brushing his cheek) and giggled behind it. 'Am I truly naughty girl?'

'Very naughty. And very truly.'

'Fact is Miss Iwai and Miss Kawai say that they will speak for Japanese delegation. They tell me not to worry. They tell me to go shopping.'

'And what have you bought?'

He was leaning forward to peer into the nearer of the two shopping bags. But Miss Shimada jerked it away with a little squeal. 'No, no! Amos-san, no!'

'Why can't I look?'

'Because' – she looked up at him roguishly – 'because these are lady's things. Private!'

Lady's things? What could that mean? He imagined

169

black silk-and-lace underwear, a bra with impertinent apertures for the nipples in its out-thrust cones, an exiguous suspender-belt with . . .

'Where you go now?' she was asking. 'I want to walk in garden. You wish to come in garden with me?'

'Well, yes, but . . .'

At that moment Mr Tu hurried towards them, a large, stiff envelope, covered in a number of carbuncle-like seals, extended in both hands before him, as though he were a waiter carrying a tray. 'I'm sorry, I'm sorry,' he got out breathlessly. 'I couldn't find a typist, so I had to type it myself. Not good typing.'

'Well, the seals look good.'

'Yes, I'm good at seals.' Continuing to ignore Miss Shimada, he asked: 'Shall we go?'

On an impulse Amos turned to Miss Shimada: 'Come with me – I mean, come with us!'

'Come? Come where, Amos-san?'

'To see the President.'

'You are going to see the President?'

'Er, yes.'

'I come!' Miss Shimada squealed in delight. At that she tripped over to the reception desk to leave her two carrier bags.

'The President won't mind, will he? She's so sweet. We can say she's part of a deputation.'

'The President has refused to see you, Mr Kingsley. So he will *not* be seeing you – or Miss Shimada.' For once, Mr Tu sounded irritable. 'But she can certainly come for the ride – if she so wishes.'


When the black Mercedes drew up outside the Presidential palace – there had been some argument between Mr Tu and one of the sentries before it was admitted – there were two men in short-sleeved shirts and black neckties standing at the top of the wide sweep of steps. As though each were vying to be the first to reach the car, they now raced down. The first of them to arrive pulled open the nearest door, the second the farthest. Each bowed as Amos, Miss Shimada and Mr Tu descended from the air-conditioned coolness into the heat. Had the men been warned that the petition was about to be delivered? Had the President changed his mind about not seeing Amos?

The man who had opened the door for Amos now extended a hand. 'I am delighted to meet you, sir.' He spoke English with a strong American accent. He shook Amos's hand as though priming a pump.

'And I am – er – delighted to meet you. This is my colleague Miss Shimada. She decided to come along too, since the Japanese are so much, er, interested in the matter in hand. And this is, er, Mr Tu.'

Mr Tu looked as stunned by this enthusiastic reception as Amos was feeling.

'Please.' Having also shaken their hands with the same relentless vigour, the second man pointed up the steps. Amos, followed by Miss Shimada and then Mr Tu, began to ascend.

The first man leading them, his shoes squeaking on the marble, they progressed down a corridor flanked by uniformed, armed guards who saluted as they passed. Amos wondered if he ought to salute back. But the only salute which he was confident of bringing off satisfactorily was a Boy Scout one. They entered a vast room, dotted with 'Empire' furniture which looked as if it had been manufactured the previous day in Taiwan.

'Please, sir. Madam. Please.'

Amos and Miss Shimada placed themselves side by side on a settee. They smiled nervously at each other, and Miss Shimada gave a twitch to her tartan skirt and a tug to her tartan tam o'shanter.

'Please.' 'Please.' 'Please.' They all began to exchange cards.

Soon after that, a young girl glided in with a tray on which were set out three coffee cups. She handed them in turn to the visitors, beginning with Amos and ending with Miss Shimada.

One of the President's aides leaned towards Amos, hands on the ebonized arms of a chair the back of which was surmounted by a brass sphinx, and told him: 'We are very happy to have you here.'

'We are honoured,' the other aide took up.

'The President is sorry to keep you waiting. He has some important business to conclude.'

'The President!' Amos squeaked. Then he recovered himself. 'Oh, that's all right. Actually, we're not in any hurry. To speak of, that is.' Amos sipped at the coffee. One would have expected better in a Presidential palace. But at least, amazingly, the President was going to see him. That was one in the eye for Margaretta and her crew!

'Meantime, while we are waiting, perhaps we can clarify certain details?'

'By all means. Yes.'

'You have the plans?' The other aide pointed to the envelope which Mr Tu had laid across his knees.

'The plans?'

'Your proposed plans for the station.' The aide turned to Miss Shimada. 'We are, of course, delighted that your country is joining the consortium. We have been hereditary enemies for too long.'

'The station?' Amos was bewildered.

The aide went on: 'The President has long felt the need for a nuclear power station in Malindi. It has now become his most urgent priority.'

Amos all at once realized that something terrible had gone wrong. But what? Then he remembered what Naylor had told him about a delegation of 'bigwigs' which had arrived from England at the same time as Laura and himself.

As he looked across at the door in mounting panic, it opened and three plump, dark-suited Englishmen were shown in.

'We're terribly sorry to be so late. No one at the Embassy warned us of the traffic-jams. I do hope the President . . .'

Mr Tu said something hurriedly to one of the aides in Malindian. He then said to Amos: 'We'd better beat it.' Even in the embarrassment and confusion of the moment, Amos was startled to hear the vulgar colloquialism from someone usually so formal in his speech.

The other aide had gone into the corridor, from where he could be heard shouting in Malindian. Two guards clattered in, guns at the ready.

Amos bowed and smiled at the two aides. Then he found himself bowing and smiling at the three plump, dark-suited Englishmen, murmuring at the same time: 'So nice to have met you. So very nice.'

'We go?' Miss Shimada asked.

'Yes, that's right.'

'We do not see President?'

But, having grasped her by the arm, Amos was already propelling her towards the door. Then suddenly he thought: The petition!

'Mr Tu . . . Mr Tu! One moment please.' Relinquishing Miss Shimada's arm, he raced after Mr Tu, caught up with him and prised the envelope from his grasp. Then he went back into the room, despite the effort of one of the guards to fend him off with his gun.

'I, er, wonder if, when you see the President, you could give him this? We haven't the time to stay to see him. It would be cutting things too fine.'

'Certainly, old boy.' The oldest and the plumpest of the three Englishmen took the envelope. He examined it. 'What wonderful seals. You don't see seals like that in England nowadays.'

'Yes, I'm good at seals.'

'I think that one can say, along with the Immortal Bard, that all's well that ends well.' Mr Tu leaned back in his seat in the Mercedes, the air-conditioning rapidly drying the sweat which had been trickling down his face.

'I'd hardly say that things had ended well after our ejection by armed guards. There was the, er, loss of face, apart from anything else.'

'Why did President-san not see us?'

The two men ignored Miss Shimada's interruption.

'You can say that you were admitted to the Palace,' Mr Tu explained. 'You can say that you were welcomed by two of the most important of the President's aides. You can say that the President was absent but that you, er, safely delivered the petition for immediate passing on to him. No one will be able to criticize you. Not even Mrs Svenson.'


In this optimistic forecast, Mr Tu was sadly wrong.

'Am I to understand, Mr President, that despite your gaining entrance to the Palace, you did not insist on seeing the President himself?' It was now not Margaretta, Frank or Heinz who was baiting Amos, but the chain-smoking Argentine. Amos, who could not remember his name, had already begun to think of him as General Galtieri.

'That was hardly something on which I could insist. I was received by two of the President's top aides with the utmost courtesy. I was offered some, er, excellent coffee. We had an, er, enlightening and, er, by and large fruitful conversation. And I then handed over the petition.'

'Surely you ought to have refused to leave the Palace until the President had received you.'

Suddenly Amos felt angry. 'Would the Argentine delegate mind putting out his cigarette? No smoking is permitted in this room . . . Thank you. Now I will answer his question. Had I taken the course which he suggests, I have no doubt that one of the armed guards

174

would have ejected me. That would hardly have been, er, consonant with the dignity either of WAA or the office of its President, now would it?'

'I beg to disagree!' Frank had jumped to his feet. He leaned on the desk in front of him, as he scowled across at Amos. 'If you had been ejected by armed guards, think of the favourable publicity for both WAA and the prisoners, and the unfavourable publicity for a government which commits the obscenity of keeping innocent writers in gaol! Did such a consideration never occur to you, Mr President?'

'Everything happened, er, so fast. In such circumstances, there is no time to weigh all the pros and cons . . .'

Amos knew that an even larger majority than before was now against him. They thought that he had been feeble, lacking equally in resource and in courage, a wet, a wimp. Did Miss Shimada share their view? There was no way of knowing. On the way back from the Presidential palace, she had insisted on being dropped off in the shopping quarter.

'What are you going to buy now?' Amos had asked her.

She had shaken a finger at him. 'Naughty boy! You are very naughty boy! Too inquisitive! I wish to buy more lady's things.'

Ah, lady's things, lady's things!


After dinner that evening, Carmen and Amos walked side by side in the oppressively scented garden of the hotel. She had suggested dinner up in her suite, but he had made the excuse that it was necessary for the President of WAA to be as accessible as possible to the delegates.

'Your trouble, Kingsley, is that you are too much of an English gentleman.'

'Well, yes, you may be right.' She was walking so

175

close to him that, to avoid a collision, he had to keep brushing against some extremely prickly bushes.

'But that is what I like best about you. . . . that, through and through, you are an English gentleman.'

'One is what one is.'

'I invite you to visit me in Costa Rica. I have a beautiful house by the sea. A paradise! There is my house, and there is a guest house. You may use the guest house for as long as you wish.' She squeezed his arm. 'You do not know what a banana is till you have eaten one off a tree in Costa Rica. Please come! Feel free!'

But Amos could not feel free. He felt suffocatingly constricted by his dependence on Laura, by his attraction to Miss Shimada, by Carmen's domineering boldness and, above all, by his duties and responsibilities as President of WAA.

'I'd love to accept. But I'm – I'm not sure about my wife. Laura's not very good at heat, and I imagine that Costa Rica is always very hot, isn't it?'

'Leave your wife behind!'

'Oh . . . I don't really think I could do that.'

Carmen's hand again went around his arm, to squeeze it even more firmly than before. 'So many young lovers here!' She pointed to a narrow bench in a clearing beyond them, where someone appeared to be lying with extreme precariousness on top of someone else. 'What are they doing? What are they doing, Kingsley? Tell me!' She gave a loud, baritone laugh. 'Happy couple! Like my people, Malindians know how to be happy.'

'Are you being bitten by mosquitoes? I am. Even if one takes the pills, I'm told one has to be extremely careful of malaria. Perhaps we ought to go in.'

'Oh, such an English gentleman!'

Carmen sounded half admiring, half exasperated.

>:> <:<

## 12

Amos had so often heard people claim that they attended WAA Congresses for the screwing; but, meditating in his pyjamas over a slice of papaya, he decided that, at least as far as the Malindian Congress was concerned, it would be more accurate to claim that they did so for the boozing and bitching. The cruel paradox was that the people whom one most wished to screw (suddenly he was intoxicated by an image of Miss Shimada dressed, or partially dressed, in her 'lady's things') invariably fluttered away from one's grasp like capricious butterflies; whereas the people whom one least wished to screw (suddenly he was overwhelmed by a memory of Carmen's ample presence crowding over him) bore down on one like juggernauts in a narrow *cul de sac*.

Well, yes, he supposed that the screwing was going on even here. Poor Mr Tong was probably being obliged to screw his grim wife as an act of contrition for having, at so many previous congresses, screwed other, more desirable women; Frank was probably screwing Margaretta, when the two of them were not discussing 'strategy'; and it was just possible that Carmen, having failed to be screwed by himself, had managed to be screwed by someone else. Laura would often enunciate as a great rule of life that, where screwing was concerned, there was always someone for everyone. But, if that were true, why was there now no one for him?

He remembered a Congress in Edinburgh. There,

most improbably, an unprecedented amount of screwing had certainly gone on. But of course one had to bear in mind that the cold of those July nights had also been unprecedented. When he had arrived – without Laura, who had had a summer flu – an efficient little Scots body with watery blue eyes and an overlarge cardigan had directed him to a ground-floor room, overlooking the garden, in the conference centre where the Congress was being held. 'It's the best room,' she told him. 'As befits our President.' When Amos opened the door on this best room, it was to find a tiny sixtyish woman, seated on the bed in nothing but a pair of combinations, cutting her toenails with what appeared to be dress-making scissors. 'Oh, I'm sorry,' he gasped and retired in confusion.

'I think there must have been some error,' he told the efficient little Scots body. 'Someone seems already to be in the room you gave me.'

'Och, that's wee Mrs McGregor again! She always tries to take the best room. I'll have her out.'

Eventually, fully dressed and flushed with indignation rather than shame, wee Mrs McGregor emerged from the room, and Amos then assumed possession of it.

The evening that had followed had been such an exhausting one of whisky, haggis, Scottish reels and Scottish ballads that Amos had been delighted first to fall into bed and then to fall into a deep sleep.

He was woken by the knowledge that someone was attempting to get into the bed beside him. Had Laura, unexpectedly recovered, raced northwards through the night to lie once more in his arms? Or could the intruder be that saucy folk-singer lassie, a bandeau round her head and a Sam Browne belt round her waist, who had so often toasted him in Glenfiddich? He sat up and reached for the light. Beside him was an elderly, grey-bearded man, totally nude. His pyjamas were on the floor. He and Amos stared at each other. Then the elderly man climbed out of the bed with a nonchalant 'Sorry, old chap, must be some mistake', picked up his pyjama trousers and, swaying slightly first on one stork-like leg and then on the other, began to put them on. 'Where would Mrs McGregor be then?' he asked, as though he were asking the way to the nearest post office.

'I think she was moved to room 201. Or it could have been 202.'

'I'm much obliged to you,' the man said, leaving the room.

For a long time Amos had lain awake, listening to the incessant sounds of slippers shuffling up and down the passage outside and of doors opening and closing. Screwing was going on all around him. Why, oh why, was he always left out?

. . . Having now once again put this question to himself, he scooped one final mouthful from the papaya and broodily sucked on it. Then he set about shaving, bathing and dressing.

It was so early that the newspaper kiosk had not even opened. A party of American tourists, clamouring for their bills and gesticulating to the bell-boys, were clearly on the point of departure. A party of Japanese tourists, slumped in chairs while waiting for their rooms to become vacant, had no less clearly just arrived. Amos wandered out through the revolving doors, into the surprising coolness of the early morning, and for a while stood staring at the cars hurtling, at eye-level, along the distant motorway. Then he strolled towards the empty swimming-pool. How wonderful it would be if, by some miracle, it was glittering with water, and there, a solitary naiad or yes! a solitary water-lily, floated Miss Shimada in the centre! But there was no water now, and in the centre of the pool was an elderly man, barefoot and naked but for some ragged shorts, who was sweeping it with a broom.

Suddenly Amos was aware that two young people, a boy and girl, were following behind him. Was the following deliberate? He left the pool and zigzagged up a woody incline beside it. The boy and girl did likewise. He sat on a bench. The boy and girl sat on another nearby bench. He circled a summer-house and circled a tennis court. They circled both. He stopped and again stared at the cars on the motorway.

'Good morning, sir.' It was the boy.

Amos turned. 'Good morning.'

They were an attractive, neat pair, the boy in an open-necked shirt and jeans and the girl in a flowered cotton dress.

'You are Mr Kingsley,' the girl said – a statement, not a question.

'Yes, that's right. How do you know that?'

'You are famous writer,' the boy explained.

'Well, not *all* that famous.'

'Very famous. President of WAA,' the girl said.

'For my sins.'

'Please?'

'Never mind.'

'I recognize you,' the boy said.

'Do you? How?'

'From photograph. Many photograph in paper.'

'Well, yes, I do seem to have figured in the local rags quite a lot these last few days.'

'We wish to show you university. Where we study,' the girl said.

'Oh, that's a nice idea.' It was a combination of the prettiness of the girl and a sense of his own isolation which made the idea nice.

'Now?' the boy suggested.

'Now! Oh, but I'm far too busy now. Our assembly of delegates – our meeting – starts at nine-thirty.'

The boy lifted Amos's wrist and looked at the fake

Rolex watch on it. 'Only quarter to eight,' he said. 'University near.'

'Come!' the girl said.

'Well . . .' There was nothing to do in the time that yawned between; and the girl *was* jolly pretty; and it would be interesting to talk to some young people who appreciated him for what he was, after all those middle-aged and elderly people who were constantly nagging and criticizing him . . . 'Oh, all right,' he said. 'Yes! Why not?'

'You will come?'

'Yes. But I must get back well before nine-thirty. It wouldn't do for the President to be late. The President has to, er, preside at our meetings, you see.'

They began to walk down a slope to a slip road below the tennis courts, with the boy from time to time putting out a hand to ensure that Amos did not fall. Such a nice-mannered young couple . . .

'How are we going to go?' Amos asked. 'By bus?'

'My elder brother is waiting in his car,' the boy told him.

'Oh good!'


'It seems to be an awfully long way to your university.' Amos peered out of the back of the car as one shimmering paddy-field succeeded another.

'Not far now,' the boy, seated beside him, told him.

Amos had long since wearied of attempting to make conversation with the trio. Previously so friendly, the boy and girl had become oddly aloof; and the boy's brother, who looked at least forty, appeared to speak no English at all.

'I mustn't be late. You know, I did tell you that – '

'Please do not worry.'

Again Amos peered out of the window. There was now not a single habitation in sight. 'Is your university out in the country?'

181

'Please do not worry.'

But how could he help worrying? It would be awful if, after all the unpleasantness of the last days, there should now be yet more unpleasantness because he had failed to turn up on time for that morning's session. Ah, well! All at once he felt unaccountably tired. He closed his eyes. If they were not prepared to make conversation, he might as well have a zizz.

He was woken by a click and the feeling of something cold and constricting around the wrist nearest to the boy. As he opened his eyes, emitting a gasp, he heard another click and felt something cold and constricting around his other wrist. Then he could see nothing, except for a bright, quivering bar of light which ran across his knees.

'Here! I say! What's going on?' His voice was muffled by the hood pulled down over his head almost to the shoulders. He struggled to jerk his wrists apart and found that he could not do so.

'Please do not worry.'

How idiotic to keep telling him not to worry! Not merely was he likely to be late for that morning's session, but these students appeared to be playing some silly kind of practical joke on him.

'It is better if you are calm.' It was the girl who said this, her previously soft, gentle voice suddenly grown hard and imperious. 'Better for us, but also for you. We will not hurt you, if you do what we tell you.'

'I should hope not!' Could they hear him, with this suffocating thingie over his head? 'What *is* all this?'

There was a long silence. Then the boy said: 'I am sorry, Mr Kingsley. You are hostage.'

'Hostage! Don't be so silly! Why should I be a hostage? I'm someone totally unimportant. And totally unpolitical. And poor.'

'You are famous novelist,' the boy said.

'You are President of WAA,' the girl said.

'But I'm not . . . And that was all a mistake!'

Had they heard that? Or were they ignoring it?

After a long silence, the boy said: 'There is nothing personal.'

'I should hope not! What harm have I ever done you?' Another long silence. 'What's the *point* of all this?'

'There are three writers in prison. You know about these three writers in prison, I think. Two do not interest us so much. But one is important. We will exchange one President of WAA for three Malindian writers.'

'But your President – the President of your country – will never agree to that! There's the whole question of face. In the East . . .' Oh, what was the use of arguing with them? The thingie over his head was making him feel not merely terribly helpless but also terribly sweaty and, yes, really rather sick.


Well, things could be worse. He might, after all, have been brought here not on the back seat but in the boot of the ramshackle Toyota; and he might have been shut up, not in this small, high-ceilinged room with its truckle bed, its square wooden table and its upright wooden chair, but in a box-room or a broom-cupboard. He had even been left some reading matter, although admittedly it consisted of nothing more exciting than an issue of the *Morning Star* several months old, a paperback abridgement of *Das Kapital*, and what appeared to be a Malindian body-building magazine. He even had a carafe of water, a tin chamber-pot, a washbasin (although neither tap ran) and a mirror to reassure himself that, despite his ordeal, he had kept his usual colour.

From downstairs there came the din of a transistor radio playing Western pop music. Laura would no doubt have been able to tell him the name of the group – not that he would have wished to know. He had eaten a bowl of rice, and he had drunk a bowl of tea.

He had also been escorted to a lavatory certainly cleaner than the one which he had been obliged to use on his visit to the prison.

It was all really rather ironical, he told himself. For almost three years he had been agitating on behalf of people imprisoned for what they had written; and now here was he, imprisoned, well, not exactly for what he had written but for what someone else had written. He only hoped that some members of WAA would now start to agitate on his behalf.

'What do I call you?' he had asked the boy.

'A.'

'A? Is that a Malindian name?'

'No. Letter of alphabet.'

Amos had not been surprised when the girl had subsequently told him to call her 'B'.

'How long are you planning to keep me here?'

'How long is President planning to keep writers in prison?'

Amos could see the bitter logic of the answer.

'Do people know what has happened to me? I mean, I'd hate my wife to worry . . . Well, of course, she's going to worry that I've been taken hostage, but she'd worry even more if she thought I'd just disappeared.' But that, of course, was precisely what Laura herself had done: just disappeared.

'Later you can talk to boss. He not here now.'

'And he, I suppose, is called "C"?'

The boy left the room without an answer.


Near the close of the afternoon, the sound of a car chugging up the narrow dirt road made Amos hurry over to the window in the hope that, by some miracle, the police had located him. But, instead, a tall, elegant man, briefcase in hand, got out of another Toyota, even dustier and more dilapidated than the one in which he himself had travelled. From the way in which both A and B rushed out of the house to greet him and from their greeting itself – legs together, arms to sides, a deep bow – Amos guessed that this new arrival must be the boss.

The boss threw, rather than handed, his briefcase to A. Then he threw, rather than handed, his panama hat to B. Without his panama hat he revealed to Amos, looking down on him, that he had a circular bald patch at the back of his head. Suddenly he looked up. A solitary gold ear-ring flashed in the light of the declining sun. His extraordinarily narrow, pale bearded face suggested an oriental Christ-Buddha just brought down from the Bo-tree on which he had been crucified.

Amos expected that either the boss would at once come up to see him or he would be taken down to see the boss. But minutes and then a whole hour passed, and still nothing happened. Bored with the weight-lifting magazine, Amos chucked it on one side and lay down on the bed. In the evening breeze from the barred but open window, cobwebs swept in capricious tides back and forth on the surface of the cavernous ceiling. What was that? He raised himself on an elbow, still looking upwards. It appeared to be the outline of a trapdoor to what was presumably a loft. He hesitated. Should he try to escape? If he failed, as he was likely to do, his captivity might well become far grimmer. Indeed, it was even possible that his captors would beat him up. On the other hand, if the President refused to release the prisoners, as he was likely to do, who knew what might not then happen? There had been a young Getty who had lost an ear in such circumstances. At the thought of it, Amos's right hand went involuntarily to his right ear and rested there for a moment. In similar fashion, many Mediterranean men touch their balls when passing a nun in the street.

He stood on the bed and raised an arm above him. Yes, it was a trapdoor. But the ceiling was too high for him to do more than brush it with his finger-tips. He got off the bed; tiptoed to the chair; then carried the chair back to the bed and balanced it on top of it. With a grunt and a creaking of springs – oh, God, he hoped they wouldn't hear him – he clambered back on to the bed and then on to the chair. Oh, this was all too silly! It was unlikely that there would be another exit from the loft, and even less likely that there would be a window in it. And if there was another exit, what chance had he of using it unnoticed? And if there was a window, he would never have the courage to climb out on to the roof, much less down to the ground. It was at the precise moment when, wobbling from side to side, he decided to give up, that the chair suddenly tipped over, and he toppled off both it and the bed, to strike his forehead against the edge of the washbasin.

When he came to, A, B and the boss were standing over him.

'Now how did you do that?' The boss spoke perfect English.

Better not to let on that he had been thinking of escaping. 'I – I can't remember. I must have tripped.'

'See that he hasn't done anything serious to himself.'

First A and then B knelt down beside Amos. A put an arm under his shoulders and raised him. B placed her hand to his forehead.

'Ow!'

Dizzily, A supporting him, Amos got to his feet. He looked in the cracked mirror of the washbasin. 'God! Look what I've done to myself.'

The boss gave an order to A in Malindian, and A hurried off. 'He'll bring you something for that.'

Amos, still dizzy, sank on to the bed.

'I'm a great admirer of your work, you know. I was delighted when *The Old Devils* won the Booker Prize.'

'Actually . . .' Oh, to hell with it! 'Well, I was rather pleased myself.'

A returned with some camphor-smelling ointment,

which he handed to B to apply. 'What is it?' Amos asked, as her fingers touched his raw skin.

'Tiger Balm.'

'What? Made from tiger?'

They all laughed. Later Amos was to learn that Tiger Balm was a patent ointment regarded by orientals as a panacea.

'I wish I had your talent,' the boss said. 'When I was up at Oxford, I had dreams of becoming a novelist. But either one's got it or one hasn't got it. I realized that I hadn't got it. So . . . I went into politics. Of a sort. But, you know, writers always excite me. Always have done. Just having you here, sitting beside me . . . So exciting! Tremendous!'

Amos wondered whether he ought to return the compliment – 'You know, terrorists always excite me.' Better not, perhaps. Who knew where that might lead? So he merely said: 'It's nice to be appreciated. Writing's such a terribly lonely profession, you see.' He was speaking not from his own experience – Laura was constantly bursting in on him, both figuratively, with requests for him to do this or that, and metaphorically, with suggestions on how to improve his typescripts, so that he never had the chance to be lonely – but from what appeared to be the experience of other, better writers.

'Before we lose the last of the sun, we'd better take the video.'

'The video?'

The boss nodded. 'Of you. Pleading for a deal.'

'Oh, I don't think . . . I don't honestly think I could plead for a deal.'

'Why not?'

'Well, it would seem so cowardly. It would be awfully bad for my reputation. Wouldn't it?'

The boss considered, a hand fiddling with his earring. 'You may be right. Perhaps it would really be more effective if you didn't plead. If you were just,

187

well, yourself. But harassed and haggard. Yes. Yes, I think that would be best.' Suddenly he burst out laughing and pointed at Amos. 'How lucky you had that fall!'

'Lucky?'

'It means we don't have to beat you up. That bump's coming up really well.'

Was he joking? Amos was afraid that he wasn't.

The handcuffs once again biting into his wrists and his forehead throbbing from the laceration across it, Amos stumbled down the narrow staircase, with the boss in front of him and A and B behind.

'You know I'm just as eager as you are for those prisoners to be released. In fact, yesterday I delivered a petition to the President. Well, not actually *to* him, but to one of his aides, one of his most important aides, *for* him.'

The boss gave a dismissive bark of laughter. 'Petitions! Do you think that Lenin achieved the Revolution by delivering petitions?'

'When I delivered that petition, it was not my plan to achieve a revolution. All I wanted to achieve was the release of those three writers.'

Had it been a mistake to attempt to answer back? For a moment, as the boss scowled back over his shoulder, a hand on the newel post at the bottom of the stairs, it seemed so. Then he once again gave that dismissive bark of laughter. 'You are what our Chinese friends call "a running dog of capitalism", Mr Amis. But, like those other reactionary writers, Eliot, Yeats and Pound, you write beautifully. So everything – or almost everything – must be forgiven to you.'

'Oh, er, thank you. It's nice of you to say that.'

The boss posed Amos against a brick wall, explaining that, since one brick wall looked very like another brick wall, it would give nothing away about their whereabouts. 'I will not say "Smile, please!"' he quipped.

'Good. I don't really feel like smiling.'

As he looked through the view-finder, the boss said: 'That bruise on your face is good, very good.'

'It's also painful, very painful.'

'You may speak now.'

'Speak?'

'Say something for the camera.'

'What do you want me to say?'

'Say what *you* want to say. Just be yourself. *Now!*'

Amos licked his dry lips. Briefly he put forefinger and middle finger to the contusion. Then he said what he wanted to say: 'I am being held hostage. As you will all know, I have been in the forefront of the agitation for the release of three writers at present held in prison. But to secure that release I cannot condone violence and blackmail. A grievous wrong is being done to the prisoners. But it would be an even more grievous wrong to release them because of terrorist threats.' Oh, lordy, lordy! What was he saying? To say what one wanted to say: for him that had so often been the prescription for saying something totally disastrous. He could not see the boss's face behind the camera; but he could see A and B glaring at him, as though eager to be ordered by the boss to knock him down and kick him. Amos gabbled on: 'Now I have a message for my wife. Laura, darling – be brave! I'm thinking of you constantly. I have faith that somehow we shall eventually be reunited. Keep that faith with me. And, er, keep your pecker up!'

Oh, why, why did his use of that last phrase make him think of Naylor?

'Good.' It was a relief when the boss, handing over the camera to A, gave this approval. 'Get that tape to the television station as soon as you can,' the boss told A. He turned to Amos. 'You look just terrible. When you appear on the screen, it'll really make people sit up and take notice . . .'

*

189

At nine o'clock that evening, Amos suddenly felt that he was about to burst into tears.

For him, nine o'clock in the evening had always been *l'heure bleue*. It was at nine that Laura suddenly irrupted into the sitting-room, as he was watching the news, to announce that the dishwasher had once again flooded the kitchen; that a sudden, acid burp forecast that he was about to suffer another night of heartburn; that Margaretta or Frank or Max rang up to discuss yet another crisis in WAA; that he realized that *Let Dogs Delight*, *My Ass and I* and *Fairest Fair Isle* would never be remembered as Kingsley Amis's, or Salman Rushdie's or even Margaretta's novels would be remembered.

Sitting on the edge of the narrow truckle bed, his hands in his lap, he suddenly decided that this was The End. Hostages usually died, didn't they? (The few who didn't, returned either physically or mentally mutilated.) Of course, he'd always known that the thought of never seeing Laura again would fill him with despair and anguish; but that the thought of never seeing the children again should have the same effect . . . Oh, how he wished he hadn't so often complained when he had found that Harry had yet again borrowed a tie, a scarf or a pair of socks, or that Vera had yet again got toast-crumbs on the butter!

He must write them all a farewell note, at once tender, forgiving and inspiring. It must be the sort of note which could be reproduced in the *The Times* or the *Independent* or the *Guardian* without any embarrassment either to them or to him. It must be the sort of note which, years ahead, would appear in anthologies; and which would provide a fitting end to the biography that someone would eventually no doubt write of him.

He had a pen in the breast-pocket of his jacket. But what was he to do for paper? Were there still some sheets of lavatory paper in his back trouser-pocket? He searched, but could find none. Somehow it seemed inappropriate to inscribe a farewell letter on a page of

the *Morning Star*, *Das Kapital* or a body-building magazine. He pulled his wallet out of his jacket. Perhaps an
Access invoice – or, classier, an American Express one
– was nestling in it? But all he found was a thick wad of
visiting cards.

Seated once more on the edge of the bed, he began
to thumb through the cards. They were of all sizes, all
thicknesses, all colours. Miss Iwai's had the texture of a
segment of bamboo. That of 'General Galtieri' had the
luxury of a photograph set into it, which did indeed
make him look, with his stern gaze and bristling moustache, like some military man of note. Carmen's, the
largest, was a shade of deep mauve, with her name
cancelled out with a single imperious stroke in green
ink and 'Love, Carmen' scrawled across it. There were
Mus, Nus, Tus and Chus galore.

What most interested Amos was the way in which
everyone sought somehow to define himself (or herself)
on this piece of pasteboard. 'Poet, publisher's reader
and folk-singer, Member of the Zimbabwean Centre of
WAA.' 'Novelist, Former President (1973–4) of the
Luxembourg Centre of WAA.' 'Playwright and Actor,
Honorary Secretary of WAA Centre of Armenian Writers Abroad.' It was partly through their usually undis-
tinguished activities but even more through WAA that
all these people sought for self-definition. But for them,
with their idealism, their indignation and their compassion, WAA would not exist. But might not the corollary
of that also be true – that, but for WAA, with its
demands on their idealism, their indignation and their
compassion, they themselves would not exist?

Amos weighed the cards in a hand.

He would also, of course, have to write a farewell
letter to WAA. Something memorable in its courage and
dignity, like the last words of Captain Scott. But something that would also make them all feel sorry and
ashamed for the way in which they had misjudged
him, nagged him and bullied him. Something that

would make them say: 'He was a good man. He was a good President. He was the best President we have ever had. How could we have treated him in that abominable fashion?'

Amos's eyes filled with tears. Then, through those tears, he glanced at his fake Rolex watch. It was two minutes past ten.

*L'heure bleue* had passed.

He'd wait until tomorrow to write his farewells. Now he'd better try to get some sleep.


The next evening, the boss, who had been absent all day, came into the little room. He crossed over to where Amos was sitting on the edge of the truckle bed staring down at pictures of stocky Malindians demonstrating their lats and their pecs, and patted him on the shoulder. Because of the heat, Amos was wearing nothing but underpants and singlet. 'Are you hungry?'

'A little. Yes.' In fact, a growing apprehension had robbed him of all appetite.

'Good. Our friends will prepare us some supper. Meanwhile we can talk. I want your advice.'

'My advice?' Why should a terrorist want his advice?

'As I told you' – taking him by the bare arm, the boss was now leading Amos out of the room and down the stairs – 'I decided that I had no talent as a novelist. But as a poet . . . Sometimes I write a poem which seems to me not bad, not bad at all. Now you are both something of a poet and something of an anthologist. So, if you will allow, I should like to read to you one or two of my poems . . .'

'Splendid!' Amos felt as insincere as when he feigned enthusiasm for some literary offering from Miss Iwai or Miss Kawai.

*

'How did you come to learn English so well?'

The boss cracked a walnut in a naked palm. He would show as little compunction about cracking a human skull, Amos decided. Then he poured what was left of a second bottle of Malindian whisky into his glass and gulped it down. 'My father – who happened to be Sultan of Buru before the Federation was created – was the first Malindian ambassador to the United Kingdom. He sent me to Harrow School. Rather a philistine school, I can't say that I enjoyed it all that much. But my years at the House were full and happy ones.'

'The house?'

'Christ Church.'

'Oh, Christ Church College!'

'No. Christ Church.' The boss cracked another walnut. 'I thought you were an Oxford man?'

'Er, no.' Then Amos remembered that for the boss he was not Amos Kingsley but Kingsley Amis. 'I mean, er, yes. Yes. I was at . . .' His voice trailed off. What the hell was the name of Amis's college?

'Well, if you've had enough to eat, let's get down to business.'

Business, it became clear, was a reading of the poems. There were a vast number of them, clamped in a file.

'Yes, yes!' Amos would exclaim when the boss, having read one, looked over to him for his verdict. Or 'Hm. Hm,' he would grunt, as though still pondering all the fascinating philosophical resonances of the poem in the recesses of his consciousness. Or he would exclaim: 'Yes, that I *do* like! A lot!' Except that they were so much longer, the poems might easily have been accepted as the work of Miss Kawai or Miss Iwai.

As the boss drank more and more of the Malindian whisky, so his eyes became more and more blood-shot and his reading more and more slurred. Amos cast a surreptitious glance at his fake Rolex watch. The second-hand was still stuck; but the other hands

193

seemed to be working, and by them it was already twenty minutes past eleven. Presumably A and B had long since retired. Amos thought of the narrow truckle bed . . .

'Now you must know a lot of publishers?'

'Well, er, yes, a few.'

'Of course you do. You must have a lot of influence with them. So I was wondering . . . Of course I know that these are not precisely the kind of poems which you yourself write. You're more of a conservative, aren't you? Some might even say a reactionary. But you have a nose for quality. I can see that.' The boss had laid a forefinger to the side of his own nose. He swayed slightly, as he leaned forward in his chair. 'Why the hell aren't you drinking? You don't like this whisky, do you? You think it muck, don't you? Well, fair enough! You've the reputation for being some sort of connoisseur and you don't want to lose it. I understand that. That's OK by me. But, maybe, when all this is over, you could perhaps see whether you could find me a publisher? Now how about that?'

'Of course. Delighted.' If the boss thought that he could find him a publisher, then he might think twice about killing him or having him killed.

Again the boss raised the bottle. This time he drank directly from it. 'Mind you, we may have some difficulty in communicating with each other in the immediate future. Once the prisoners and you are released, I'll have to do a bunk. Over the border. All set up. But I'm not going to tell you *how* it's all set up. You might tell other people, mightn't you? Stands to reason.'

'Oh, I wouldn't want to . . .'

The boss squinted at him. Then he leaned across the table: 'You know, Kingsley, I *like* you. I like you a lot. Great writers have always had that effect on me. I remember when I once asked Richard Adams to sign *Watership Down* for me at Harrods . . . I found him quite

194

irr-irr-irr' – he hiccoughed – 'quite staggering. Does that seem awfully kinky to you?'

'No. No, not really.'

'Then there was the time when C. P. Snow came to a lecture to the Oxford Literary Society. I absolutely fell for him. The intellectual power of the man! It had a quite devastating physical effect on me. To be frank, a *sexual* effect. John Braine was another. Not quite in the same intellectual class as Snow, of course, but tremendously attractive. And of course Norman Mailer . . . Do you despise me for all this?'

'Of course not.'

'Of course not! You're a man of the world! Anyone who reads your novels can see that. Shocked by nothing. A true man of the world. *Nihil humanum* . . . How does it go?'

'I'm afraid my Latin's rather rusty now.'

Amos felt the boss's hand close on his bare knee, squeeze, and then move caressingly upwards. 'Has anyone ever told you that you have the most incredibly g-g-glabrous skin? I've never encountered a skin like yours. In a man, I mean. I bet there isn't a hair on your body.'

Suddenly there flashed on Amos a recollection from his days at a minor public school. A prefect in his house had sent him, a skinny fag, with a note to a prefect in another house. The note had been opened in such a way that Amos had been able to glimpse its contents: THIS IS HE, in gigantic capitals. Nothing else. The recipient had stared at Amos, as Pope Gregory might have stared at his '*Angeli, non Angli*'. Then he had run a hand up Amos's cheek. 'I don't imagine you've ever had to shave.' Not caring what punishment might later be in store for him, Amos had taken to his heels.

It was this recollection, rather than any thought of escaping, that now made Amos push back his chair and jump to his feet. 'Must, er, take a leak,' he said. 'Too much of that gut-rot.' He spoke as he imagined that

Kingsley Amis would have spoken in a similar situation. 'Back in a mo.'

'Right you are! But don't be too long! You know, that incredibly g-g-glabrous skin of yours is almost as much of a turn-on as your l-l-literary reputation.'

Amos left the room. He opened the door of the lavatory, without going in, then shut it. He went through a small room, its door open, and out through a door, also open because of the heat, on to a porch. He jumped off the porch, almost twisting his ankle.

Then, barefoot and in nothing but underpants and singlet, he began to run through a dark night noisy with the croaking of bull-frogs from the paddy-fields all around him.

# 13

>:> <:<

This was totally different from chasing a bus in Tooting
Broadway. His arms pumping and his eyes stinging
and almost blinded with sweat, Amos gulped the
metallic-tasting air. Running along a path jagged with
stones had been as excruciatingly painful to his bare
feet as running along the shingle of Brighton beach; but
he preferred that to his present running across a paddy-
field, where snakes might be lurking. Hadn't Mr Tu
told him that, nervous creatures, snakes would usually
slither away at hearing the smallest noise? But even the
smallest noise was inadvisable when the boss, A and B
were probably all already in pursuit.

A dark, flat sky pressing down on a dark, flat
landscape, there was not a light to be seen. Perhaps the
inhabitants of this district were so poor that they did
not have lights? Perhaps there were no inhabitants? It
was wise to have left the main road initially; but it
might now be wise to return to it, in the hope of
flagging down a car or truck. But *where* was the main
road? He had no idea. Oh, if only Laura, with her
infallible sense of direction, were with him! But perhaps, on second thoughts, it was as well that she
wasn't. When the two of them chased a bus in Tooting
Broadway, she invariably missed it and so caused him
to do so.

Against the grey horizon, something of a darker grey
moved. Oh, God, was it one of them, waiting for him?
Armed perhaps? A terrorist was sure to be a first-class

shot. But in this thick darkness could he be relied on merely to wing his quarry? Amos halted and, body almost bent double, hands on knees, drew one rasping breath after another. If they heard him, he just did not care. He would wait here until they came to fetch him. He was certainly not going to risk a bullet.

His next rasping breath seemed to be echoed by that dark-grey shadow ahead of him. Were they making fun of him? Then, even without a rasping breath from him, there came another and another from in front. Amos moved stealthily forward, until he all at once realized that the rasping breaths were coming not from a human being but from a donkey. A donkey! He'd better try to ride it. That way he would progress more quickly, and there would be no danger from snakes. Besides – the idea suddenly flashed on him in the way that ideas suddenly flash on writers at the darkest and therefore most improbable moments – he might even gather the material for a book entitled *My Ass and I Again: A Journey By Donkey Through Malindi*.

Unfortunately, this donkey was far less compliant than dear old Pepita. 'Come on . . . Good girl . . . I mean – er – good boy . . . I'm not going to hurt you . . .' But the real question at issue was whether the donkey was going to hurt him. A carrot would have been useful, or even a sugar-lump. Finding the tether, after some groping on the ground – oh gosh, oh golly, let there be no snakes! – Amos tugged on it. The donkey reared up, its bared teeth luminous in the surrounding gloom. Amos gave another tug. Eventually, somehow, he was astride the animal, having extemporized some reins from the tether. Twice the donkey reared up again in an attempt to unseat him, but each time, by clinging to its mane, Amos managed to frustrate it. Then, as though it suddenly acknowledged a will stronger than its own, the animal became wholly docile. Amos kicked at its flanks, and they began to jog off across the scrub.

'Good girl . . . I mean, er, good boy . . .' Already he felt quite attached to the creature.

If there was a donkey, there must be an owner of the donkey; and if there was an owner of the donkey, then there must be a house or at least a hut in which the owner lived. But the countryside seemed eerily uninhabited. Well, he'd let the dear old girl – er, dear little fellow – be his path-finder. Set loose, animals usually made for the place where their owners could be found.

They came to a track, and the track then widened until it was almost a road. They passed first the ruins of what must once have been a barn, and then a stone drinking-trough, from which the donkey insisted on drinking. Then they reached what presumably passed for a main road, despite its fissured surface. Soon after that, they came on a battered Dormobile, parked on the verge. As they trotted up, Amos saw, with a mingling of relief and astonishment, that it had a plate with 'AUS' on it hanging askew from its back bumper. He dismounted from the donkey and tethered it to a bush. Then he walked up to the Dormobile and knocked at its door. There was no answer. 'Anyone at home?' he called. He repeated it more loudly: 'Anyone at home?'

The door opened and, at the moment when he was taking in a young woman's face with a mass of dishevelled hair about it, he felt the gun cold against his temple.

'Don't shoot, please! I'm a fellow countryman. Well, not precisely a fellow countryman. But a – a Pommie.'

The woman did not remove the gun. 'Jesus! What the hell are you doing here?'

'Let me in and I'll tell you.'

'What the fuck is it?' a sleepy voice called from the interior.

'Don't ask me. Some half-naked bum. Says he's English.'

By this time the donkey had begun to crop the scant vegetation of the verge.

'You wouldn't have a telephone, would you? No, of course you wouldn't.'

A man now appeared in pyjama trousers, his tattooed chest bare. He scratched at the hair on his chest (however the boss may have intended it, that epithet 'glabrous' had been insulting, Amos thought) and scrutinized the newcomer. Then he said: 'Looks harmless to me. Harmless but daft. All right, you can come in, mate.'

Two children were snoring in a bunk.

'I must get back to Batu as soon as possible. Or to a police station. We've got to move fast. I was taken hostage by some terrorists. I managed to escape. Please help me.'

The man said: 'We're dead tired, mate. Driven more than two hundred miles over these crappy roads. We need a good night's sleep.'

'Please! *Please*! If they find me here . . .'

'There's no way we're going back to Batu. We've just come from there,' the woman said.

'I'd make it worth your while.'

Both of them looked at him with pitying derision. Amos realized how unprepossessing he must look, barefoot, in underpants and singlet, with a badly bruised face.

'I'm President of WAA.'

Clearly that meant little to them.

'I'll reward you just as soon as you get me back to Batu.'

Clearly that meant even less.

Suddenly he had a brain-wave. He held out his right wrist. 'Do you want a Rolex watch?'

The man grasped his wrist and looked at the watch. 'You'll give me this to take you back to Batu?'

'Or to a police station. If that's nearer.'

'You've got yourself a deal.' The man began to remove the watch. Then he squinted. 'This bloody second-hand is stuck.'

'Oh, that's all right. Anyone can fix that. I'll pay to have it fixed for you just as soon as you get me somewhere safe.'

The man at first seemed reluctant. Then he handed the watch to the woman: 'Keep that safe,' he told her. 'I'll put on some clobber and then we'll get started. You'd better come up in front with me,' he told Amos. 'I don't want any funny business with the wife, while my back is turned.'

'Oh, I wouldn't dream of . . .'

'No, but the wife might. You don't know the wife.'

Well, come to that, the man didn't know Laura.


The battered Dormobile drew up at the hotel behind a Cadillac from which three obese Arabs and a skinny Malindian, clearly their interpreter, were taking a long time to descend. Eventually, both arms extended in front of him, the Malindian was carrying, piled on top of each other, all three of the Arabs' immaculate brief-cases as well as a shabby one of his own.

The two Australian children were the first to jump down from the Dormobile. Both were barefoot, both were sunburned to the colour of a ginger-nut, and both had long, tangled blond hair. The boy wore nothing but a pair of ragged khaki shorts, and the girl nothing but a pair of ragged khaki shorts and a singlet. The boy was carrying a toy rifle and the girl a toy pistol, with which they at once threatened the uniformed commissionaire as he was in the act of bowing the Arabs into the hotel. 'Stick 'em up! You're under arrest!'

With surprise, Amos recognized that toy pistol. It was the one which, so terrifyingly, the Australian woman had held to his temple.

'Come back in here, you perishers!'

The perishers paid no heed to their father. They were now miming their version of the St Valentine's Day Massacre, with the commissionaire and the bell-boys as

201

their victims. 'Bang! Bang! Bang! Take that, you creeps! Take that, you bastards!'

For the first time Amos noticed that the back window of the Dormobile was covered with cut-outs of kangaroos leaping, each with a baby kangaroo in its pouch, over a sticker which read: 'AUSSIES DO IT DOWN UNDER.' Do what? he vaguely wondered, before turning to the man. 'Thank you so much for your help. A good deed in a naughty world. I feel, er, bad about the second-hand of the watch. Are you sure you wouldn't like me to see if the jeweller in the hotel basement arcade . . . ?'

'Nah, nah! Don't give it a thought. Haven't got the time. We want to push on – or, rather, push back. In any case, you'll want to have a bath and a kip, after all you've been through.' He patted the watch. 'I've always dreamed of having a Rolex.'

'Oh, by the way – if you go back by the same road – I think I left my donkey tethered up. Perhaps, if you should happen to see it . . .'

'Haven't time for that, mate! Sorry! Must make Tongu by nightfall.'

Amos sighed. 'Well, it was, er, nice meeting you.'

'And it was nice meeting you too. President of WAA! Can't think why I'd never heard of WAA before. I'll be sure to look out for it now . . . Get back in here, you bleeders!'

Eventually, the bleeders having been dragged back on board – their mother was still asleep in her bunk – Amos limped towards the entry of the hotel. The huge commissionaire took in lacerated forehead, dirty bare feet, and begrimed underpants and singlet. He shook his head decisively. Then he grunted: 'Beat it!'

'Don't you recognize me? You opened the car door for me only two days ago, you opened it a number of times. I'm staying here. Room – room number . . . seven hundred and something. I'm President of WAA.'

Whether the man understood any of this, it was

202

impossible to say. He merely scowled at Amos, hands on massive hips, like a Sumo wrestler preparing to floor an opponent. Then he repeated: 'Beat it!' Perhaps that was the only English phrase he knew, other than 'Yes, sir', 'No, sir', 'Please, sir', and 'Thank you, sir.'

Suddenly Amos, by now an object of scornful or pitying interest to anyone passing in or out of the hotel, was saved by a screech. 'Amos-san! Amos-san!' Abandoning her two shopping bags, Miss Shimada raced towards him as fast as the constriction of her elaborately flowered silk kimono allowed. 'You are not dead! I thought that maybe you are dead!'

'Well, not quite.'

Suddenly, in totally unJapanese fashion, she had flung her arms around him, hugging his grubby, malodorous body to her own immaculate, perfumed one. He was being smothered in magnolia petals, he was drowning in extract of lemon.

'When I am unhappy, I always go to shop. I am so unhappy about you that I buy many, many things this morning. I am naughty girl. I do not go to assembly of delegates. But do not be cross with me. Miss Iwai and Miss Kawai . . .'

'How could I be cross with you!'

After this rapturous greeting and the fortuitous arrival of one of the Mr Mus, Amos was at last admitted to the hotel.


Madam was upstairs in the room, Amos had been told. What he had not been told was that Naylor was with Madam.

'Amos! Pettikins! Tweetlebug! Honeycup!' It was years since Laura had called him any of these things, and so in a way it was gratifying. But in a way it was also embarrassing, with Naylor watching and listening from his place by the window, while the two of them went into a clinch and she continued to burble her endearments. Half crying and half laughing, she eventually got out: 'I thought you were dead!'

'Why should everyone think I was dead?'

'Everyone?'

'Well, Miss Shimada did.'

'Miss Shimada?'

'I met her as I was coming in.'

'Oh. Well, after that incredibly brave speech of yours on television, we all just thought . . . You know what terrorists are like. Of course you do! You now know far better than any of us.' She put a hand up to the laceration on his forehead, just as Miss Shimada had done. 'Oh, you poor darling! What you've suffered for WAA!'

'Being President of WAA has brought me nothing but suffering.'

The telephone rang. Officiously Naylor picked up the receiver. Why the hell couldn't he, in the words of the commissionaire, beat it? And what the hell was he doing up here in any case?

'Yes . . . Yes . . . He's here. Looking rather the worse for wear, but quite able to talk . . .'

It was Mr Tu. 'Oh, Mr Kingsley! Congratulations! A thousand congratulations! When you are ready – you will probably wish to have a bath and change your clothes – the press wish to interview you. And there is also the Director of the Department of Criminal Investigation. I know you spoke briefly to one of his men downstairs in the lobby, and a widespread search has already started. But he himself now wishes to talk to you. There is the task of looking at photographs of well-known, er, anti-social elements. Well, I am sure you will understand. So can you be ready as soon as is possible? Shall we say at eleven-thirty?'

Amos looked at his watch. But the watch was not there. Oh, of course, he'd given it to that Australian!

'Yes, eleven-thirty will be fine.'

When he had replaced the receiver, Laura cried out:

'Amos, what's happened to your watch? The watch I gave you.'

It was at that moment that, so long a prisoner on the treadmill of non-fiction, Amos Kingsley was at last released and became a novelist – like, well, er, Kingsley Amis. 'They took it from me.'

'The brutes!'

'I fought to keep it. Because' – his voice broke – 'it was all I had with me to remind me of you. You gave it to me. That's how this' – he touched the laceration on his forehead – 'happened to me. In the struggle.'

'Oh, Amos!' Laura ran to him, where he had sunk on to the bed, threw her arms round him and kissed him passionately on the lips. Then she hurried over to Naylor. 'He'd better have that one.' She pointed to the Rolex which she had given to Naylor on his birthday.

'My watch?'

'It's all right, Laura. I can wear the Cartier – or the Longines.'

'No, darling.' Deftly Laura was removing the watch from Naylor's wrist. 'You must have a Rolex.'

Amos felt that there was something symbolic, retributory and, yes, holy about this action of transferring the watch from Naylor's hairy wrist to his own hairless one.


Amos had had a bath and, with Laura's assistance – Naylor had at last been persuaded to go – had got dressed. A doctor then arrived, not the hotel doctor but (so Mr Tu told him) the American-born Professor of Traumatology at the Medical School of the Municipal Hospital. While dressing the laceration, the doctor told Amos that it would be advisable if he were both to have an X-ray and see a psychiatrist colleague of his – a brilliant young man, who had trained in New York and whose patients included no less than three contributors to the *Village Voice*.

'But why should I want to see a psychiatrist? I feel perfectly sane. Never saner.'

'Victims of experiences like yours often express that view in the first euphoria of their release. Subsequently, they pay the price of their stoicism. Such stoicism is similar to leaving a blind abscess unlanced. Do please think again about it . . . May I take a look at your feet?'

Amos reluctantly removed his shoes and socks.

'Tsk, tsk! The soil of this country is notably tetanic. I think it would be a wise precaution if I gave you an injection.'

'But injections always make me faint. I know it's silly of me but ever since . . .'

The doctor, clearly not believing Amos, laughingly injected him. Amos fainted.

When he came round, the Director of the Department of Criminal Investigation and Mr Tu had joined them in the room. The Director first questioned Amos relentlessly, if admiringly, with Mr Tu acting as his interpreter, and then produced a vast album of photographs. Amos turned the pages: 'That one looks rather nice . . . Oh, he looks rather like an oriental Gore Vidal . . . Heavens, I wouldn't like to meet *him* on a dark night . . .' But of his three abductors he was unable to find a single likeness.

As Amos closed the album with a melancholy shake of his head, Mr Tu leaned towards him to say that the Director of the Department of Criminal Investigation wished to know whether, perhaps, he was frightened of identifying anyone for fear of subsequent retribution.

'Certainly not!'

'He asks to be forgiven for putting such a question to a man who has shown such remarkable courage. But it would be natural if you were frightened. After all, terrorists of that kind stop at nothing when they want their revenge.'

Amos began to feel relieved that none of the photographs had been familiar to him. 'Yes, I can understand that.'

'If you were to recognize someone, of course you would at once have a twenty-four-hour guard put on you.'

'I can't recognize a single face. Honestly.'

'Are you sure, Amos?

'Of course I'm sure! I think it might be better if you didn't interfere, Laura – *if* you don't mind.'

Amos had never spoken to Laura quite like that before. But she looked gratified, instead of indignant.


Eventually, supported on the one hand by the Director of the Department of Criminal Investigation and on the other by Laura, with Mr Tu behind him, Amos emerged from the suite. With a scream, he threw up an arm and attempted to retreat. But it was not the guns of terrorists that were flashing at him but the cameras of innumerable press photographers.

'You see,' Laura said, when Amos had recovered his equilibrium, 'that doctor was right. The psychological effects of your experience have been far more serious than you ever realized.' She turned to appeal to the photographers, many of whom were walking backwards, still flashing their cameras, as Amos and his party advanced towards them. 'Please . . . *Please*! . . . My husband has been under the most terrible strain. Don't you realize? He was tortured! They nearly killed him!' But the cameras went on flashing.

In the foyer people stopped in their tracks to stare and even point. 'Hey! That's the guy who was hijacked!' Amos heard one excited, elderly member of a Sunset Holidays group shout to his fellow members. The commissionaire who had previously attempted to keep Amos out of the hotel now rushed forward with a grubby and crumpled piece of paper which, Mr Tu explained, he wanted Amos to sign. Mrs Tong, who was presumably waiting for Mr Tong, actually beamed and waved at him.

The room set aside for the press conference was crammed with journalists of every nationality, seated, squatting on the floor, or leaning against the walls. The first to speak was the young American who had been so snide and supercilious when interrogating Amos at the airport. Now, instead of lolling in his chair, his legs stuck out ahead of him and his hands deep in his trouser pockets, he stood up, gave a small introductory cough, and then declared in a reverential voice that, on behalf of all the press corps, he wished to congratulate Amos both on the high courage with which he had spoken on the video and the miracle of his escape.

'Well, that's very handsome of you all. Of course, I'm, er, delighted to be back here – with all of you, with my fellow members of WAA, but, above all' – he looked across at her and they exchanged a fond smile – 'with my loving and beloved wife.' Laura extended a hand and Amos took it and, on an impulse, kissed it. The cameras once more flashed, and the whole press corps broke into delighted applause.

'After the terrible ordeal through which Mr Kingsley has passed, I am sure that none of you would wish to impose any further strain on him.' Heads nodded sympathetically at Mr Tu's words. 'But, within reason, he has expressed his willingness to answer your questions.'

Amos told the story of how two young people – 'they seemed so thoroughly *nice* at the time' – had engaged him in conversation; of how he had woken up with a start to find the handcuffs round his wrists and the hood over his head; and of how he had been incarcerated in a stifling room with bars on the windows. When asked about the wound on his forehead, he repeated his tale of the fight for the watch – 'You understand, I wasn't concerned about the loss of a Rolex watch *as such*. What concerned me so deeply was that the watch had been a present from my dear wife – whom I was then wondering if I'd ever see again.' Laura flashed him a grateful smile.

'You showed great courage on the video,' a French journalist commented.

'Thank you. Of course, as you know, I am eager – as every member of WAA is eager – that those three unfortunate writers should be freed. But no government should give way to that kind of blackmail. If it does, then civilization as we know it collapses. There was a principle involved. I had to fight for that principle – whatever the cost.'

A respectful silence followed.

'Any more questions?'

'Would Sir Kingsley like to tell us something about the manner of his escape?' The journalist was Norwegian. *Sir* Kingsley! In a moment of self-indulgence, Kingsley wondered: Could that be prophetic? Then he put the thought away from him as unworthy.

Amos once again assumed his new role of novelist. He elaborated the story as – yes, why not? – Kingsley Amis might have elaborated it. One of his gaolers had been conducting him to the, er, toilet, when he had seized his opportunity. There was no paper there, he had pointed out, and as the gaoler had then stooped to examine the dispenser, he had quickly administered a karate chop. Faced with the second gaoler in the passage-way to the front door, he had head-butted him before the man had had time to use his gun. He had then raced off into the night.

And how had he eventually been transported back to Batu?

Well, he had run over totally deserted country for a long time. (Should he tell them about the donkey? No, better not. It sounded, well, rather unheroic.) And then, at long last, he had come on this Australian family asleep in their Dormobile. They were perfectly ordinary people, simple people, with absolutely no interest in culture. In fact, they had never even heard of WAA, let alone his name! But they could truly be said to be the salt of the earth. Yes, he had not the slightest hesitation in saying that – the salt of the earth. They at once took him in and tended to him. Then, without a thought, they had retraced their long journey all the way back to Batu. Refusing any recompense and unwilling to face any publicity, they had left him at the hotel and had then once more set off on their travels. When such people existed in the world, one could not wholly despair of its future.

'What are now your plans, Herr Kingsley?'

Amos gave a deprecatory smile. 'My immediate plan is to have a long talk with my dear wife here.' For a dark second, Amos thought of Naylor. 'But of course the WAA Congress must go on. We have the problems not merely of the three writers in prison in this country but of a multitude of writers in prison in many parts of the globe. And of course there is the perennial problem of censorship. Constantly in my mind at present is that book by that, that Indian – or do I mean Pakistani? – author – '

(Oh, golly, he had forgotten both the man's name and the title.)

'*The Satanic Verses*. By Salman Rushdie,' Laura prompted.

'Thank you, my dear.' He put a hand to his forehead. 'I'm afraid that my lapse of memory is due to fatigue. I'll be forgetting the title of the Koran and the name of its author next. Please, please forgive me.'

After he had posed for yet more photographs – at one point the journalists even insisted that he simulate for them his first rapturous embrace with Laura on his return – Amos left the room to yet another round of applause.

'I imagine you would now like to go upstairs again and rest?' Mr Tu said.

'Yes, come on, Amos!' Laura cried. 'Etslay uckfay – ontopray!'

But energy was surging through Amos, as though all those admiring journalists had coalesced into a dynamo to transmit to him a huge psychic charge. He ignored Laura. 'Is the assembly meeting?'

'Yes, the assembly is meeting. At present it is still discussing literatures in languages of lesser currency.'

'Then I should certainly be there. You know how interested I am in literatures in languages of lesser currency. When I was once on a holiday, as a student, in Pwllheli, a Welshman whom I met – purely by chance in the YMCA – persuaded me to join him in some translations from the *Mabinogion*. Our best effort concerned – if I remember rightly – the association between Manawyddan and Pryderi. Not at all bad.'

'How interesting! You are a polymath, Mr Kingsley.'

'Oh, I wouldn't say that. Just a case of "These fragments have I shored against my ruin . . ."'

'Ah! I understand.'

When Amos entered the assembly, with Laura and Mr Tu following, he was astonished to see Margaretta presiding in his chair. What was *she* doing there? She wasn't even one of the Vice-Presidents of WAA. But this was not the time to be ungracious. So he smiled at her and called out from the door: 'Don't let me disturb you in your deliberations, Margaretta!'

Margaretta jumped to her feet, to be followed by even the most aged and the most comatose of the Vice-Presidents on the dais and then by all the delegates in the body of the hall. 'Amos! We were so happy to learn of your escape!' She jumped off the dais, raced down the hall, and threw her arms around him. 'Thank God, thank God that you're safe! Your courage! Your resource!'

Delegates began to pat him on the back and shake him by the hand.

'Please . . . Please . . . I'm tremendously touched by your reception. But I only did what any of you would have done in similar circumstances. I just happened to be, well, lucky.'

'Junk the modesty!' Frank's violent thump between Amos's shoulder blades all but doubled him up. 'Hail the conquering Hero! All Hail!'

'Well, er, again – thank you all. Now shall we get on with business?' Amos advanced to the platform, clambered on to it and repossessed the Chair. 'Item number eleven – is that right? Literatures in languages of lesser currency. I'm particularly interested in this subject, since as a student, when I was once on holiday in Pwllheli . . .'

Amos was not fated to preside for long on the subject of literature in languages of lesser currency. Suddenly one of the Mr Mus irrupted into the hall. 'Mr Kingsley! Mr Kingsley!'

'Just one moment, please, Mr Chu – I mean, Mr Mu. The delegate from Baluchistan has just raised an interesting point about – '

'Mr Kingsley! You must come at once! The President wishes to see you! At once! The car is ready!'

'Well, in that case . . . Margaretta dear, do you think you could bear once again to take over the Chair in my absence?'


The same two aides, in short-sleeved shirts and black ties, were standing at the top of the steps when Amos and Mr Tu arrived in the black Mercedes. But, as they raced down and vigorously pumped Amos's hand, they gave no indication that they had ever set eyes on him before.

'Please!' one said, pointing to the steps.

'Please!' the other repeated, doing likewise.

Once again guards, posted at intervals down the wide corridor, saluted Amos as he passed. This time he was ready for them, not saluting but giving each a brief, authoritative nod.

One of the aides said something in Malindian to Mr Tu, and Mr Tu then translated: 'The President awaits you.' This time there was to be no exchange of visiting cards and no nervous sitting in Taiwan 'Empire' chairs.

'Mr Kingsley! Mr President of WAA!' The short, chubby, white-haired President rose, circled from behind his desk and advanced with disconcerting nimbleness. 'I am happy, happy, happy!'

The two men shook hands. Then the President grasped Amos by the shoulders, leaned back and beamed at him: 'Bravo, bravo, bravo! A hero!'

Amos was conscious that he was smirking. He wished that he could think of something self-deprecatory and off-hand to say.

'Please!' One of the aides was pushing a heavily upholstered armchair towards him.

'Please!' The President pointed.

Either talking slowly and, as far as possible, in words of one or two syllables, or turning to Mr Tu for a translation, Amos again told his story. The President nodded his head. At one point, when Amos related the incident of the karate chop, he clapped his plump hands together. At another moment, as though to reward Amos, he proffered a box of chocolates. Amos shook his head: 'Thank you, Mr President, but I try not to eat sweet thing between meals.' He patted his stomach. 'My wife's always nagging me about my figure.' Did the President know the meaning of the word 'nagging'? At all events, he laughed.

At the close of Amos's narration, the President turned to Mr Tu and spoke briefly in Malindian.

'The President wishes to thank you and congratulate you. He hopes that the rest of your stay in Malindi will be happy. He wishes to present you with the Order of the Tiger Second Class.' Then Mr Tu added hurriedly: 'Second Class is not what you may think, Mr Kingsley. Second Class is high, high class. First Class is only for heads of states, you understand.'

'Please tell the President that I'm extremely grateful.' As he said the words, suddenly an idea, self-effacing and quixotic, came to Amos. 'Extremely grateful,' he repeated as he asked himself: Shall I give way to the idea? Then, having decided to do so, he went on: 'But, rather than acccept the Order of the Tiger – tremendously honoured though I should be by it – I should like to ask the President for a gracious favour.'

Mr Tu translated and then turned back to Amos: 'The President wishes to know the nature of this favour.'

'I beg him to grant an amnesty to the three writers now in prison. Not as a right,' he hurriedly added, remembering all that he had heard in the past week about face, 'and not as an admission that they were wrongfully imprisoned, but as an act of clemency.'

The President pondered, his jowls sagging and his small, alert eyes almost disappearing under lowered lids. Then he looked up and grinned: 'OK! Mr President of WAA, you have your wish. Provided men are not dead, I order release.' He extended a hand towards his desk and pulled out a drawer. 'But I also wish present you Order of the Tiger. Second class.'


'Mr Kingsley?'

'Yes.'

'Mr Amos Kingsley?'

'Yes, that's right.'

'Oh, good! I was in Tangu, trying to find out something about the nuclear power station which a consortium of British and Japanese are rumoured to be about to build there. So I missed your press conference. Do you think you could possibly spare me a few minutes of your valuable time for an interview?'

'Well, er, yes. I suppose so. What is your paper?'

'*The Times.*'

'*The Times of Malindi*?'

'Good God, no! *The Times* of London.'

*

214

'Now we come to the final item on the agenda. The election of your President for the next three years. As you will know, we have, er, five candidates of which I am, er, one. Since that is the case – I mean, since I am one of the candidates – I shall now vacate the Chair, calling upon your senior Vice-President, Señor Gabriel Lopez Martinez of Chile, to take it in my place.'

The senior Vice-President staggered to his feet. He bowed to Amos stiffly, then cleared his throat. 'Mr President – all the other four candidates have withdrawn in your favour.'

Amos was unable to conceal his stupefaction. 'Has Mrs Svenson withdrawn?' That the other three should have done so, he could believe; but that Margaretta, so implacable in her enmity and so ferocious in her ambition, should also have done so, was as though Edward Heath had joined Mrs T.'s Cabinet.

'Yes, I have withdrawn, Amos! With no hesitation and no regrets!'

The senior Vice-President tottered forward and all but fell off the dais. 'Then, messieurs, mesdames, fellow members of WAA, may I assume that Mr Amos Kingsley has been elected our President for the next three years by universal acclaim?'

A roar of approval confirmed that his assumption was correct.


Laura and Amos were dressing for the farewell banquet.

'What I just don't understand is why you told me that you were going to be in Tongu when you were clearly *not* in Tongu.'

'We were in Tangu.'

'In Tangu? Is there such a place?'

'Of course there is. They once had one of their massacres there. I wrote Tangu in my note. Tangu is the Florence of Malindi. Tongu is its, well, Viareggio.

Everyone knows that. And now there's this possibility that a British and a Japanese consortium – ' She broke off, a hand raised to her mouth. 'Oh, bugger! I shouldn't have let that out. Bob particularly told me not to let that out. That's why he went to Tangu.'

'What do you mean? Are you talking about this nuclear power station?'

'So you know about it! Oh, darling, you are clever! Yes, that's it. Bob – as you probably also know – isn't *really* employed by the British Council. Well, not entirely. That's his cover. You know how it is with so many of these British Council types. His work is really, well, hush-hush.'

'So that's why there wasn't a single book in his house and why, when I referred to *Tom Jones*, he began to talk about Las Vegas!'

'He's not a *total* philistine. He does, in fact, know *something* about ELT.'

'Anyway, what I want to know is what precisely was going on between the two of you?'

'Oh, darling, don't be so idiotic! I don't find him in the least bit attractive. He's so hairy, it would be like going to bed with a kelim. I just wanted to get away from WAA. That was all.'

'So you promise me – '

'Oh, darling, please! Can't we leave the subject? In a way it's flattering that you should be so possessive and jealous, but really . . .'

Later, as they were about to leave the suite, Amos asked: 'Why aren't you wearing that dress?'

'Which one?'

'The one you said was for special parties. The one we queued in the rain to buy at the Harvey Nichols sale.'

'I don't know which one you mean.'

'The one that looks like a giant cigar tube. You know!'

'Oh, that one!'

'Yes, that one.'

'Oh.'

Amos rushed to the wardrobe. 'Here it is!' Then he saw that, with what appeared to be a single slash, it had been bisected from the top of the bodice to the bottom of the skirt. 'How the hell did this happen?'

Laura was confused. 'I – tore it.'

'Like *this*? Don't be silly.' Amos went across to Laura, dragging the dress behind him. He held it out to her. 'Tell me, Laura! How the fuck did this happen?'

Laura looked terrified of him. It was the first time that she had ever done so. 'Semba,' she said.

'*Semba*?'

'She took her kitchen devil to it.'

'But *why*?'

Laura shrugged. 'Mad. She's mad.'

'But what was the dress doing in Naylor's house?'

'I, er, left it there.'

'Why?'

'Well, I wanted to keep my luggage as light as possible. And Bob said that there'd be no need of an evening dress in Tangu.'

'Do you mean that Naylor and Semba . . . and that Semba was . . . ?' But there were things that it was better not to know and therefore better not to ask. 'Oh, come on! Let's go! We're late already.'


Amos thought of those kangaroos on the back window of the Dormobile as he and Carmen hopped round the dance-floor. This, a samba, was the third dance which she had claimed from him, and he had not yet had one dance with Miss Shimada or even with Laura. Breathless, he conducted her back to her table, where a number of diminutive Costa Ricans jumped up to attention for her majestic arrival. 'Please sit for a moment, Amos.'

'Well, I really ought to see what my wife is up to . . .'

'Please – sit!'

Amos sat, perching himself on the edge of a vulnerable-looking gilt chair and looking around him for Miss Shimada. Oh, God, no, no, no! She was dancing with Naylor . . .

'Kingsley, I think of you as one of a long line of English writer men of action.'

'Oh. Er. Do you?'

Carmen nodded. 'There was your Sir Sidney. There was your Lord Byron. There was your T. E. Lawrence. You belong with them.'

'I wish I could write like them.'

'To celebrate your courage, I have something for you.' She stooped, picked up her massive crocodile leather handbag, and clicked it open. From its jaws she extracted a long buff envelope. Oh, God, another poem! 'Please!' She held it out to him.

'Thank you. Thank you very much, er, Carmen. That's most kind of you. I'll look at it later.' He stuffed the envelope into a pocket of his jacket.


Perhaps it was the *botni*; perhaps the liberal gulps of champagne as delegate after delegate came up to drink his health; perhaps the nervous strain of watching Miss Shimada dance not just that once but again and then again with Naylor. At all events, suddenly Amos had to dash to the loo.

It was only when he had finished that he realized that the paper-dispenser was empty. He might be not in the most expensive hotel in the capital but back at that prison.

Suddenly a solution came to him. He pulled out Carmen's envelope. But instead of the expected poem, it contained a thousand dollars in hundred dollar bills.

Recklessly, he used one of the bills.

\*

In the bar, after the dance was over, Amos asked Max and Mr Tu for their advice. Would it be *ethical* to accept such a present?

'You cannot return the money,' Mr Tu said. 'Impossible. Mrs Mendoza would at once lose face. In Latin America to lose face is almost as disastrous as it is in the East.'

'No, you can't offend Mrs Mendoza,' Max took up. 'That would be most unfortunate. The Costa Rican Centre wants to host a Congress next year, and she will be largely responsible for the financing of it. Of course,' he added, 'there *is* that little problem of those four Costa Rican writers in prison . . .'

'Well, in that case . . .' Amos smiled to himself. 'Toy boy,' he murmured.

'Toy *what*? Max asked.

'Toy boy. Secretly, I've wanted to be a toy boy all my life. And now, at forty-six, I've become one.'


Late that night the telephone rang in the suite. It rang for a long time before Amos had sufficiently disengaged himself from Laura to answer it.

A gruff resonant voice began: 'I have not become the King's First Minister in order to preside over the liquidation of the British Empire . . .' Then it broke off and Mr Nu's light, nasal voice took over: 'Mr Kingsley, when you return to England tomorrow and meet again with the Queen, you will not forget me?'

Amos felt in generous and all-powerful mood. 'No, I won't forget you.'

'You promise me?'

'I promise you.'

## 14

>:> <:<

'Laura! *Laura*! That's the bell!'
   'Well, answer it then.'
   'I can't. I'm in the loo.'
   'Bugger!'
When Amos emerged from the loo, Laura held out a
parcel to him. 'I didn't look properly when the postman
gave it to me. It's addressed to Kingsley Amis. And it
seems to have been posted months ago.'
   'Kingsley Amis!' Would he never escape from Kings-
ley Amis? Amos examined the parcel. 'From Hanoi.
I've never had a parcel from Hanoi.'
   'I don't imagine that Kingsley Amis has either. Oh,
do hurry up, Amos. You haven't even pulled up your
zip. We'll be late!'
   Amos was so flustered that, as he tore open the
parcel, its contents, innumerable closely typed sheets
of yellowing, flimsy paper, scattered across the floor.
But one sheet, a letter, remained in his hands:

Dear Mr Amis
I was sorry that our friendship was so abruptly
broken off – although I could appreciate your
reasons.
   It would have been pleasant to have discussed with
you such questions as whether more really means
worse, whether the arts really do not benefit from
subsidies, and whether Kipling (now there is a writer
to whom I thrill as much as to you or C. P. Snow or

Norman Mailer!) was really a closet gay. Perhaps at some future date, in happier circumstances . . .

Meanwhile I am taking the liberty of sending you some copies of my poems, in the hope that perhaps you can do something to assist me with their publication in England. Sadly and, to me at least, surprisingly no one here seems to be greatly interested in them.

As you will know, there is no WAA Centre in Vietnam. When you write, please send me full information about how I should set about trying to establish one . . .'

'Amos! For God's sake leave that! You can read it later. We can't keep *her* waiting!'


'Oh, dear! I do wish I'd gone before we left.'

'You did go, Mummy!' Laura said crossly, as she jumped another traffic light at amber.

'Not immediately before I left. Do you think I can go there?'

'I imagine so,' Amos said. He would probably have to go himself, he felt so nervous.

'You know, Amos, I really do think that you should be wearing morning dress.'

'If I possessed morning dress, I'd be wearing it, mother. But to hire it would have been rather, er, squalid.'

'This car is rather squalid. Most people hire cars as well as morning-dress for these occasions.'

'I've no wish to appear to be something other than I am – a man who owns a single dark suit and a beat-up Ford Cortina.' Amos was lofty.

'I really don't know why Queenie didn't make it a knighthood. It's thoroughly mean of her.'

'Laura, please!' Laura's mother tugged at the brim of her pink straw hat, pulling it down yet lower over her forehead. 'It's so childish – and so disrespectful – to speak of the Queen like that. Particularly when we're on the way to, well, visit her at her home.'

'Amos *deserved* a knighthood. Think of all he went through!'

'Well, it's very nice to get an MBE,' Amos said. 'After all, I'm the first International President of WAA ever to have become a Member of the Order of the British Empire.'

'Since you're the first British International President, that's hardly surprising,' Laura answered tartly. 'Some other International Presidents have been awarded the Nobel Prize.'

'Anyway, Kingsley Amis has never got a knighthood.'


Having parked the car in the courtyard of Buckingham Palace, Amos and the two women were separated. Amos was conducted into a vast, high-ceilinged room, in which future KBEs, CBEs, OBEs, and MBEs were corralled, each group in its own pen, and were then instructed in what would be expected of them. The two women were ushered to seats in the main hall.

Amos was later to learn from Laura why she and her mother had both been absent at the awesome moment when he had advanced towards the Queen and had been invested with his honour.

'I've got to go,' Laura's mother had hissed.

'You've been!'

'I've got to go again.'

'Not now! In a moment Amos will be – '

'I must! We don't want an accident. Not here – in Buckingham Palace.'

'Oh, very well!'

The two women had begun to scrape past knees as they had hurried for the exit. 'Really, mother!' Laura was exclaiming, when she was not saying 'Excuse me!' or 'Thank you.'

There was an elderly, uniformed, heavily bemedalled man at the doors, now closed, through which they had entered. A retired admiral? A retired general?

'I wonder if we could slip out? My mother's not feeling very well.'

The man had opened one of the doors, had let them through and had then followed them out, closing the door behind him. He had pointed to a chair. 'Please sit down, madam.' Then he had summoned one of the two lackeys standing at the head of the grandiose staircase. 'Bring this lady a glass of water.'

'Oh, no, no, Laura! *Not* a glass of water!' At that Laura's mother had simultaneously burst into tears and drenched a *petit point* chair-cover worked by the Duke of Edinburgh.

Meanwhile Amos, the backs of his knees trembling uncontrollably, was approaching the Queen.

He heard a strangely girlish voice: 'Now let me see – you're a writer, Mr Kingsley?'

'That's right, ma'am.'

'And are you writing anything at present?'

'Well, yes, ma'am. As a matter of fact, I'm writing two books simultaneously. One is about some recent adventures I had in Malindi, when I was taken hostage. You may have read about the incident, ma'am. Not at all pleasant. And the other book is a new departure for me, in as much as it's a novel – I've never before attempted a novel. My theme is the sense of alienation which overcomes . . .'

Suddenly Amos became aware of a look of growing panic in the bright, azure eyes fixed on him.

The Queen leaned towards him. She grabbed his hand. 'How nice, how very nice!' she said in those high, bell-like tones of hers. At that, she gave him a shove away from her, so violent that he all but fell over.

Amos took two steps backwards, as he had been

instructed. Then, all at once, he seemed to hear Churchill's voice, once more reverberating as it must so often have reverberated through this palace: *'An iron curtain is drawn down upon their front. We do not know what is going on behind . . .'*

Amos took a step forward. He must, yes, he must keep his promise!

'Oh, Your Majesty, ma'am, excuse me, there was just one other thing . . .'

But someone had taken him firmly by the elbow and had begun to march him away.